A CHRISTMAS KISS

Ann heard laughter as she descended and she followed the sound to the rose parlor. She entered to find Ruston on the floor, with Noël on his stomach, worrying frantically at his waistcoat buttons. Mossy gaily grasped her kitten and danced away. "I'm going to take him upstairs now. He hasn't had his dinner yet."

"Please, don't let me interrupt," Ann said.

Ruston clambered to his feet as Mossy skipped from the room with Noël. "Let her go." He brushed himself off.

Ann realized she was watching his broad hands straighten his breeches and quickly looked away. She was shy, suddenly, not knowing what to say.

He stepped in front of her, reached in his pocket, took her hand and placed one berry in it. "I think I will claim one kiss now."

"Why are you doing this?" she asked, looking away. She didn't think she could bear another of his soul-shattering kisses.

He clutched her shoulders and drew her near, not answering. He tipped her face up with one hand and kissed her, possessing her lips with a gentleness that seared her soul. She shivered, and despite all her resolutions found herself responding, opening to him like a flower to warming sunshine . . .

from "Noël's Christmas Wish," by Donna Simpson

BOOK YOUR PLACE ON OUR WEBSITE AND MAKE THE READING CONNECTION!

We've created a customized website just for our very special readers, where you can get the inside scoop on everything that's going on with Zebra, Pinnacle and Kensington books.

When you come online, you'll have the exciting opportunity to:

- View covers of upcoming books
- Read sample chapters
- Learn about our future publishing schedule (listed by publication month *and author*)
- Find out when your favorite authors will be visiting a city near you
- Search for and order backlist books from our online catalog
- Check out author bios and background information
- Send e-mail to your favorite authors
- Meet the Kensington staff online
- Join us in weekly chats with authors, readers and other guests
- Get writing guidelines
- AND MUCH MORE!

**Visit our website at
http://www.zebrabooks.com**

STOCKING STUFFERS

Judith A. Lansdowne
Jeanne Savery
Donna Simpson

ZEBRA BOOKS
Kensington Publishing Corp.
http://www.zebrabooks.com

ZEBRA BOOKS are published by

Kensington Publishing Corp.
850 Third Avenue
New York, NY 10022

First Printing: October, 2000
10 9 8 7 6 5 4 3 2 1

Printed in the United States of America

CONTENTS

A CACHE OF
MAGICAL KITTENS

by

Judith A. Lansdowne

One

The Honourable C. Archibald Pope cursed under his breath, raised his collar against the wind and trudged wearily onward. His ears had begun to burn so badly from the cold that he had resorted to placing his muffler over his hat and tying it beneath his chin. Although his hands were gloved and stuffed deep into the pockets of his greatcoat, his fingertips were becoming quite as numb as his toes, and there was no telling at all where his nose had gone. It had left his face long ago. He was certain of that, for he felt its presence not at all. Truly, this had become the most frustrating and torturous journey. And now, of all things, it was beginning to snow.

Likely I shall die out here on this gawdforsaken bit of ground before I ever do locate Wyndhover, he thought, peering squinty-eyed across Marston Moor into the fading daylight. *I have been walking for hours and not so much as one barn to shelter in have I seen, much less a cottage, much less Wyndhover Manor. Ought to have turned about and sought out the road to Haworth the very moment that Feather stumbled.*

But he had ridden east of Haworth an hour or more before Feather had gone lame and then thought to find shelter much closer than that hour's walk back the way he had come. He had assumed that he was a deal nearer his journey's end, expecting to come upon Wyndhover in no time at all. Of course he had assumed, as well, that after nine years and more, a direct and usable road would have been built to cut directly across the moor to Wyndhover and the village of Wynd beyond, but apparently it had not. "Unless I have missed the road somehow," he muttered through frigid lips. "Though how anyone but a blind man can miss an entire road. . . . It is all my fault, my gallant Feather." His sad, hazel-eyed gaze turned back upon the little bay mare who hobbled determinedly behind him. "It is all my fault, my darling, and I do apologize for it." Pope's heart lurched the tiniest bit at the sight of the little mare shivering, blowing cold vapor through her nostrils, and limping badly. Still she attempted to keep pace with him as best she could. He went to her upon the instant and took her bridle in both hands. "You are the bravest horse in all the world, Feather," he whispered, rubbing his cheek against hers. "Brave and noble and true. I will not give up on you, m'dear. Never."

Pope feared that the bay with the solitary stocking had done herself greater harm than he could plainly see and that, in the end, he might well be forced to put her down. But until it was proved to him that she had done such serious damage to herself, he would look after the little mare, continue to walk slowly so that she might not become separated from him, and when at last he found them shelter, do his very best to attend to her injury properly. And C. Archibald Pope's best was not a thing at which to scoff. He was a gentleman never inclined to surrender easily. No, he was not. Fate and bad fortune might beat him mercilessly about the head for an eternity and more before he would bow to either of them. He had proved it to be so any number of times before, and he would continue to withstand their buffets as far as he was able for the years that remained to him.

We might be safe and warm now, if we did not need to hobble along at such a pace as this, he thought, rubbing the mare's neck with fingers he could not feel. *But then again, we might not. Perhaps my memory has failed me and I am far wide of Wyndhover. Perhaps there is no shelter to be had in this direction at all.*

"It is all my fault that we stand here shaking and shivering, Feather, m'dear," he whispered. "Had I been more circumspect, you would not have stumbled at all. But we shall not turn to ice, either of us. I promise you that. We have a promise to keep, you and I, and we cannot keep it if we freeze to death on this moor, m'darling girl."

The mare shivered again, her muscles quivering like a blanc-mange, and Pope had an idea. He lifted the handle of his portmanteau from off the saddle bow, set the small case upon the ground and opened it. At the very top, folded carefully, lay his best coat—a coat of style and precision, so deep a blue as to be almost black with three diamond buttons down the front—a coat that had been made precisely to his measurements by the grand tailor of London, Weston. A gift from his elder brother, Samuel, it was the only true bit of luxury he had brought with him. It was, in fact, the only true bit of luxury he actually possessed, and it was also the warmest thing in his portmanteau. He plucked the coat out and tossed it over one shoulder as he unsaddled Feather. Then he arranged the coat along her back atop the saddle blanket and put her saddle back on to hold it in place. "That will help a bit, I hope," he said to her, stroking her sturdy little neck. "Come now, Feather. It is only a bit farther, I think. Only a bit farther."

Rebecca, Lady Wraithstone peered out into the swirling snow and sighed. The flakes were smaller than before and falling in greater numbers. The wind had increased, the daylight was almost gone, and still there was no sign of him. Had he not written that he would arrive today? She thought to go and reread the missive the gentleman had sent, but then decided against it, for she knew precisely what it would say. It would say that he was privileged to accept the position she offered him and would arrive at Wyndhover on the afternoon of the second day of December.

"But the afternoon turns into evening and there is not yet a sign of him," she whispered to herself as she drew the heavy draperies across the windows and turned toward the hearth. "Perhaps he could not hire a vehicle at the Yellow Packet in Wynd to drive him here. Perhaps the vehicles are all spoken for or none of the drivers will take their teams out because of the snow." Or perhaps he has not enough money to hire a vehicle, she thought then with a frown. "What a gudgeon I am not to think of such a thing. The gentleman is a tutor and likely his pockets are not so very flush. Perhaps Mr. Pope thinks to walk from Wynd to Wyndhover. Oh, dear, I ought to have inquired of him. How stupid of me not to inquire of him!"

With mittened hands unaccustomed to such tasks, Rebecca lifted one of the logs from the stack upon the settle and attempted to toss it onto the fire. It was so cold in this room. So very cold. But the log, a deal too large for the stack of skeletal sticks beneath it, rolled off to one side where it lay with one end vaguely near the tiny blaze and the other well away.

"Pshaw," she muttered in frustration as the long-lingering ache in her stomach blossomed into true pain and most unwelcome tears began to sting at the back of her eyes. "Is there nothing I can do correctly? Must I prove a failure always? Anyone can place a log upon a fire. Anyone but me, it appears."

Beneath an enormous layer of quilts upon the bed behind her, a tiny body stirred and whimpered. She hastened at once to the little lump beneath the bedclothes. "Do not cry, William," she whispered and, without thinking, leaned down to bestow a kiss upon her son's pale cheek.

The cheek turned quickly away before her lips could touch it and hid itself beneath the counterpane. The boy whimpered again, then turned back toward her. Two enormous blue eyes peered fearfully out from beneath the quilts.

Rebecca's mittened hands fluttered helplessly in the air before her. She longed to take her son into her arms and hold him safely and comfortingly against her breast, but she knew from grim experience that she dare not. "You wish me gone, dearest. I can see as much. And I shall go in just a bit," she managed, struggling against her tears by nibbling at her lower lip. "It is merely that . . . that . . . I have been so very lonely, William, without your papa, and though you never do say, you must be lonely too. And I did think that together we might . . . we might . . . comfort each other." Her tears escaped her and glided soundlessly down her cheeks. She turned away from the boy quickly so that he would not see and stepped haltingly back toward the hearth.

He is not coming, she thought, the many slashes that criss-crossed her heart opening and closing with each despairing beat. *Mr. Pope has had word from Mr. Parker or Mr. Rathmore and reconsidered the entire thing. He has chosen to decline the position. I shall receive his missive stating as much with the next mail.* "What am I to do?" she murmured, watching the flames flicker in the fireplace. "If Mr. Pope has changed his mind, I shall be forced to advertise the position again. And no one will take it. A position advertised in all the London papers six times in a year must clearly be suspect. I doubt even the neediest of tutors would consider such a position."

Rebecca attempted to maneuver the misplaced log onto the fire with the tongs, her hands shaking. *Mr. Pope must come,* she thought. *He is my last hope. Oh, please, Richard. You are William's papa. Whatever has happened to Mr. Pope, cannot you reach down from the heavens and help him? If he has changed his mind, cannot you make him change it back again? And if it is merely that he waits without a ride at the Yellow Packet, well, I shall send our own coach to rescue him at once. That much, at least, I can do. I do think he will have gone to the Yellow Packet, do not you, Richard? If he booked passage upon the mail?*

"I have sent James and Michael to light the flambeaux at the gate, madam," announced Buzzerby as he placed a bowl of chowder upon the dining table before Lady Wraithstone.

"Just so, Buzzerby. An excellent idea. I am so very stupid not to have thought to send the coach before now. But Mr. Pope did not mention it and it did not occur to me that he might be unable to hire a vehicle at the inn to bring him to us. He will not have attempted to walk out from Wynd, do you think, Buzzerby? Not in such weather as this."

"No, madam, I cannot think so," Buzzerby replied, standing stiffly behind her. "Mr. Bumpers would inform him of the distance involved at once and our new tutor would think better of it."

"Perhaps he has hired a vehicle, Buzzerby, and John will miss him upon the road."

"John will recognize any of the vehicles from the Yellow Packet, my lady. Knows each and every one of the drivers. Does he meet with one along the way, he will stop and inquire if our tutor is aboard the vehicle. John is to be trusted to bring the gentleman to us, I assure you."

Rebecca bent her head over her chowder and seemed to study it intently as she smoothed the linen napkin upon her lap. "You do not think, Buzzerby," she said in the softest voice, "that Mr. Pope has changed his mind about accepting the position and has remained in London?"

"Never, my lady," declared the butler bracingly. "More likely the mail has been delayed. It has snowed a good deal just to the south of us. The gentleman will come just as he promised, my lady, and John will bring him to us. You may depend upon it."

Buzzerby was merely attempting to be kind, of course. Rebecca realized that. She spooned a bit of the tepid chowder into her mouth and gazed down at the empty dinner table in silence.

"I fear Mr. Pope has had second thoughts about coming to us, Buzzerby," she said as the chowder was replaced by a substantial portion of lamb with potatoes and peas. "John has driven all the way to Wynd on a fool's errand."

The butler did not respond. It was not that he did not wish to respond, merely that he could think of not one more thing to say to raise her ladyship's spirits. Winter was a dismal time in the West Riding and it made for dismal feelings. *Her ladyship ought not to be here,* Buzzerby thought. *Her ladyship's life is discouraging enough without spending the winter in this drafty old house.* But he could not say such a thing. Never. "The gentleman's name is Mr. Pope, madam?"

"Indeed. I am certain I mentioned his name to you, Buzzerby. Several times."

"Just so. His lordship was used to know a Mr. Pope," offered the butler. "A young gentleman with six elder brothers, he was. Spent his summers here at Wyndhover when he was a lad. But then, that particular Mr. Pope was drowned at sea years and years ago."

"You do not think, Buzzerby, that perhaps this is one of his brothers who comes to us?"

Buzzerby had, in fact, pondered that precise question any number of times since he had first heard the new tutor's name, but he could not think it to be the case. "No, madam," he said, "I think not. Their father is the Earl of Severnshire. I cannot think that any of his sons would be forced to hire out as a tutor, madam. But perhaps this Mr. Pope is some distant relation. One never knows unless one makes it a point to inquire."

Night and the snow swirled around Pope in the most confusing manner. But then, everything had grown confusing. He could not feel his legs and feet trudging on beneath him, though he knew they must be doing so, for the landscape around him continued to alter appreciably. He could not feel his arms or the wiggling of his fingers inside his gloves, but when he glanced to see, they were indeed there. And he no longer knew in which direction he walked, though he believed that he was still bound across the moor in the direction of Wyndhover because his increasingly foggy mind told him that it must be so.

I shall just sit down for a moment, Pope thought as he noticed himself stumble. *My legs are not working quite properly. I will rest for a moment or two—merely until I can get my bearings and regain some energy.* He settled himself upon the cold, wet ground with his back against a twisted, leafless oak and sighed. "I have never been so weary in all of my life, Feather," he told the little mare as she came to a standstill beside him. "We shall pause here for a bit and then strike out again, eh?" His eyes, weary from squinting into the snow and the night, closed of their own accord and his head nodded down onto his chest. He would have been deeply asleep within moments, but a peculiar skittering sound—very near his ear—startled him into full awareness. "Did you hear that, Feather? No? Well, I did. And a good thing, I think. Almost I fell asleep, m'dear, and got us both froze to death."

"Brrrr," responded a tiny voice.

"Brrrr? What the devil?" Pope looked about him, curious. "Well, you did not say it," he stated quite plainly to Feather. "I am not so muddled that I believe horses say 'brrrr.' "

"Brrrr," said the tiny voice again, and another joined it, and a third and a fourth, a fifth and a sixth. And then Pope actually felt something—tiny rufflings against the back of his greatcoat collar.

"What the deuce?" He pushed himself slowly away from the twisted old oak tree and squinted at it with some perturbation. "What the deuce?" he mumbled again as a tiny gray head, eyes golden with reflected shards of moonlight, peered at him from some three feet above the ground. "A tiny ghost?" He stretched a hand toward the head and it disappeared immediately.

Feather nickered and moved closer to the oak.

Pope ran his gloved hands along the tree bark. "Ahhh," he said with satisfaction as he came upon a small opening in the trunk. "Nothing ghostly about it, Feather. We have come upon a nest of some sort." He reached down inside the tree trunk and at once tiny claws seized upon the back of his glove and clawed upward until they reached the sleeve of his greatcoat. A kitten appeared, scrabbling upward toward his shoulder. Pope plucked it from the coat sleeve and held it up before his eyes. "Poor thing," he murmured. "Barely bigger than a minute, you are, and shaking with cold. It cannot be much warmer inside that tree than it is out here, eh?"

Pope's lethargy departed. It occurred to him that such a tiny kitten as this was not likely hiding in the oak alone. He put the fellow gently into his greatcoat pocket, reinserted his hand into the hollowed trunk and one by one scooped five more kittens from the hiding place. "Now," he said, the kittens divided evenly between his pockets, "we must only discover your mama, eh? And then we will all of us find a warmer place to shelter from this confounded cold." With considerable doubt—for if the mama were in the tree with them, would she not have shown herself long before now?—Pope reached into the aperture one last time, straining to reach all the way to the bottom. He felt something, but could not tell what. He pulled back, divested himself of his gloves and stuck his hand back into the cavity. Fur? Yes, it must be. With his gloves on, he had thought it to be a layer of leaves, but it felt more like fur, though how could one tell when one's fingertips were near frozen? He stood upon his toes and reached farther, his entire shoulder now inside the hollow trunk. Clasping as much of the stuff as he could in his hand, he tugged it upward and out of the opening. "Oh," he sighed, staring at the lean body that he had grasped by the scruff of the neck.

The mare moved even closer and nudged at the body. It wiggled the least bit. "Mrrr," it responded weakly.

"She is not dead, m'girl," said Pope, rubbing his hand tenderly along the cat's tangled fur. "We will see what can be done for her, eh?" Swiftly he buttoned the near dead cat inside his greatcoat. "Either we will all discover shelter soon, m'dears, or we will all perish upon this moor before the sun rises, but none of us shall cross the River Styx without making a concerted effort not to do so, I promise you that."

Two

Buzzerby stood upon the threshold of the winter parlor, only the paleness of his complexion suggesting that he had moments ago received a grave shock. "Mr. C. Archibald Pope, madam," he announced, in a voice that trembled the merest bit.

"Mr. Pope?" Lady Wraithstone's heart leaped at once into her throat, making her voice catch. He *had* come! Oh, thank goodness! He had *not* altered his plans and decided to turn down the position. In her relief, Lady Wraithstone rose at once from the chair before the fire and crossed the room to offer her hand to the fellow in welcome before she had even truly taken one good look at him.

"I shall not step into your parlor, Lady Wraithstone, if you please," declared Pope as he bowed awkwardly over the proffered hand. "I have been walking across the moor since before sunset and am travel-stained beyond belief. But I did think it best to inform you at once and in person that I have arrived safely. Mr. Buzzerby did attempt to persuade me otherwise, but I would not listen. And so here I am, still wrapped against the cold, but hoping to set your mind at rest."

"Oh," responded Rebecca, her lovely blue eyes studying him for the first time—and with considerable concern. This was the new tutor she had hired for William? This diminutive being, no taller than she, drowning inside a dismally wet and muddied greatcoat? With a long, very red nose, and an equally red muffler tied over his high beaver and down under his chin, he reminded her at once of the stories her papa had told her long ago, stories concerning a rambunctious and very mischievous elf.

"My lady?" said Pope, into what had grown to be a very long silence.

"Oh! Oh, you must pardon me, Mr. Pope. I just did not expect . . . that is to say . . . Mr. Pope? The pockets of your greatcoat are . . . wiggling?"

"That will be the kittens, my lady."

"The kittens?" Rebecca stared at him in the most bewildered fashion. "And your arm, Mr. Pope," she said then, deciding to ignore what she could not truly have heard him say. "Have you injured your arm in some way that you hold it so tightly against your chest?"

"No, I am fine, Lady Wraithstone," he assured her. "It is merely that I am supporting Mrs. Oakwood inside my coat."

"Mrs. Oakwood?"

"Indeed. I hope you will not mind that I have brought the entire family with me, but they were in dire need of warmth and food, you see. I shall not bother any of your staff with the care of them, I assure you."

Rebecca's mind twirled and tilted in the most bewildering fashion. Had he truly said that he was carrying a Mrs. Oakwood beneath his coat? And that he had brought his entire family with him? No, that could not possibly be.

I must learn to pay strict attention when people speak, she admonished herself in an uneasy silence. *I cannot allow my mind to go wandering.* "You came across the moor, Mr. Pope?" she asked, deciding upon that as the most reasonable of the questions whirling about in her brain. "How came you to be so far to the west of us as to find yourself upon the opposite side of Marston Moor, sir? You did not come upon the *Regent* from London, then, certainly."

"No, my lady, and I regret that I did not. But I could not have brought Feather had I come by the mail."

"Feather?"

"If you will pardon me," Mr. Pope said, taking not the least note of the fainting tones in which his new employer had uttered the word "Feather." "I am rather wet and chilly, Lady Wraith-stone, and I—"

"How thoughtless of me! Buzzerby will lead you directly to your chambers and see that the fire is kept ablaze the entire night. You will get one of the boys to keep the fire blazing, will you not, Buzzerby? Yes, and you must see that Mr. Pope is provided with towels and hot water and all the quilts for the bed that he requires and . . . What is it that gentlemen drink to warm their bones, Buzzerby?"

"Brandy, my lady," offered the butler in less than stentorian tones, his countenance not yet restored to its natural color.

"Just so. You must see that Mr. Pope is provided some brandy . . . and food. You must be very hungry, Mr. Pope. I shall send James up with a tray. Go at once, Buzzerby, and show Mr. Pope to his chambers. Only see how he shivers standing about so."

"Yes, but I ain't dead, Buzzerby, so do get over it," advised Pope as he rubbed warmth and a bit more life back into the mother cat and then set her on the settle before a saucer of warm milk and some scraps of meat pie. "I do thank you for the use of Richard's robe, by the way. I had no room to pack my own. She is very sad, Richard's lady, is she not?"

"Very sad, Mr. Arch— Pardon me, Mr. Pope."

"No, no, Mr. Archie is quite good enough, Buzzerby. You were always accustomed to call me Master Archie when I was a lad. Mr. Archie is equally acceptable."

"But you are a lad no longer and—"

"Mr. Archie will do nicely, Buzzerby. And do not persist in staring at me in that most unnerving fashion, if you please. I am not a ghost and I have not come here to haunt the household."

"No, Mr. Archie. Why . . . why have you come?"

"To be of help, Buzzerby, to Richard's lady and to his son. I heard the most distressing rumors about the lad in London. And then I happened to speak to a Mr. Rathmore. You will remember a Mr. Rathmore, Buzzerby," Pope said, staring down into the clothes press at the kittens flailing about in a nest of towels.

"Indeed. He was the last of his lordship's tutors," replied Buzzerby, gathering up Pope's sorely stained traveling clothes to give to the little scrub girl.

"No, you are mistaken there. *I* am the last of his lordship's tutors, Buzzerby. Mr. Rathmore was the tutor before me."

"But you are not a tutor, Mr. Archie."

"I beg to disagree. I am a tutor. I have agreed to accept the position and Lady Wraithstone has agreed to have me. What is her name, Buzzerby, Lady Wraithstone?"

"Her name, Mr. Archie?"

"Yes, her Christian name. What is it?"

"R-Rebecca."

"Rebecca. And his lordship is called William?"

"Just so, Mr. Archie."

"And Lady Wraithstone did not exaggerate in her letters to me? Little Lord Wraithstone has truly not spoken to anyone or let anyone touch him since the day of his father's death, not even Lady Wraithstone or his nanny?"

"He will not so much as be kissed upon the cheek by his mama, Mr. Archie. And he will dress himself any which way and bathe himself as best he can, but no one is to touch him with so much as one finger."

"Or what, Buzzerby?"

"Well, if one appears as though one is going to touch him, he runs and hides under his bed and will not come out until everyone is gone. Or . . ."

"Yes, Buzzerby?"

"Well, if it is not possible for him to escape and hide, he screams the most hideous screams and runs 'round and 'round so a person cannot catch him. His behavior has driven every tutor Lady Wraithstone has managed to acquire quite mad, let me tell you."

"And her ladyship fears the child has run mad, I have not the least doubt."

"She is most frightened for the boy," nodded Buzzerby uneasily. "She was terrified, Mr. Archie, when you did not arrive before dark, that you had changed your mind and decided against accepting the position."

"Yes, well, I have not decided against it."

The sun had barely risen the following morning when the creaking of the door to his bedchamber roused a bleary-eyed Pope. He peeked out from beneath an enormous stack of quilts and blinked in the most befuddled manner at one interesting blue eye as it peered at him through a crack between the door and its frame. For a moment, Pope could not for the life of him think where he was or to whom such a clear blue eye might belong, and then he realized.

"Do come in, my lord," he offered, uninhibited by the fact that his nightcap slanted down over one eye, the collar of his nightshirt was rumpled up about his neck and he was battling to suppress a yawn. "I am far more interesting to gaze upon close up, I assure you. Especially my nose. To view my nose close up, Lord Wraithstone, is a veritable entertainment in itself."

The gap between door and frame did not, however, widen, nor did the one blue eye appear to respond in any noticeable manner.

"Well, then, I expect I shall need to rise without company this morning. How early is it? Shadowy in here." Allowing the suppressed yawn to flow from him at last and stretching mightily as well, Pope climbed from beneath the covers. "Brrrr," he said, his bare feet dancing across the carpet to the washstand. "I do wish that I had some bedroom slippers. Even with the fire still ablaze, my feet are freezing."

No response was forthcoming from the vicinity of the blue eye, though it remained steadily fixed upon Pope as he performed his morning rituals. Pope did hear a tiny gasp when he cut himself shaving, but the gasp was not accompanied by any movement of his chamber door.

Donning his second best pair of breeches, a clean shirt and a most extravagantly embroidered waistcoat, Pope tugged a silver-backed brush through his dark curls, tied a blue cravat around his neck and strolled to the clothes press. He tugged the middle drawer, which had not been closed entirely, a bit farther open. "You look greatly improved, Mrs. Oakwood," he said quietly. "Feeding the urchins, are you? What a splendid mother. Only be patient for a bit longer, m'dear, and I will bring more of that excellent milk and meat pie we shared last evening."

Pope heard his chamber door creak even as he spoke, and he smiled to himself. So, he thought, his lordship is at least as curious as most boys. No doubt wishing to know why his new tutor speaks to a clothes press. Pope turned toward the door, intending to welcome the lad into his chamber and introduce him to the mother cat and her kittens, but no sooner had he done so than the child, in a blur of rumpled nightshirt and flopping slippers, lunged back out through the doorway.

"No, my lord, do not run away," Pope called after the hastily retreating little figure. "Only come back and I shall introduce you to the most amazing . . ." But the child had disappeared before Pope could finish his statement.

C. Archibald Pope was not a gentleman to be daunted by such rude behavior upon the part of an aged duke, much less a six-year-old viscount. He took a moment to shrug into his morning coat, tucked his timepiece into his waistcoat pocket, slipped into his shoes and then strolled through the doorway into the adjoining chamber in which he discovered a bed quite equal in size to his own enormous four-poster.

Ah, so I have been given the nurse's chamber, he thought, *and thus connect with the nursery.* In silence, he studied the room. A fire sputtered upon an ancient hearth. Heavy gold draperies were drawn tight against the cold. A badly scarred chest made from pine was polished to a bright shine despite the letters and lines carved impertinently into it by children of ages past. In one corner sat a ladder-backed chair. In another, a three-legged stool. On the far wall, beside a door opposite the one through which he had entered, a clothes press and an armoire reigned, separated only by a tiny washstand.

Pope grinned. It was just as he remembered it, this chamber he had shared with the boy's father through any number of summers. He had no doubt that the schoolroom which lay beyond remained much the same as well. But where had Lord Wraithstone gone? Pope strolled across the maroon and gold carpeting, opened the opposite door and peered into the schoolroom. It *was* just as he remembered it, but it contained no Lord Wraithstone. "Well," he said quietly, "unless you have run off into the corridor in nothing but your nightshirt and slippers, which is a most unacceptable thing to do, my lord, you are under your bed. Are you under your bed?"

With careful steps Pope made his way back to that piece of furniture and knelt down beside it. He tossed the sides of the bedclothes up onto the mattress and peered under the thing to spy a tiny figure huddled there. "Good morning, my lord," he said in a pleasant voice. "I am your new tutor, Mr. Pope, but you may call me Archie if you wish."

The little boy scooted farther toward the head of the bed—as far away from Pope as he could get.

"I am quite certain that I am not *that* intimidating, William," Pope drawled. "You are surprised to see a strange gentleman in the house is all. Did not anyone tell you that you were to have a new tutor?"

A nearly inaudible whimper answered him, the sound scratching across Pope's heart like a needle across silk.

"I expect your mama did tell you, but you have forgotten," whispered Pope to himself. "Lord Wraithstone," he began again, "I intend to be a good deal more than your tutor, you know. I intend to be your friend. I am sadly in need of a friend myself, you see, and since I have definitely decided upon you to fill that position, I must do as much for you in return."

The little bundle of humanity under the bed wriggled a bit and made a tiny grunting sound.

"Yes, I am aware that it must be uncomfortable under there at best, but then I was not the one who suggested it. I expect you did not think that I would awaken when you peeked in at me, eh? But I did, and here I am. And here I will remain until you have come out from under your bed to greet me properly." Pope left his knees and sat smack down upon the carpeting. He rested his back carefully against the nightstand and stretched his legs out before him. "I had the devil of a time finding this place, you know, William. I was accustomed to come here in the summers and play with your papa when we were boys, but the moor does not look quite the same in winter."

"Uhmmm," responded the tiny being under the bed.

"My horse, Feather, and I got lost on the moor, and if it had not been for the cache of magical kittens we discovered—why we might never have reached Wyndhover at all. Saved my life, those kittens did, and Feather's as well." Pope listened to the gentle stirring beneath the bed and smiled to himself. "I will lay you odds, William, that you have never seen such fine kittens as I have brought with me in all of your life. They are tumbling about in my clothes press even as we speak. Should you not like to meet them?"

"Hmmuh," grunted William.

Pope resisted the urge to gain his knees and peer under the bed again because he was certain that the slithering sound accompanying that grunt was Lord Wraithstone crawling toward him.

I shall just pretend that I do not care if he crawls out or not, he thought, fishing his watch from his waistcoat pocket. With a flick of his thumb, he popped open its cover and it began to chime whimsically, just a bit of a song. "And good morning to you as well, Throckmorton," Pope said in response. "You always know when it is time for me to be doing something, do you not? And you are correct, as always. It is time for me to be feeding the kittens' mama. I do thank you for reminding me of it. You will wonder, no doubt, my lord, that I address my timepiece as Throckmorton," he continued, avoiding the urge to look straight at the little blond head that poked out from beneath the bed to stare at his pocket watch. "Any number of people wonder at it, but that is his name, you see. Throckmorton. So he was named when my grandfather bought him, and so he remains to this day."

Little Lord Wraithstone in rumpled nightshirt, sans nightcap, blinked bright blue eyes at the timepiece. One small finger reached out toward it. Pope closed the cover and sprung it open again, causing the thing to chime once more. "Gracious, but

Throckmorton is extremely vocal this morning," he said as the boy's mouth opened in delight.

Just then, with a click and a clump, the door from the schoolroom to the nursery opened. William scrambled immediately from sight. Pope gained his knees to gaze up over the mattress and discovered a rather dour, middle-aged woman frozen upon the threshold. "Let me guess," he said pleasantly, peering up at her like some demented elf. "You are his lordship's nanny?"

Three

"Sent me off, he did, my lady," complained Nanny Montcliff loudly. " 'Tis not a tutor's job to be dressing his lordship. Will not get him dressed properly without me, I daresay."

Lady Wraithstone, who had risen from her own bed only moments before, played nervously with the ribands upon her robe and gazed vaguely at the nanny. It was likely true that William would not let Mr. Pope help him to dress, but then, he would not allow Nanny Montcliff to help him to any great extent either, and so Rebecca did not at all recognize the significance of the situation.

"I cannot think . . ." Rebecca began. "I cannot think why Mr. Pope should . . . He was kneeling upon the floor, you say? And William under the bed?"

"Frightened his lordship was of that odd little man," grumbled Nanny Montcliff. "His lordship does always hide beneath the bed when he is frightened."

Lady Wraithstone sighed. It was all beginning badly again. Obviously, William was as frightened of Mr. Pope as he was of everyone and everything else. It would likely take weeks before the gentleman could even approach the boy. *And Mr. Pope will give up long before then,* she thought. *He will toss his hands into the air and depart in a huff like all the others. I would do so myself if I were not William's mother. No, I would not! What a thing to think!*

"Well, you must just go down to the kitchen, Nanny Montcliff," she said, realizing that the nanny remained before her. "You must just go down to the kitchen and fetch William's breakfast up to him when it is prepared. We shall give his lordship and Mr. Pope that length of time in which to become acquainted. It will not matter that his lordship eats his breakfast in his nightshirt. Not this once."

"Just so, my lady," nodded Nanny Montcliff with a sniff, and took herself off directly.

"I shall wear the old brown velvet, Dorothea," Rebecca murmured distractedly. "Whatever can Mr. Pope be thinking to approach William with no one to introduce them properly? And after we have corresponded for months upon the subject of William's . . . illness. Is the gentleman mad?"

Dorothea, who had been lady's maid to Lady Wraithstone for ten years, knew at once that the particular question of the new tutor's sanity was not truly intended for her and so she ignored it completely and crossed into the adjoining chamber to fetch the dress her ladyship had requested.

I shall ask Nanny Montcliff to send Mr. Pope down to me as soon as she takes William his tray, Rebecca mused. *Yes, and Mr. Pope will join me in the breakfast room and we shall take some time to become acquainted ourselves. Then I will remind him that William is not just any lad, that he is . . . ill. Although I am quite certain that I made everything perfectly clear in our correspondence. I know that I did. And Mr. Pope indicated that he understood precisely.*

"He is dressed?" Lady Wraithstone stared in amazement across the breakfast table at the long-nosed, diminutive gentleman with the blue cravat tied rakishly about his neck. "No, he cannot be. I did not hear one scream from the nursery."

"Gentlemen, my lady, do not scream upon donning their morning clothes. At least, I do not know of any who do. I and my brothers did not." He smiled at her as he raised a cup of tea to his lips.

His hazel eyes lit with such good humor that Rebecca could feel a smile spring, all unwittingly, to her own face.

"Or did you mean that *I* did not scream?" he added, his own smile widening. "Because I should be telling you an enormous farradiddle to say that I did not think to do it. But there, I am courageous if nothing else and stood my ground admirably despite any number of things flying through the air at my head. Not so much as the most minuscule of screeches passed my lips, I assure you, even when the hairbrush hit my stomach. His lordship appeared quite impressed with me for that."

"Oh!"

"No, do not frown. And just when I have got a smile to play about upon your lips, too."

"But William . . . attacked you."

"I should hardly call it that, my lady."

"What would you call it?"

"A mere scuffle at most. And that, I think, because he did not wish any assistance at all. He wished to dress himself by himself, and would have done, too, except that laces at the back of one's breeches are very hard to tie when one is six. And buttons, though they will succumb to one's will, are not always inclined to enter the proper buttonhole. Still in all, I was most careful not to touch him, only the laces and the buttons, and his lordship did an admirable job of the rest. He looks quite the dandy this morning, let me tell you."

"Am I to conclude, Mr. Pope, that you have decided to accept the position permanently?" asked Rebecca, her blue eyes filled with the oddest mixture of hope and despair. "William's actions have not swayed you from your decision? You are not about to call up your horse and ride away from us?"

"Of course not. What sort of a gentleman should I be if I were to do such a thing as that? I came here for the precise purpose of teaching your William, and teach him I will. Do not worry, my lady," Pope added softly, one long-fingered hand reaching toward her across the table, though he was careful not to reach too far. "I have given you my word to stand by the boy and I will."

"But you . . . you did not come by coach and you brought only one portmanteau with you. And there was barely anything at all in it, Buzzerby said."

"Oh, as to that, the rest of my things will arrive upon this doorstep in a fortnight at the very latest. I had not much with me in London. Most of my things must be sent from my father's house at Leeds and so I did make a stop there on the way here but I could not carry a trunk on horseback, you know."

"That is why you came to us from across Marston Moor!"

"Yes. It seemed the most logical thing to ride cross-country from Leeds. I had done it numerous times when I was a fledgling. My horse did never go lame on me then, however, nor was it winter and the night descending. Buzzerby did tell you, did he not, that I am precisely the C. Archibald Pope he thought drowned at sea? I assumed he would do so the first thing this morning."

"You were a very good friend of my late husband's."

"Say rather that Richard was a very good friend to me." His eyes searched her face in the most peculiar way and Rebecca felt her cheeks begin to burn like a schoolgirl's because of it. "What, Mr. Pope?" she queried, moving uneasily in her chair.

"You are not at all the sort of woman I pictured you to be," William's new tutor replied thoughtfully. "No, not at all. Apparently Richard developed a modicum of sense over all the years we spent apart. And now, if you will pardon me, my lady, I expect his lordship has quite finished with his breakfast and is waiting upon me to begin his lessons."

Richard? Rebecca thought as she watched Pope rise and leave the room. Richard did never suffer any gentleman to call him by his given name. And to say that Richard developed a modicum of sense? What on earth did Mr. Pope mean by that?

Pope took one determined step from the corridor into the schoolroom and halted.

Lord Wraithstone ceased to spin the globe behind which he stood and stared up at the gentleman.

Pope took a second step.

Lord Wraithstone glared and held his ground.

Pope took a third step.

Lord Wraithstone rocked from heel to toe to heel to toe.

Pope took a fourth step and little Lord Wraithstone's courage betrayed him. He spun about, bolted across the entire length of the room, dodged into the nursery and slammed the door with great vehemence behind him.

"I am aware," whispered Pope to the empty schoolroom, "that I have bitten off a great deal more than I can chew, Richard, but I shall persist in nibbling away at it until it is a more manageable size. I promise you." Whereupon, he crossed the room himself, opened the door that had been slammed against him and stepped into the nursery. "No, do not go under the bed again, sir," he ordered just as the soles of Lord Wraithstone's shoes disappeared from sight under that particular piece of furniture. "Truly, you are far too old to be hiding away beneath your bed every time you wish to avoid things, my lord. Such a peculiar method of coping will not do at all. I did not harm you this morning, did I? And I have not the least intention to harm you now, you rascal. Do be brave, William. I will lay you odds that your papa did never hide away under that bed. No, not your papa. Why, he was as brave as he could stare."

A tiny mutter emerged from somewhere near the far end of the bedstead and Pope shook his head in mock despair. "William," he declared quietly, "I know that you can speak, and quite properly too. Your mama wrote to me that you were accustomed to chatter away from morning till night, without the least inhibition, to anyone who would listen to you."

Only a grunt reached Pope's ears in reply.

"You cannot go through the remainder of your life, my lord, without speaking to a single person. Believe me. I once attempted the thing and it doesn't work. Try as I might to keep my silence, there was always something that demanded to be said to someone. Do come out now, eh? Say 'yes,' William."

"Rmmmph."

" 'Rmmmph' is not 'yes.' It is not so much as an acceptable word as far as I know."

"Rmmmph."

Pope grinned. He could not help himself. "You are the most outrageous rapscallion, Lord Wraithstone. Even more outrageous than your papa. Do you not think so, Throckmorton?"

"Ding, ding, dingle-de-ding," answered the pocket watch as Pope opened it.

"There, you see, even Throckmorton thinks that you are outrageous."

The slight murmur of knees whisking across carpeting was heard from beneath the bedstead.

"Like to hear Throckmorton talk, do you? Well, come out then, and you and he shall have a bit of conversation. You need not bother about me, either one of you. I shall just sit down here upon this stool and concern myself with lofty thoughts and righteous ideas while the two of you do whatever it is you wish to do." Whereupon, Pope set the watch on the washstand and took a seat upon the stool which was so very low to the floor that his knees came near up around his ears.

William appeared bit by bit from beneath the bedstead. He checked most carefully to see that Pope was indeed sitting upon the stool. He located the watch upon the washstand, then glanced back to see that Pope had not moved. Taking an enormous breath for one so tiny, the boy scurried out into the open, seized Throckmorton, and dashed back under the bed.

Pope watched from beneath lowered eyelids but moved not an inch and said not a word. For two hours and more, he sat upon the little stool and listened to his watch chime melodies and Lord Wraithstone grunt and hum and mutter incomprehensible syllables whenever the boy deemed it his turn to uphold the conversation.

"I cannot think, Mr. Pope, what benefit lies in sitting beside a bed under which my son is hiding," Lady Wraithstone said uneasily as Buzzerby exited the drawing room. "And to sit there for hours on end, doing and saying nothing—"

"Nanny Montcliff has been spying upon us, I take it," Pope responded, accepting the cup of tea Rebecca offered him and leaning back against the flowered upholstery of the sofa upon which he had seated himself. "Never trust a nanny, I say, if you have business with her charge. A jealous lot they are."

"Nanny Montcliff was not spying upon you. She simply

stepped into the nursery to . . . to . . . Well, she did not actually say why she stepped into the nursery. But she did say that she discovered you upon the stool and heard William mumbling to himself under the bedstead and that you both remained so for hours. She continued to peek in at you, you see."

"I was pondering William, nothing more, my lady. He is a bit of a puzzle, your son, and demands some contemplation."

Rebecca staved off a sigh and ignored the nervous pain once again blossoming in her stomach. William was more than a bit of a puzzle; he had become the Gordian Knot of late, defying all attempts to untie him. She raised her teacup to her lips and sipped daintily, wondering all the while what she could say to this gentleman that she had not already written to him in her letters. "You are . . . you are not among the general run of tutors, are you?" she blurted out. "You are the son of an earl, Buzzerby tells me, and—"

"The seventh son of an earl," clarified Pope. "An odd son driven to prove himself capable of independence. Though some may frown upon my seeking a position anywhere but with the military or the church, still, tutoring is not so despicable as shopkeeping or actually working with one's hands, is it? I might have become a secretary to one of the more powerful lords and not an eyebrow would have tilted at it, you know. But I would not make a good secretary. I will make an excellent tutor. It is because of you that such a position occurred to me."

"Because of me? When . . . when was it that you decided to become a tutor, Mr. Pope?"

"Oh, about the time that I noted your fifth advertisement for a tutor in the *Times,* I should say."

Rebecca lowered her teacup and stared at him, her brow furrowed with sudden suspicion. "Do you mean to say, sir, that William is your very first pupil? Mr. Pope, you led me to believe—"

"Yes, I know precisely what I led you to believe, Lady Wraithstone. I led you to believe that I was a tutor who could perform miracles. I deduced from the frequency of your advertisements, you see, that you required precisely such a gentleman."

"But you are *not* a tutor at all?" The teacup tilted precariously in her ladyship's hand. Pope stood hastily and reached across the table that separated them to keep it from spilling its contents onto the carpet.

"Thank you, Mr. Pope," Rebecca whispered hoarsely, taken aback at her own inattention. "I was not paying the least heed, I expect. I shall just set it down and—"

"Your hands shake as though you have just spied a perfect horror sitting across from you," observed Pope, taking the cup from her and setting it down himself. "But that cannot possibly be. Me, a horror? Something of which to be frightened? Never. You are not frightened of me, my lady. How could you be? A fellow of such unimposing aspect and humble demeanor? A fellow with such short legs and such a very long nose?"

A smile wavered across Rebecca's face.

"Just so. Much better. No, do not send that smile scurrying away. A lady as lovely as yourself ought always to smile."

"Mr. Pope!"

"I do beg your pardon," said Pope, once again taking a seat upon the sofa.

"As well you ought."

"It is merely that I have not yet adjusted to this thing."

"What thing, Mr. Pope?"

"Being a tutor, my lady, and the very awkward subservience necessarily involved in it. It is a rather precarious subservience at best, is it not? I am the son of an earl; you are a viscountess; and yet, you are my employer and I your employee. But I shall muddle through and get it all properly sorted out. And I assure you, Lady Wraithstone, though this may be my first attempt at tutoring, it is not my first attempt at miracles."

"Truly, Mr. Pope, you are the most unsettling creature."

"Yes, I know, but you will grow accustomed to me. You may even come to like me. Richard did . . . come to like me, I mean."

"The l-letters of reference you forwarded to me," Rebecca began. "If you have never been a tutor, how—"

"Wrote them myself."

"Mr. Pope, how dare you write letters of reference for yourself?"

"Forced to do it. Never been a tutor. Had no one to apply to for a reference. Most expedient thing, really."

"Why did you not just write to me and say that you were a friend of Richard's lately forced to seek a position and wished to apply?"

"Because likely you would not then have offered me the position. You advertised for a tutor; clearly, you wished to hire a tutor; and so, I thought it best to become a tutor."

Pope sipped at his now tepid tea. His eyes sought hers over the rim of the cup . . . clear, honest eyes, Rebecca thought them, despite the manipulation of facts to which he had just admitted.

But he has lied to me! she told herself. *He has admitted that he has lied to me. And am I now to entrust William to a gentleman who . . . who . . . ?*

Rebecca could not think what she ought to do or how she ought to feel. Had it been one of the maids, or the cook, or even the butler who had come to her with false references, she would have dismissed that person upon the instant without the least thought, without the least care. But she found that she could not do likewise with Mr. Pope. No, she could not. Perhaps it was a great foolishness upon her part, but in her heart, Rebecca *wanted* to believe that this most peculiar gentleman before her was a kind and fundamentally honest man possessed of the best intentions. She wanted to believe that he could help William, that he could restore to her the happy, loving child she had once known. She *wished to believe*, heart and soul, that C. Archibald Pope, despite his admitted lack of experience at tutoring, despite his mild deception to gain entrance to her household, despite his odd demeanor, *could* perform miracles.

Four

"And with whom ought I to eat my dinner, Buzzerby?" asked Pope with a hint of a boyish smile. "Certainly not with her ladyship. Will you force me to eat in the nursery with his lordship? Or alone in my chamber? For the entire time that I remain? It could be years, you know. I should like another slice of that beef, by the way, if you would be so kind."

"I cannot think how you come to present yourself into this household as an employee," muttered Buzzerby, cutting the gentleman another slice of beef.

"He is his lordship's tutor," offered the housekeeper as she passed the beef down the table to Pope. "Certainly he is welcome at our table, Horace. He cannot be expected to dine with the lower servants."

"Certainly not," agreed Dorothea, helping herself to another slice of bread and butter. "That would be most exceptional."

Buzzerby glared them both into silence.

"A tutor's lot, I am discovering, is uneasy at best," Pope commented, cutting into the beef. "Apparently tutors do not quite fit in anywhere."

"No, they do not," acknowledged Buzzerby. "And you, Mr. Pope, do not fit in at all. How can you call yourself a tutor?"

"You did agree to call me Mr. Archie, Buzzerby."

"Yes, but—"

"And you, lovely ladies," he added, setting both the housekeeper and her ladyship's maid to blushing girlishly, "you must call me Mr. Archie as well."

"You are the son of an earl," declared Buzzerby in a clearly disapproving tone.

"Yes, but a most inconsequential son, I assure you. Besides, Buzzerby, I am not come here as a guest, you know. I am come here to earn a salary."

"Bah! You are come here for some reason, but to earn a salary is not that reason."

"Just so. You are correct," acknowledged Pope. "You see through me as you always did, Buzzerby. It is not to earn a salary that I have come. I have come to help his little lordship to make his way back into the world. I have promised myself to do so. But I am not averse to earning a salary, Buzzerby. I have my own way to make in the world. A seventh son cannot be dependent upon others for his livelihood or he is like to starve one day."

"You will be with us for years," murmured the housekeeper sadly. "His lordship's case is most dire. Not one of the physicians or surgeons her ladyship has called upon can think how to help the lad. The boy has run mad, they say, and must be locked away for his own good and his mama's as well."

"Do not say so," protested Dorothea. "Oh, Martha, do not say so. I cannot bear to hear it said aloud. Certainly something can be done. Something *must* be done. Every day he grows more distant. Every day another piece of her ladyship's heart is cut away. She will die if this illness does not part from his lordship soon."

The three upper servants grew still at the thought and three pairs of eyes gazed despairingly at Pope.

"What dour pusses," Pope declared, glancing from one to the other of them in turn. "Have you no faith? Has hope deserted this entire household? Where has your courage gone, to give up on such a small boy so easily? Lord Wraithstone will be well by Christmas. I give you my word upon it. Now, Buzzerby, indulge me in another slice of that beef. I shall need to be well-fed if I am to attack this problem with all the power at my command."

* * *

"All the power at my command," muttered Pope as he checked Feather's fetlock, approved the poultice, and reached up to pat the mare's neck. "What a thing for me to say, Feather. Just as if I had some power at my command. Still, their eyes did light up when that phrase tumbled from between my lips. Hope filled their souls again on the instant. I could see it alighting there. And hope is a very good thing to have, ain't it? A damnably good thing. Only think what straits we should have been in if I had given up hope while crossing the moor, Feather, eh? Statues of ice, you and I would be at this very moment. Yes, and that wretched cat and her kittens equally frozen, though forever quite overlooked inside that tree as they were. We should none of us have reached safety without a good helping of hope and an equal portion of persistence."

Feather nickered softly and nuzzled at his shoulder until he took her muzzle into both hands and gave it a thorough rubbing.

"And I have put my word on the line, too, Feather," he said, resting his forehead against the blaze that marked her face. "I have said that Lord Wraithstone will be well by Christmas. A fool thing to say, because it gives us so little time, and if I do not succeed, they may lose hope again and sink even further into despair. And when Lady Wraithstone notices that they do, she may lose heart as well. Bah! So what if I did say by Christmas? Christmas is a good three weeks away. Plenty of time to discover what must be done. I shall just set my mind to it, though you will need to assist me, my girl. You and Mrs. Oakwood and her cache of kittens. All of us must put our hearts and our souls into making the boy well again, Feather, and that's a fact."

Rebecca mounted the staircase to the second floor, stood debating for a moment, then mounted to the third floor and let herself into the nursery. William was already a tiny lump beneath the bedclothes. She noted with dismay that his eyes were squinched tightly closed. *He is pretending to sleep,* she thought, *so that he need not deal with me. Why? Why?*

Instinctively, her hand reached out to smooth the golden curls from his brow, but she brought it back at once. "My sweetest William," she whispered. "I love you with all my heart. Why will you not let me so much as touch you?"

The child curled himself into the tiniest ball he could and squinched his eyes more tightly closed. Rebecca's breath came in short little gasps to see it. She turned away and walked with measured steps from the nursery, back along the corridor and down the staircase. She made not one sound until she was safe in her own chambers, where she gasped once as though an arrow had pierced her heart and then sat down upon the edge of the small settee in the sitting room and buried her face in her hands. But she did not cry. She told herself over and over that she would not cry. She had cried for far too long and it had done nothing to improve the situation. After a bit, she rose and rang for Dorothea to help her into her nightrail.

"Do help me out of this confounded dress, Dorothea," she muttered when her maid appeared. "I am at wit's end with the wearing of it. It is so heavy and dark and depressing."

"Just so, my lady," replied Dorothea, following Lady Wraith-stone into the adjoining dressing room. In a matter of moments the tabs were undone and Lady Wraithstone was stepping out of the offending dress and out of the shift she wore beneath it and Dorothea was helping her into her flannel nightgown and then into her robe. Her ladyship sat before the tiny vanity and allowed the maid to take the pins from her hair and brush out the long blonde tresses. "That is enough, Dorothea."

"But, my lady."

"I do not wish to have my hair plaited tonight. I cannot think why, but the mere thought of it appalls me."

"Yes, my lady."

"You may go now."

"Yes, my lady." But Dorothea did not perform her usual curtsy nor take one step toward the doorway.

"What is it?" asked Rebecca, gazing at her maid's reflection in the looking glass.

"It is . . . it is . . . him, my lady."

"Him?"

"Mr. Archie, my lady."

"Mr. Archie? Mr. Pope, do you mean? You call him Mr. Archie, Dorothea?"

"He expressly requested us to do so at dinner this evening. Oh, madam, he is the one!"

Rebecca studied Dorothea's drab countenance in the looking glass and discovered something she did never think, after so many years, to see there . . . a softening of the face, a flush of excitement, a particular glow about the eyes.

"He is the one? The *one,* Dorothea? Oh, do not say that you are enamored of Mr. Pope?"

"Enamored? Oh my goodness, no, my lady. I should never think to . . . Mr. Archie is the one who will bring Master William back to us, is what I mean, my lady. I know it to be true. There is something about that gentleman. You must put your faith in him, my lady, and all will be well," Dorothea said in a rush. And then, fearing that she had overstepped her bounds by saying a good deal more than she had ever said to Lady Wraithstone in all the years that she had served her, she raised one hand to her lips, curtsied abruptly, and exited the chamber.

Pope had opened the door between his bedchamber and the nursery and called in a whisper to William. Now, sitting upon the edge of his bed, he watched as William in a nightshirt, nightcap and slippers stood in the open doorway, eyes round with amazement.

"They are magic, you know," Pope said quietly as one by one Mrs. Oakwood carried her kittens from the clothes press to the middle of the bedstead. "A regular cache of magical kittens, they are. Their mama is magic, too. Saved my life on the moor, the lot of them. Kept me from falling asleep and freezing to death. I do hope," he added as Mrs. Oakwood set the last of the kittens into the nest she had kneaded for them in the middle of Pope's quilts, "that you do not intend for all of us to spend the entire night together, Mrs. Oakwood, because that will not do at all."

"Mrrph," replied Mrs. Oakwood, peering over her kittens at

Pope and then at William with wide, golden eyes. "Mrrrrrr mrrrph brrrphst."

"Oh. Well, that will be quite all right then," nodded Pope. "If it is merely for a bit of an outing. May I say, Mrs. Oakwood, that you are looking much more the thing this evening?"

"Mrrgle frrstz."

"I am? Well, I thank you for the compliment. May I introduce William, Lord Wraithstone, madam? You will come to like William, I assure you." Pope grinned as little Lord Wraithstone wiggled with excitement and took three careful steps into the room. "Do come closer, rascal, and make Mrs. Oakwood's acquaintance. Yes, and the acquaintance of this litter of reprobates she has given birth to as well. Only see how rambunctious they are. Uh-oh, there goes one over the edge."

Pope snatched at the wandering kitten, seized it before it tumbled to the floor and held it up before him. Its little kitten feet scrambled at the air as he rubbed its nose against his own. "I am hoping that one of them has the magic to make my nose shrink a bit," he smiled at Lord Wraithstone. "Should you like to hold this fine fellow, William? Apparently, he is not a nose kitten. Perhaps his magic is intended for you."

The boy shook his head adamantly and stepped away.

"Well, perhaps another time. Do not run off. We shan't force you to touch them if you do not wish it, shall we, Mrs. Oakwood?"

"Mrrphst mrrrr."

"No, of course not. Mrs. Oakwood says that you must just do as you like in the matter, my lord. But you may watch them play until she tucks them away for the night, may he not, my dear?"

"Brrrrr-murrgle."

"Exactly so. Until their bedtime."

Little Lord Wraithstone dashed back into his own bedchamber and returned at once with his three-legged stool. He placed it carefully at the foot of the bed, stepped up onto it and stood holding to the bedpost with both hands, staring down at the cat and kittens. There he remained, silent, wide-eyed and happy as a lark for a full hour before Mrs. Oakwood decided it was time to carry her kittens back to the clothes press.

"What the devil am I going to do?" Pope whispered as he returned from seeing William safe into his bed and collapsed into the chair before the fire. "How am I to rescue such a tiny boy from whatever ghosts haunt him if he will not speak to me about them? If he will not speak at all?"

"Mrrrow," offered Mrs. Oakwood, leaping up onto his lap and settling comfortably there.

"You and the kittens have won a place in his heart, my dear. I could see that from the very start."

"Brrrrrrrr," replied Mrs. Oakwood cozily.

"But how the deuce am I to win a place in his heart so that he will speak to me and tell me what it is that he fears so? I have promised to make him well by Christmas, Mrs. Oakwood. Given my word. And Christmas is merely three weeks away."

"Mrrrow-muffle mrphst!"

"Well, but I must do it by Christmas. Whatever ghosts haunt the boy, I must banish them by then or Richard's lady and her son will have the most dismal holiday. And I find that I wish above all things for their holiday to be bright and shining and filled with joy. She is the most deucedly alluring female, Mrs. Oakwood. However did Richard come to marry such a deucedly alluring female—so gentle and stoic and strong? I should have thought Richard bound for the altar with the most outrageous, dreadful little hoyden he could find."

"Do cease screeching and tugging upon the knob, William. You shall not have your way in everything—not without making decided concessions at the least," declared Pope a full three mornings later. "We shall make no progress at all if you persist in hiding under your bed each time I ask you to do something that you do not wish to do, you know. That is precisely why I locked the door up tight from the other side," he explained, leaning comfortably against the only other door that gave exit from the schoolroom. "If you wish to hide beneath your bed-stead now, you must come directly here and say as much."

The little boy turned to glare at him.

"Just so," nodded Pope. "You must only stand before me and say, 'Mr. Archie, I wish to hide under my bed now,' and the door to your nursery will open like magic."

William turned back and gave the door to his nursery three more tugs and a kick, then faced Pope again and shifted from one foot to the other, doing a tiny jig of his own making.

Pope folded his arms across his chest and rested his shoulders against the solid oak of the door. At least the lad was giving the matter some consideration, he thought. That was a step in the right direction. And then the door against which Pope leaned opened and he tumbled backward out into the corridor.

"What are you doing to my boy?" cried Nanny Montcliff, sidestepping Pope's flailing arms and falling body, then glowering down at him as he thumped down upon the floor. "How dare you to make his lordship scream so? You are an unfeeling brute!" And with that, she stepped over Pope and into the schoolroom. "What has that cruel gentleman done to you, my dearest?" she crooned, crossing to William. "Well, whatever he has done, he will not do it ever again. I shall see to that m'self. What is it you wish, Master William? To go into your nursery? And that horrid person has locked the door, has he? Well, Nanny has keys, my darling. Nanny has her own set of keys. Wait just a moment, dearest."

"Do not you dare open that door!" growled Pope, hurriedly gaining his feet and rapidly closing the distance between them. "I will open it when I am ready and not before."

"Bosh. He is an infant and he wants his room. What can it hurt to give the poor child what makes him happiest?"

"If you open that door," Pope threatened, coming to a halt barely inches from the woman, "I shall cut off your head and serve it with hummingbird tongues for dinner!"

Lord Wraithstone gazed up at Pope from beside his nanny in something approaching wonder.

"How dare you to threaten me!" protested the nanny, though she read correctly the anger in the gentleman's eyes and edged away from the nursery door. "I will tell her ladyship. I will have you dismissed."

"Fine. Run off and tell her," urged Pope. "But do it now. And close the hall door as you leave."

Nanny Montcliff did precisely that, slamming the door with such vehemence that, for an instant, everything in the room appeared to shake. One of the globes actually crashed to the floor. William stood and stared up at Pope, his mouth open wide.

"You do not want to see your nanny's head served at table with hummingbird tongues, eh, William? I, for one, do not blame you a bit. Such a sight would ruin my appetite for a month."

A grin flickered across little Lord Wraithstone's face.

"Oh my," Pope whispered. "Have you inherited your papa's sense of the absurd, then? How he and I were accustomed to laugh at the most dreadful things. Only think of it, William. In comes Buzzerby at the front of the dinner parade carrying a great silver platter. Off comes the cover and there, surrounded by hummingbird tongues—"

A sound slipped into the space between the two. It was merely a giggle, tiny, soft and gone in a moment, but Pope thought it the most pleasant sound to reach his ears in decades.

"So. I thought there must be something of your papa in you. I will bet you are fond of horses as well. Your papa was always very fond of horses."

Lord Wraithstone smiled widely and nodded.

"Well then, would you like to walk out with me to the stable, my lord, and meet my mare? Feather will be overjoyed to make your acquaintance at last. I have told her ever so much about you. That is my mare's name, Feather, and she is most fond of young gentlemen—as long as they do not screech in her ears. You will not screech in Feather's ears, will you?"

Lord Wraithstone shook his head most seriously from one side to the other.

"No, of course you will not. What a gudgeon I am to even think of it. But you must put on your coat and hat and gloves and even a muffler, I expect, because it is cold outside. Do you know where they are, your outside clothes?"

Lord Wraithstone nodded and pushed at the door to the nursery. Pope searched in his pocket for the key and opened the lock. He thoroughly prepared himself for the sight of William dodging past him and scurrying under the bed, but in his heart a hope that it would not be so fluttered into being.

Lord Wraithstone dodged under Pope's arm just then, and scuttled across the carpeting—but not under the bedstead. No, he did not. He skipped to the armoire and tugged both doors open to reveal to Pope, with considerable enthusiasm, precisely where his outdoor clothing hid.

Five

"I cannot understand, Mr. Pope, why you should attempt to help William by frightening him all the more." Rebecca paced the length of the sunroom, her hands gripping each other tightly behind her back, her head bowed. "He is a child. He struggles with some horrid illness that not one of the physicians or surgeons I have consulted dares to put a name to, and yet you think it your duty to upset him more by locking him out of his nursery. And, when his nanny comes to his aid, you threaten her life right in front of him. What is wrong with you, sir, to do such things?"

Pope, who stood respectfully before the sunroom windows, shoved his hands into his pockets and noted how the dark green velvet of Lady Wraithstone's gown whispered around her with each step she took. It was, he thought, the most respectable and yet most enticing gown he had ever seen. It actually had a waist where the waist should be, and long, close-fitting sleeves, and cream-colored lace decorating cuffs and collar and ranging down the bodice in a soft, quiet V. Above it, her hair glowed like a golden halo around her pleasant, though presently scowling, face.

"Have you nothing at all to say for yourself, Mr. Pope?" Rebecca asked, coming to a halt directly before him. Truly, she hoped he did have something to say for himself. Something perfectly intelligent and defensible. How long had he been at Wyndhover? Four days? So short a time? Yet it felt to her as if she had known this decidedly odd little gentleman forever, and she had not the least wish to send him away.

Please say something, she thought as her eyes met his. *Oh, please! Tell me I am not mistaken in you.*

"Well, Mr. Pope?"

"There is not much to say, my lady. Merely that after his nanny left us, his lordship and I decided to go to the stable so that he might make Feather's acquaintance," he said quietly. "He allowed me to hold his coat so he might slip into it more easily, and to tie his muffler. He put his own hat and gloves on. Missed a few fingers in his gloves, but I could not argue that that was of any great consequence, so we merely observed the fact then chose to ignore it. After he and Feather had thoroughly studied each other, we strolled off across the park, your son and I, and stomped about in a pile of leaves that your gardener was kind enough to gather together for us."

"William went outside with you, Mr. Pope?" Such a clear glint of hope rose into her eyes that Pope was forced to smile. "He played in the fallen leaves?"

"Yes, my lady."

"Then all that Nanny Montcliff related to me about your confrontation in the schoolroom was untrue?"

"Well, no, his lordship and I were involved in a minor battle. And when she chose to take his side and thus undermine what little authority I have so far gained, I am afraid that I lost my temper. She did not tell you that I threatened to behead her and serve her head at dinner with hummingbird tongues, eh?"

"Mr. Pope!"

"I did not actually intend to do it, of course."

"Of course not."

"No, but I did hurt her feelings. I know that I did."

"She wishes me to dismiss you, Mr. Pope. At once. It is her view that you have already—in so short a time as you have been here—done William great injury."

"I see. And do you generally take Nanny Montcliff's advice in all matters concerning your son?" He studied her up and down in the most audacious manner. "No," he said then, "you do not."

Rebecca knew that she ought to be perturbed with him for studying her so boldly, ought to be righteously angry at his callous treatment of Nanny Montcliff, but she could not be anything of the sort because— "William accompanied you outside to play? Willingly?"

Pope nodded. Only once. But in that single nod Rebecca read a self-confidence that sent goose bumps of expectation up and down her arms. She thought to herself that here before her— with the sun at his back bestowing a particular brilliance upon his dark curls and emphasizing a heretofore unnoticed sturdiness in his slight stature—here before her—hidden behind his admittedly long nose and beneath his well-worn jacket of rust and his old buff breeches—here before her stood the only man in all of England capable of saving her son.

"He would not take my hand," said Pope, the very tone of his voice filling her imagination with visions of some secret power he kept hidden within his breast. "He did not pet my horse or ask to sit upon her. But he did smile to see how Feather nibbled at my ear and he did laugh when he jumped into the leaves. And he ran about the park like an imprisoned fawn set free."

Buzzerby was highly disturbed. Lady Wraithstone could tell as much simply from the manner in which the tips of that kindly old butler's ears were turning red as he stood stiffly before her in the drawing room that evening.

"I have discussed the situation with them both, and I have decided, Buzzerby, that John shall drive Nanny Montcliff into York to spend Christmas with her sister."

"She is crying in the kitchen, my lady."

"I have told her that she is not dismissed, that she shall return to us after Christmas, but she will not be consoled."

"No, my lady." Buzzerby's back straightened even more—a feat Lady Wraithstone would have thought impossible.

"John is to drive her directly to her sister's door, and you are to give her a bonus of sorts, Buzzerby, so that she will have some pin money about her. And from now on, his lordship shall be solely in Mr. Pope's charge. You will make the staff aware of that. They are not to interfere in anything that Mr. Pope attempts to do with William."

"Yes, my lady."

"You think I am wrong to send Nanny Montcliff off?" Rebecca's hands played with the arms of the chair upon which she sat. Her neck was getting a definite kink in it from looking up at Buzzerby, but he would not sit down in her presence. It was not done, and Buzzerby never did what was not done. "You must tell me the truth, Buzzerby. You *know* Mr. C. Archibald Pope. Do you think me mad to set him over my son without Nanny Montcliff to keep her eyes upon them?"

"No, my lady."

"No. Then why do you look at me with such an odd expression upon your face, Buzzerby? Speak up, for now is the time to say what you think upon the subject. I am inviting your opinion."

Buzzerby lowered his chin the slightest bit. He nibbled at the inside of his lower lip. He shuffled his feet and rearranged the hands he held behind his back. "Mr. Archie is not a nanny, my lady. There is a good deal to be done, looking after a little one, and Mr. Archie cannot possibly realize. The boy must be bathed and dressed and fed and—"

"Yes, yes," interrupted her ladyship impatiently. "But Mr. Pope desires to hold all authority over his lordship for a time. If there is anything that William requires, Mr. Pope wishes to be the person to provide it. We shall all of us help him if he requests it, of course. All he need do is ask and we shall come to his aid."

"But it does seem odd to dismiss Mrs. Montcliff when she might easily provide any assistance that Mr. Archie requires."

Rebecca nodded. "Just so. But Nanny Montcliff is jealous of William and has set herself against allowing Mr. Pope the least power over the boy. She cannot bear to have him near William, Buzzerby. She will be more of a hindrance than a help, he says, and I believe him."

"Yes, my lady."

"What I am saying . . . what I wish for you to tell me, Buzzerby . . . Can . . . Is . . . Ought I to give Mr. Pope such authority over my son? You *know* him, Buzzerby."

Buzzerby took a step backward. His hands came loose from behind him and swooped up to wring each other before his slightly protruding stomach. His brown eyes blinked and blinked again and his lips parted, but no sound emerged from between them.

"Buzzerby? What is it? Is there something about Mr. Pope that you think I ought to know?"

"It is merely that . . . that . . . Mr. Archie was always a most unpredictable young gentleman, my lady."

"Unpredictable?"

"He is. . . . One never knew, my lady, what to expect of him."

"Do you mean to say that he is not dependable?"

"No, no, I do not mean to say that. Our late Lord Wraithstone was accustomed to depend upon Mr. Archie in everything, my lady. The grandest of friends they were. Mr. Archie did spend all of his summers here from the time of the . . . incident . . . at Harrow until he went off to university."

"What incident, Buzzerby?"

"Well, it was most bizarre, my lady. Most bizarre. And one cannot . . . that is to say . . . I cannot be certain, you know, that Mr. Archie had the least thing to do with the incident, but—"

"What incident, Buzzerby?" Rebecca asked again.

"The . . . the blowing up of the headmaster's bed, my lady. Gunpowder. Blew the mattress clear up to the ceiling. Stuck there, too, it did. At least, his lordship said it did. Stuck there for a good hour and more. Had to climb up and pry it down, the boys did. Covered in honey, the whole of it."

"And Mr. Pope was blamed for it?" queried Rebecca.

"Indeed, my lady. All fingers pointed in Mr. Archie's direction, so to speak. Sent down for it, Mr. Archie was, and invited never to show his face at Harrow again. Invited never to show his face at home again, either, when his mama and papa learned of it. They relented, of course, though Harrow did not."

"Well, well," coughed Rebecca, covering a giggle that escaped her. "I do see what you mean by bizarre, Buzzerby. But certainly Mr. Pope has outgrown such tendencies by now. How odd that I should never once have met Mr. Pope. I should think that Lord Wraithstone might have mentioned the gentleman to me, that Mr. Pope might at least have come to call upon us."

"His lordship thought Mr. Pope deceased by then, my lady."

"What? So long ago? Before we were married?"

"A full year before. Held a funeral for the lad, his family did, though there was no body to be had. Of course there cannot have been a body, for he is here among us, is he not?"

"He is definitely here among us, Buzzerby."

"Just so. And not so much as a word has he said about where he has been for the past nine years. Merely, 'How do you do, Buzzerby. Pleased to see you again' as if we had seen each other only last summer, my lady. That is why!" exclaimed the elderly butler abruptly with a quick snap of his fingers.

"Pardon me, Buzzerby?"

"Oh, I do beg your pardon, my lady. But it did just now occur to me. That will be why Mr. Archie came to us from across the moor. He rode first to Severn Hall at Leeds to inform his family that he has risen from the dead."

"Risen from the—"

"Merely a manner of speech, my lady. Of course, he could not have done. People do not, you know."

"No, of course they do not." Lady Wraithstone was close to laughing aloud, and indeed was forced to cover her mouth with one hand to avoid doing so. How startled Buzzerby must have been to see this particular gentleman arrive. And Mr. Pope, so pale and ragged and wet, coming off the moor looking quite like the ghost of the drowned gentleman Buzzerby thought him to be. And then, Buzzerby introducing him as though there were nothing at all exceptional about him—wondering all the while whether the gentleman was truly human or a ghost! And then Rebecca did laugh. She waved Buzzerby from the room, leaned back in her chair and laughed loud and long, laughed as she had not done since the death of her husband and the subsequent illness of her son.

"Mrrow," Mrs. Oakwood greeted as Pope, having tucked Lord Wraithstone into bed, arrived at his own chambers. "Mrrrr mwow," she said, sticking her gray-striped head up from the drawer, ears perked in expectation.

"Mrrr mwow, yourself, m'dear," Pope replied, untying his cravat and tossing it negligently upon the top of the clothes press. "I am worn to the bone with the charge of but one rap-scallion, and there you sit entertaining six of them. I cannot imagine where you find the patience to do it."

"Mrrrph mwow mrrrrrr," Mrs. Oakwood responded quite happily, hopping from the drawer to rub against Pope's legs. "Mrrrr brrrphst."

"Yes, I know they are *all* willful and energetic, but William is a particularly difficult kitten. And puzzling. Though the answer is most likely right beneath my nose."

"Rrrrrrow mrrrphlfst."

"Yes," Pope laughed, "I do realize that to be right beneath a nose like mine is not to be so very close as it might sound. There is a reason for William's aversion to being touched and touching, and it cannot be a very complicated one. The boy is merely six, after all. How complicated can a six-year-old's mind be, do you think?" Pope unbuttoned his old rust-colored coat, pulled the wing-backed chair before the fire and settled down into it with a grateful sigh. "Well, Buzzerby will be happy at least," he told the mother cat as she leaped up to settle in his lap. "So long as I am in charge of William, I need not sit down to dinner with the upper servants. He will see that my dinner arrives upon the tray with William's every evening, I think. Oh, yes," he murmured, leaning back to search in his coat pocket with one hand. "I have saved you something to munch upon, my dear. Yes, here it is." And with long, slim fingers, Pope opened up his knotted handkerchief and began to pull a lamb chop into pieces, offering them to the cat one by one.

He smiled as he watched her eat. He had always been fond of cats, though his brothers had persecuted him mercilessly for such an utterly female tendency. "Female tendency. Ha!" he said aloud, causing Mrs. Oakwood to stare up at him questioningly.

"Nothing, my dear. It is nothing. I am merely commenting upon the fact that gentlemen are meant to despise cats. You did not know that, did you? No, of course you did not. Well, but it is true. Gentlemen may be fond of hounds and horses, it seems, but felines such as yourself, Mrs. Oakwood, must be most studiously avoided."

"Mrrrrrr."

"Just so. A most unfounded prejudice. But not to fear. I am fond of cats nonetheless. And hounds and horses as well. And hares. And hedgehogs. By Jove, I am fond of everything that is capable of looking at me with wide-eyed innocence. I suspect that is why I am fond of William and his mama, do not you?"

"Mrrrph brrrrr mrrrow."

"Here, have another bite and then I shall fetch the pitcher from the washstand and pour you some fresh water to wash it down, eh? The thing of it is, Mrs. Oakwood, that I find myself inclined to grow very fond of William and his mama. I came to help them for Richard's sake, because we did promise each other that we would always help each other out, no matter what. And I did expect to discover something of Richard in the boy and therefore to like the lad. But I did never think to develop a fondness for Lady Wraithstone. I thought she would be . . . well, someone other than what she is."

"Rrrrrrr mrrrrow mrrrrfpgle?"

"Well, but I was not only very far away. Richard thought me dead. I did tell you that. He would have come directly to my aid else. I am convinced of it."

"Mrrrph mrrrphgle."

"Yes. He was just that sort of fellow. And therefore, I am obliged to do all I can, you see, for the boy and for . . . Rebecca. By Jove, but Richard's lady is a veritable temptress, Mrs. Oakwood."

"Mrphgle?"

"No, no, not in that way. It is merely that she is . . . she is so fine a woman. I need merely glance into her eyes and. . . . Well, she is not some peagoose fluttering mindlessly about, you see. No, nor some spoilt beauty intent upon her own pleasure. She is gentle and intelligent. You need only look into her eyes, Mrs. Oakwood, to see the sort of woman she is. I vow, Richard must have drowned himself in the sheer beauty of those eyes. I would be delighted to drown in them myself. Well, I would, if I had not gone and developed such an aversion to drowning."

Six

Invited by Mr. Pope to do so, and with such a pleading look in his eyes at the time, Rebecca began to rise early each morning in order to break her fast with her son and his tutor at the little table in the schoolroom at the ghastly hour of seven. She developed the habit of dropping in on them at odd moments during the day to watch Mr. Pope draw the letters of the alphabet for William to copy, listen to Mr. Pope read, watch him and her son spin tops, make toy swords from sticks and hold mock fencing matches. And whenever Mr. Pope laughingly begged her, she would sit down at the pianoforte, which he had contrived to get carried up to the schoolroom, and play the jolliest songs she could remember so that William and Mr. Pope might hop, skip and prance about the schoolroom pretending to dance. She sat with her son for hours on the schoolroom floor watching Mrs. Oakwood and her kittens play, accompanied Mr. Pope and William on walks about the park and went with them at least fifty times to see Feather in the stable. She would giggle as girlishly as she had ever done when the mare invariably nibbled at Mr. Pope's ear, licked his nose and tugged at his pockets in search of a treat. And when one afternoon William giggled right along with her, smiling up at her with the most pleasant of smiles, her heart soared toward heaven.

"I wish to thank you, Mr. Pope," she said one evening, having invited the tutor to join her in the drawing room and provided him with a glass of her late husband's brandy.

"To thank me?" Pope stared into the deep golden liquid as he swirled it slowly in his glass. "I have done nothing, my lady."

"You have given William the joy of his childhood back."

"No. I only get him to taste of it from time to time."

"It is a great deal, Mr. Pope. He is no longer the sullen child who sat and stared from his window and hid away at the first sound of someone approaching. He plays at games again, and he giggles. If you knew how long I have lived without that endearing sound—"

"Yes, but he does not yet say a word. And he will not touch or be touched by anyone or anything. He will not pet Feather, though I can see that he wishes to do so, and he will run to the opposite side of the room, you know, if Mrs. Oakwood or one of the kittens should come too near to him."

"But he will speak, Mr. Pope. You will bring him to do so in time. And he will cease to shrink away from touching Feather and the kittens and then people as well."

"You say it with such confidence."

"Yes, I do. You are a remarkable gentleman, Mr. Pope, and I have come to believe in you with all my heart. You will give me back the son I once knew. I have no doubt of it."

C. Archibald Pope glanced up to meet Rebecca's gloriously happy blue-eyed gaze and wondered how best to extricate himself from the drawing room—the sooner the better.

"What is it, Mr. Pope?" Rebecca asked, detecting a whisper of his uneasiness in his glance. "Is there something you require of me? You need only say and—"

"No, no, nothing, my lady. You are the best of all employers, I am certain."

"But . . . there is something. Come, Mr. Pope, speak the truth. In the past twelve days, sir, you have had sole charge of my William and you have done wondrous things for him. Certainly, if there is anything—anything at all—that I may do for you. . . ."

Pope smiled in the most lopsided fashion. His neckcloth had grown suddenly tight, his brow abruptly hot and his heart pounded against his ribs like a lion caged. "Truly, there is nothing. You are a most remarkable lady."

"Re-remarkable? I am most ordinary, Mr. Pope. So ordinary

that I was especially surprised that Richard should take notice of me in the least. He was so very handsome, my Richard."

"As William will be."

"Oh, yes. And Richard was quite the dandy, too."

"I should like to have seen that—Richard as a dandy."

"You were *very* close friends with my husband?"

Pope shifted uneasily upon the settee. "Very close," he managed as the brandy slipped quietly over the edge of his glass and slithered between his wrist and shirt cuff. "But fate separated us for a very long time," he continued, ignoring the sticky liquid entirely because she had obviously not noticed and he did not wish to bring his awkwardness to her attention. "I was devastated when I returned to England and learned of his death."

"Returned from where, Mr. Pope? Your family and friends thought you drowned, Buzzerby said."

"Yes, well, I was nearly. It was a close thing. The ship I served upon went down with all hands."

"You were a sailor, Mr. Pope?"

"In a manner of speaking."

"In a manner of speaking?" Rebecca studied him with great curiosity. She leaned toward him, causing Pope, most unaccountably, to lean back and attempt to meld himself with the back of the settee. "How does one become a sailor merely in a manner of speaking, Mr. Pope?" she asked, her eyes wide with interest.

"W-well, one has an argument with one's father, storms off to London, purchases a merchant seaman's clothes right off his back so that one may wander the docks and look at the ships without drawing the least attention to oneself and then one gets knocked in the head by a press-gang and tossed aboard one of His Majesty's warships," Pope blurted in a great rush, unable to keep himself from noting how seductively her lips parted, how temptingly her breasts nudged the golden velvet of her bodice, how hot the blasted room had grown.

"Oh, Mr. Pope!"

"What? Oh! Just so. But I did manage to get word to my family of what ship I was on after a month or two." *Oh, dear lord, if she continues to stare at me with just that particular tilt to her*

*chin, I will forget that I am Richard's friend and her employee
and William's tutor and take the woman in my arms and—* "B-but
then the ship went down, you see, and so everyone thought me
dead," Pope gasped out into the space between them.

"Oh, poor Archie! Oh! I did not intend to . . . but William
and the servants, you know, all call you Mr. Archie and I. . . ."

C. Archibald Pope was so discomposed by her use of his
Christian name that he nearly stood up and ran from the room.
He recovered himself, however, and though his brandy glass
scraped across the wood as he set it upon the table and the
flowered settee made the oddest squeak as he pretended to re-
arrange himself upon it, he was nearly certain that she did not
notice his discomposure. "You may c-call me Archie if you
wish. I should be honored by it."

"Then you must call me Rebecca," Lady Wraithstone replied.

"No. No. I c-could not do that. You are the lady of the house
and I merely a tutor."

"No, Archie. You are Richard's best friend come to save my
William. We need pretend no longer that the gap of employee
and employer exists between us. At least, I do not intend to
engage further in that pretense. You are William's savior, Archie,
as you are mine. But you were saying that the ship went down."

"What?"

"The ship. It went down with all hands aboard."

"Oh, the . . . the . . . ship. Yes. But I could swim, and I did.
Swam and floated and swam again for days on end. I was determined not to d-drown. At last, I was rescued by an American
privateer out of New Orleans."

"An American ship?"

"Yes."

"And so you were carried to the colonies?"

"No. Not pre-precisely. She was a slaver, and so I was carried
to the coast of Africa."

"You . . . you participated in the slave trade, Archie?" Rebecca's breath caught in her throat as she said the words. Horror
turned her blue eyes gray. Her teacup rattled against its saucer.
"I cannot believe it! Not you!"

"No! No!" exclaimed Pope hurriedly. "Not made for such.

Not me. Did the most dastardly thing. Freed the wretches in the hold. Helped them to scuttle the ship. Swam for my life. Got stranded in Mozambique."

The astonishment in Rebecca's eyes set Pope's stomach leaping straight up into his throat.

"Mozambique?" she whispered in awe.

"You will not have heard of the place before, I expect. C-Captain Stergeon and his men floated up in Mozambique as well and they were that put out with me, let me tell you," Pope continued, attempting to ignore the perspiration running down the side of his nose as her gaze fixed upon him in utter fascination. "Never was such a game of h-hare and hounds as raged through that city and across the continents and seas then. Followed me everywhere, did C-Captain Stergeon and his crew. Thought they would catch me and kill me in the end. Thought I should die on one foreign shore or one foreign ship or another. Didn't. Took me nine years, but I arrived home safe. If . . . if you will excuse me, Re-rebec . . . ah . . . Lady Wraithstone, I had b-best take myself up to my bed now." Bed? Had he actually *said* bed? Pope's ears turned bright red upon the spot. He stood straight up without the least ceremony and battled with his feet at every step to keep them from actually dashing across the carpet, out into the corridor and up the staircase.

"I wish you were truly magical," Pope mumbled to the kittens as they tumbled about upon his bed while he donned his nightshirt. "Then one of you would have the power to make me tall and another to make me handsome and a third to make me wise. And you," he said, chucking one of the gray-striped ones beneath the chin, "you would make my nose shrink and my investments grow. And you, you rascal," he continued, lifting a black and white spotted kitten into his arms. "You would weave a spell that would make me appear alluring and mysterious to the lady of the house."

"Mrrrrow murrgle phstz," Mrs. Oakwood advised him quite seriously from the foot of the bedstead. "Rrrrrrr mphh murggle."

"Well, I know that, Mrs. Oakwood. It is merely that at times a gentleman has dreams. Gentlemen have as much right to dream as ladies do, do not you think?"

"Mrrrrrph."

"Ah, well, perhaps not. Especially a gentleman like myself who has nothing at all to recommend him. You would have been quite put out with me had you seen the fool I made of myself in the drawing room this evening, Mrs. Oakwood. Quite put out. I behaved absurdly. But Lady Wraithstone—Rebecca—did set such thoughts tearing through my head. Yes, and any number of odd sensations ripping through my body as well."

"Mrrrow?"

"No, I cannot explain it. She just did. And then she called me Archie and gave me leave to call her Rebecca. Well, I could not then, though I wished to do it with all my heart—especially I could not when she began to stare at me as though she were particularly fascinated with my every word. I did attempt to call her Rebecca, but it came out dreadfully odd."

Mrs. Oakwood leaped down from the bedstead to rub around Pope's bare ankles consolingly as he lifted her kittens one and two at a time and carried them back to the clothes press. She jumped up into the drawer once he had placed them all inside and watched him as he solemnly climbed up into his bed and lowered the wick upon his lamp. She set about nursing her brood, but she listened for Pope in the darkness. "Brrrrrrr," she whispered each time she heard him mutter and toss and turn. "Brrrrrr-rrup."

Rebecca no longer thought of him as an odd little man. She could not believe that she had ever done so. "He has survived a shipwreck, scuttled a slaver and freed a galleon full of slaves," she whispered into the night. "He has been to a place called Mozambique. He has sailed upon the sea for nine entire years, eluding villains in every port, and he has arrived back on British soil victorious over all the evil and all the hardships that hounded him upon his way. What stories the gentleman must have, as yet untold. What adventures yet unrevealed! And still he is so humble and so unpretentious that one would never guess he possessed such sagacity, such courage. One would never suspect at first meeting he should prove so very mysterious, so extremely bold. Is it any wonder that Richard loved him?"

No, she smiled to herself, *it is not the least wonder that Richard loved him. Richard would have loved him from the moment the headmaster's bed rose to the ceiling and remained suspended there. And I love him,* she thought. *I have loved C. Archibald Pope from the very moment William giggled in the stable. Oh, how crushed Richard must have been when he believed Archie to be drowned at sea. And how much I rejoice that it was all a mistake and he was not.*

"Archie," she said aloud in the tenderest voice. "Oh, my dearest Richard, what a gift you have sent to us this Christmas! I believe, now, that you are looking down upon William and me from heaven. I know that you are. And I shall never think of your Mr. Pope as an odd little man again, not in any way. I shall no longer think of him as *your* Mr. Pope either. From this moment on, I shall always think of him as *Our Archie*—yours and mine and William's."

For the first time in a very long time, Rebecca, Lady Wraithstone, closed her eyes against the night without the least fear for her son's welfare. Her confidence in C. Archibald Pope as a worker of miracles was complete. If any gentleman in all of England *could* restore William fully to himself, this was the gentleman—a gentleman of imagination, experience, steadfastness, determination, wit and joy. The despair that had nibbled at Rebecca's vitals for so very long rolled right over and died. Even the deep, aching slashes that crisscrossed her heart began to heal. The sweet balm of faith and hope covered them over. That night Rebecca, Lady Wraithstone, wandered into sleep with a smile upon her face and a soul so overwhelmed with trust, expectation and joy that she fairly hovered in her dreams amongst clouds lined with shimmering silver, halfway to heaven.

"Ow!" Pope cried dramatically for a second time the next morning, holding to the arm upon which little Lord Wraithstone had just landed a well-placed hit with the tip of his toy sword.

"I am grievously wounded, my lord. I am certain of it. You are a demon at swordplay!"

Little Lord Wraithstone beamed up at him, aglow with pride, as a veritable herd of kittens pounced around his feet. "A demond!" he declared ecstatically.

Pope's heart fluttered on the instant. The boy had *spoken.* He had actually said two *words.* "Precisely," Pope uttered in as nonchalant a tone as he could manage, not wishing to draw William's attention to the fact that two actual words had slipped from between his lips. "A regular demon."

"A *regular* demond!" William reiterated just as three of the kittens attempted to scramble up his stockings and into his arms. William dropped his toy sword upon the instant, pushed the kittens away, covered his mouth with both hands and ran through the door into his nursery where he crawled hastily under his bed.

Pope dashed after him. "William," he called. "William, what is it? Is it the kittens? Did they hurt you? But they did not intend it. They have sharp little claws and sometimes—"

"Mrrrrow mrrrr mrphle mrrrr," interrupted Mrs. Oakwood in a rush, scrambling full-speed under the bed herself, her kittens tumbling after her as fast as they could go.

And then, in the time it took for one of the kittens to twitch its tail, little Lord Wraithstone began to screech and squeal and cry.

"My gawd, what is it?" cried Pope, descending directly to his stomach and wiggling his way under the bedstead to see his little lordship huddled against the wall beneath the very head of the bedstead, his hands clutched tightly against his little chest and his eyes squinched shut as Mrs. Oakwood and the kittens gathered about him, attempting to rub against him, to climb up into his lap and stand with paws upon his shoulder to scrub away the tears that rolled down his cheeks and dripped from his chin.

"William, my dearest boy, you are not afraid of Mrs. Oakwood and her kittens. They are merely attempting to make you feel better, William."

"Go 'way," shrieked Lord Wraithstone, dropping his hands to shove frantically at the lot of them. "Go 'way! Go 'way!" and he sobbed all the harder as he attempted to free himself from them.

Without any further thought, Pope plucked the kittens from the child, seized Lord Wraithstone by an arm and, wiggling hastily backward, tugged the boy out from under Mrs. Oakwood's hovering nose, out from under the bed and into his own arms. He sat flat upon the floor with the child in his lap and hugged the boy against his chest. "Do not scream anymore, William. Mrs. Oakwood and the kittens will not touch you again if you do not wish it. I promise you they will not. But they are merely kittens, William. They will not hurt you."

"No!" screeched Lord Wraithstone, struggling in Pope's arms. "Do not you touch me, too! Do not!"

But Pope would not let go. He could not bring himself to let the boy go. He held William all the tighter, hugging him against his chest, rocking him. "Hush, rascal," he whispered, his lips moving against the golden curls. "Hush, my dear. I will not hurt you. Mrs. Oakwood and her kittens will not hurt you. No one in this entire house would think to hurt you. We all love you."

"You will be dead!" cried little Lord Wraithstone, his fists beating at Pope's ears and cheeks and chin. "You will all of you be dead!"

"What? We will all be what, William?"

"You w-will b-be dead," sobbed the boy more quietly as his flailing fists ceased to hit quite so hard and his head rested against Pope in exhaustion. "You w-will all b-be dead."

Pope began to croon in the boy's ear, to blow upon William's hot red cheeks, and all the while his own mind grasped at the child's words and sorted through them. "We will be dead?" he asked quietly when the sobbing became more intermittent. "Me, William? Mrs. Oakwood and her kittens? Each and every one of us?"

Lord Wraithstone, all of his energy expended, nodded wearily and buried his wet face, in despair, deep in Pope's neckcloth.

"But why will we be dead? No, do not cry anymore, my dear. You must simply tell me why we will be dead. Do you not like us, William? Do you wish us dead?"

"I l-love you," sobbed the boy. "But I have . . . I have spoked to you. An' I have . . . I have touch-ted you! An' now you will die. Ever' one of you!"

Seven

"William," whispered Pope, his breath rippling the soft, golden hair on the head pressed beneath his chin. "William, my dearest little rapscallion, you have said the worst of what will happen, have you not? Now you must tell me the rest."

"The r-rest?" asked William, wearily, still snuggled tightly in Pope's arms.

"Um-hmmm. You must tell me *why* we are all going to die."

"I saided it."

"Did you? Then you must say it again, my dear, for I fear I did not understand the whole of the thing."

"I spoked to you an' I touch-ted you."

"Yes?"

"An' you kiss-ted me, too. You did."

"Indeed I did. Right on the top of your head, and on your cheek and on your ear, but I do not understand precisely what that has to do with my dying, William, or with Mrs. Oakwood and her kittens dying."

Lord Wraithstone turned the merest bit, put his arms around Pope's neck and whispered in his tutor's ear.

A cold shiver made its way down Pope's spine. "Oh, William," he murmured, his arms tightening even more around the boy. "Oh, my dearest, sweetest William. All this time you thought . . . but it is not true, rascal."

"Uh-huh," sobbed little Lord Wraithstone, his tears flowing once more. "I *did* spoked to my papa. An' I *did* touch-ted him."

"Yes, but . . . you did not kill your papa, William."

"I d-did."

"No. Never. Your papa was gravely ill. It was that vile illness took his life, not you."

"I spoked to him," wailed the boy, clinging desperately to Pope. "I touch-ted him an' then he died! I kill-ded my papa, an' now I have kill-ded you an' Mrs. Oakwood an' her kit-tens."

The child truly believed it. Pope's heart came near to bursting with the compassion that lodged there. C. Archibald Pope came very near to tears himself. He readjusted William upon his lap and snatched the black and white spotted kitten from the floor. "I do beg your pardon, my lord," he said softly, "but is this not one of the kittens that you touched?"

Lord Wraithstone wiped the tears from his eyes, stared at the kitten and nodded.

"Well, unless I miss my guess, William, this kitten is yet very much alive."

"Mrrrrrr," agreed the kitten, batting at William's nose.

"And look here, my boy. Mrs. Oakwood is come to lick away your tears again. She is very much alive as well."

"Brrrrrow," agreed Mrs. Oakwood, leaping into Lord Wraithstone's lap, placing her forepaws upon his shoulder and beginning to scrub at the child's cheek with her rough little tongue.

"And I do not feel the least bit ill, William. We have been sitting here together, you and I, touching each other for a considerable time, yet I am feeling just the thing."

"Y-you are?"

"Indeed. How do you account for that?"

Lord Wraithstone thought most seriously for a long time, wriggling around in Pope's lap until the back of his head rested against Pope's chest. "It is because the kit-tens are mag'cal," he said at last. "Mrs. Oakwood an' her kit-tens. You tolded me so. A catch of mag'cal kit-tens what save-ded your life."

"And me, sir?"

"You are mag'cal, too."

The first footman, who had carried a luncheon tray up to the nursery, came dashing down the stairs as fast as his feet would carry him and whispered in Buzzerby's ear. Buzzerby, his eyes bright with hope, hurried off to inform Lady Wraithstone. Lady Wraithstone abandoned her knitting at once, gathered her skirts about her and climbed the staircase all the way to the third floor. She literally ran down the corridor, her slippered feet sliding, her heavy skirts swishing madly about her ankles. She halted, her face flushed, upon the nursery threshold to discover Pope— just as Buzzerby had said—seated cross-legged upon the floor beside the bed, her son resting contentedly in his arms. C. Archibald Pope was rocking slowly back and forth and whispering into William's ear. Mrs. Oakwood rubbed against them and her smattering of kittens tusseled and tumbled about on the floor.

A glistening of tears rose in Rebecca's eyes and blurred the images before her. She quickly cleared her vision with a swipe of her hand. *Archie is holding William,* she thought. *He is rocking William. My William.*

Just then the tutor shifted the child, freeing one hand, with which he reached out and seized one of the kittens. "Open your eyes, do, William," he said gently, "and hold this wiggly rapscallion for me. Hurry, William, take him. There is another one attempting at this very moment to eat my shoe and yet another threatening at my back. And three more planning something equally naughty amongst them. I can tell from the look in their eyes."

Rebecca watched with apprehension as the kitten was offered to her son. *Will he take it?* she wondered. *Oh, William, my dearest, take the kitten from Archie, do. It will not harm you. Archie would never do anything at all to harm you.*

"Take the kitten, William," instructed Pope. "Hurry. We have watched for hours and it is still not the least bit dead. Not even sickly. Damned rambunctious is what it is."

"Dam-ded rambuckshous," grinned William, turning a bit in Pope's lap to grasp the kitten in both hands. "Mag'cal kitten."

"Just so. Magical. Ow! Cease digging those pinprickers into my back, you rascal," exclaimed Pope, reaching behind him with one hand and attempting to dislodge the bravest of the gray-striped kittens who had begun a climb to his shoulder.

Rebecca's lips curved quietly upward.

"Tarnation, I cannot quite reach him, William, and he is pricking me no end." Pope began to wriggle about in the most amazing manner.

Rebecca's lips curved even farther upward. She stepped into the room and strolled hastily to Archie's aid, scattering kittens about her and brushing William and Pope with her skirts as she leaned down to scoop the kitten from the tutor's back and lift it into her arms.

"Only see what a lovely kitten is this one, William," she said, kneeling down with her prize before her son. "And he is gray with stripes, not at all black and white like that one. Is this kitten magical as well, Archie?"

"William thinks that they are all of them magical. Each and every one. Mrs. Oakwood as well. And me. I am magical, too."

Little Lord Wraithstone gazed questioningly up at Pope, then at his mama.

"I am certain that she is perfectly safe, William," Pope stated with great authority. "Your mama, sir, is holding one of the kittens in her very hands."

"Mama?" whispered Lord Wraithstone cautiously.

"Yes, dearest." Rebecca longed to reach out to her child and pull him from Archie's hug into a hug of her own, but a particular glance from the tutor warned her against it.

"Do not say anything at all for a moment, my lady," Pope cautioned. "We are waiting to see what happens."

"What happens, Archie?"

"Shhhh. Just sit down upon the floor and wait with us."

"Do not let go the kit-ten," added little Lord Wraithstone in a tiny voice. "Do not, Mama."

"No, no, I will not," Rebecca responded, her skirt creasing around her as she arranged herself upon the carpeting and set the kitten to play in her lap. In a matter of moments, four more kittens had hopped up to roll on the velvet of her dress as well, reveling in feel of the material.

She looked such a vision, seated there in a wide beam of sunlight, her hair beneath a fine lace cap glittering gold, her eyes bright with unshed tears, the soft folds of her dress flowing smoothly over her fine figure. Pope thought for a moment that he might well reach over and tug the mother into his arms as he had the son. "You do not feel at all ill, do you, my lady?" he asked instead, after a full minute had passed.

"Ill? Not at all. I am feeling just the thing."

"There, you see, William. Your mama is feeling just the thing. Fine as fivepence. I should think you might say something else to her now. As a matter of fact, my dear, I should think you might even give her a hug and a kiss."

Lord Wraithstone studied his mama most seriously. "You do not feeling bad, Mama?"

"No, William. Not at all."

"You do not even got no sniffles?"

"Not even the sniffles."

Very slowly, holding carefully to the kitten that Pope had given him, William, Lord Wraithstone, transferred himself from his tutor's lap to his mama's, displacing and scattering frisky kittens everywhere. Once he had snuggled down against the velvet of her gown, he allowed himself to be thoroughly hugged and kissed as he had not been in eighteen months.

As unobtrusively as he could, Pope gained his feet and, with a word to Mrs. Oakwood to remain and watch over the kittens and Lord and Lady Wraithstone alike, he left the nursery for his own chambers and closed the door quietly behind him.

I shall need to explain to him that Mrs. Oakwood and the kittens are not magical, Pope thought, standing with one foot upon the window seat in his chamber, staring out into the dying afternoon light. *And that I am not magical either. I have not the least idea what made him conclude that I am magical, but I shall need to make it clear to him very soon that I am not. That none of us are—that he has not the least need for any of us. He cannot go through life, after all, fearing to speak to or to touch anyone unless he has one of the kittens or Mrs. Oakwood or me beside him, but it is quite enough for today that he kisses his mama and allows his mama to hold him in her arms.*

"And once I have made us all unmagical in William's eyes,"

he mumbled to himself dejectedly, rubbing his hand against the back of his neck, "I shall need to absent myself from this place and discover some other way in which to get on about my own life. If only Rebecca were not so very kind, so very appealing, I might well remain William's tutor until he is sent off to school as I planned, but I cannot," he whispered. "I cannot."

"A poltroon, Mr. Archie?" asked a quiet voice from behind him, startling Pope into turning about so quickly that he came near to losing his balance and sitting flat upon the floor. "I did knock, but I expect you were deep in thought and did not hear me, eh?"

"Buzzerby."

"I must have a word with you. A private word," said the butler, stepping into the chamber and closing the door behind him. "I have never known you to be a coward before, Mr. Archie."

"Yes, well, and I never have been. Nor am I a coward now, Buzzerby. What put such a thought into your head?"

"You were speaking aloud, Mr. Archie, just now."

Pope's ears grew suddenly red. "I was?"

"Not all that you were thinking. I am quite certain it was not all of it, Mr. Archie, but I did hear enough to realize that you intend to abandon her ladyship and our little lord."

"Never. Not abandon them, Buzzerby. I will not take my leave until all is well with them."

"You intended to remain until his lordship toddled off to school. You are the last of his lordship's tutors, or so you informed me. He was not to have another now that you had arrived."

"Yes, but that was before I—"

"Before you what, sir?"

"Before. . . ." Pope turned back to the window, stuffed his hands deep into his pockets and shrugged. "What was it that you wished to speak with me about, Buzzerby?" he asked after a long silence. "Something private, you said."

"Oh! Yes! About the pond!"

"The pond?" C. Archibald Pope turned back to stare at the

butler as though that gentleman had lost his mind. "The pond, Buzzerby?"

"Well, it is merely a . . . a thought . . . Mr. Archie. John Coachman and the grooms have informed me that the pond at the far end of the paddock has frozen, and we all wondered . . . knowing that his lordship is recovered from his illness, Mr. Archie—"

"You know already?" interrupted Pope.

"Indeed, sir. Why, at this very moment her ladyship and his lordship are down in the kitchen, hand in hand, stirring the Christmas pudding."

"They are?" A smile flickered across Pope's face.

"Yes, Mr. Archie. Her ladyship and his lordship and a black and white kitten with green eyes which his lordship insisted upon bringing. At any rate, Mr. Archie, we wondered, you know, if . . . the pond being frozen at last . . . well, his lordship has never been skating and—"

"You want me to teach Lord Wraithstone to skate, Buzzerby?"

"His papa did so love to skate. And her ladyship is fond of it as well. At least, she did used to be, Mr. Archie. And we all thought that, since his lordship is on the mend and the skates are ready to hand. . . . John and the grooms have gotten them out and cleaned them up good as new, Mr. Archie."

"Good as new," drawled Pope. "Sharp and shining, I expect. Just waiting to glide over the ice."

"Just so. A pair just his lordship's size from when his papa was young and a pair that will fit you, Mr. Archie, and her ladyship's skates from two winters past."

"Ahh."

Buzzerby studied the peculiar look upon Pope's face. "We do not any of us intend to interfere, Mr. Archie. You have done so very much for his lordship and Lady Wraithstone. If you think it a poor idea, well, it *is* merely an idea and I did promise to . . . to . . . suggest it to you."

"And you have done, and very nicely, too," nodded Pope. "Can you skate, Buzzerby?"

"Indeed, sir. I was used to be excessively fond of skating

when I was a lad. It made the winter so much less depressing, you know, to glide across a bit of ice now and then."

"Indeed. And William would like it?"

"His papa always did, Mr. Archie, from the very first moment he stepped upon the ice when he was his lordship's age."

"And Lady Wraithstone would be happy to see her son following in Richard's footsteps, would she not?"

"Oh, as to that, Mr. Archie, Lady Wraithstone is so very happy at this moment that I cannot think she has room for much more happiness. But she did so love to skate with her husband, and to skate hand in hand with her son would be—"

"I will do it then," agreed Pope abruptly. "Tomorrow afternoon. Lady Wraithstone goes to pay her weekly call upon the parson and his family tomorrow afternoon as usual, does she not?"

"I should think so, Mr. Archie. It being so close to Christmas, she will not think to—"

"Good," interrupted Pope. "Tomorrow afternoon Lord Wraithstone gets his first skating lesson. But you must not say a word to her ladyship about it, Buzzerby. None of you. It will be our secret until his lordship has got the gist of the thing and can escort his mama onto the ice himself."

The smile that wreathed Buzzerby's face did much to instill a bit of excitement in C. Archibald Pope. "It will be a present to her ladyship for Christmas. What think you of that, Buzzerby? It will be a present from his lordship and the entire staff."

Buzzerby left the room in high gig. In the anticipation of the joy that would fill Lady Wraithstone to be escorted upon the ice by her son, he forgot completely the words he had overheard Pope muttering to himself when first he had entered the chamber, nor did he take notice of the manner in which Pope now stood biting at his lower lip, his gaze fastened thoughtfully upon the flower design in the carpeting.

Eight

C. Archibald Pope, the red muffler his mother had knitted for him wrapped jauntily around his neck, his high beaver pushed back upon his head allowing his dark curls to scatter across his brow and the seat of his breeches exceedingly cold, sat in the middle of the pond and laughed uproariously at himself.

"You is not hurted?" asked a wobbly Lord Wraithstone, standing most unsteadily above him on his own little skates.

"Only my dignity, William."

"Is that what they calls it where you come from?" asked Lord Wraithstone seriously, sending Pope off into whoops again.

"It has been nine years and more since I donned a pair of skates, my lord," Pope managed as his laughter dwindled and he set himself to standing upright again. "I did think that I could still manage the thing well enough to teach you. But perhaps not. Perhaps not."

"We has skated all the way to the middle of the pond," Lord Wraithstone offered encouragingly, grabbing hastily at the tail of Pope's coat as his own skates began to slide in opposite directions and pulling himself fully upright again. "I did almost hurted my dignity," he announced, his ankles bending first outward and then inward.

"Indeed. Shall we attempt to reach the other side, do you think? William, look. Mrs. Oakwood has shepherded all of her kittens onto the ice. Uh-oh, that one is sliding on his bottom.

And look there. That, my lad, is how one skates upon one's chin."

"An' Archie is tippy-toeing on all four feets at once."

"Archie?"

Lord Wraithstone nodded. "I asked Mama an' she said it would be all right to name him Archie, af'er you."

"Oh." Pope studied the black and white kitten. "I expect you named him after me because he is the oddest of the lot, eh? All the rest have stripes and he has spots."

"Uh-uh," denied William, placing his tiny gloved hand confidently into Pope's. "I name-ded him Archie because he is my most favoritest."

"Oh," murmured Pope, clasping the hand with which he had been entrusted tightly. "Well, I am honored, my lord."

They played upon the ice for an hour and more and entered the house by way of the kitchen door, red-cheeked and laughing, William riding on Pope's shoulders with all the kittens in a sack made of Pope's muffler tightly in his grasp and Mrs. Oakwood pattering along behind. The cook welcomed them with cups of hot chocolate and gingerbread men and scraps of meat and bowls of cream for Mrs. Oakwood and her brood.

"And did ye learn to skate, then, my lord?" asked the cook, her eyes sparkling with hope that after all the silent months, this time she would receive an answer.

"I haved learned to skate good," declared Lord Wraithstone with a deal of braggadocio, his little chest sticking out with pride. "I did not fall on my dignity but only six times. Mr. Archie falled lots more than me."

"Only because I kept lunging to catch you, you rascal," protested Pope playfully.

"Yes, but I stayed-ded up an' you did not."

"Just so," agreed Pope with a grin for the cook. "His lordship wobbled; I lunged; he remained upright; and I went chin-skating upon the ice over and over again. Careless of me."

"Uh-huh," nodded Lord Wraithstone, giggling bubbles into his chocolate. "Careless of you."

* * *

Rebecca was not the least bit suspicious. It did never occur to her for the entire week before Christmas that the members of her staff required her advice or assistance precisely at the hour of one and that she was then drawn into a thoroughly engrossing discussion, or expedition, or decorating session until the precise hour of three every afternoon. She was, in fact, enjoying every moment of it. The Yule log was cut and placed in the winter parlor. Ivy and mistletoe were gathered, hung from the chandeliers and draped, with red bows, up the main staircase. She oversaw the placing of pine boughs upon the mantelpieces and the packing of jams and jellies, breads and cakes to be distributed among the poor of Wynd on Boxing Day; she saw the wassail bowl taken safely from storage and polished to a glistening silver; and it did never once occur to her that for the same two hours every afternoon, whatever must be done about the house could not be done without her.

She had not been involved in such a flurry of activity since she had gone into mourning for Richard. And though this Christmas she would certainly grieve at the absence of her husband, the grief, she was certain, would not be so deep, so all-encompassing as it had been.

"I shall miss you, dear Richard," she whispered as she set the last stitch into a pair of bedroom slippers and set them aside. "I shall always think of you and miss you, my love, but William is so much improved that this Christmas must be spent in bringing him joy and not in mourning for all that we lost when we lost you. Oh, Richard, you would not believe what our Archie has done for William. He is the most wonderful man—so kind, so wise, so filled with love. He is truly everything that a gentleman should be, just as you were yourself. He tells William the most amazing tales of his adventures every night. I sit upon the bed beside William and listen myself because they are so exciting. And he does have a way about him when he spins a tale."

He does have a way about him, thought Rebecca, Lady Wraithstone, as she lifted the bedroom slippers from the floor and studied them, smiling softly. How could a grown man pack three entire trunks full of the most necessary things to be delivered to him by his father's coachman and still forget to pack his bedroom slippers, and in the midst of winter at that?

They attended church in Wynd on Christmas—Lady Wraithstone and Lord Wraithstone's tutor with little Lord Wraithstone seated strategically between them. And because her ladyship's pew was at the front and not at all enclosed, the villagers stretched and wiggled to get a glimpse of that almost legendary tutor. It had taken only two days for the news of his success on Lord Wraithstone's behalf to reach Wynd. It had come with Mary, the little parlor maid on her half-day visit to her mum. It had come with Dorothea, who had been sent to the village to purchase some yarn for her ladyship, and it had come with John Coachman, who had driven them both. Word of it had traveled from villager to villager, and each time the tale of the tutor's success had been related, Mr. Pope's image and character and power had grown, until now he had become a legend in his own time.

"Do ye see him?" whispered Mrs. Montog to Mr. Montog. "He be a miracle worker that 'un."

"Aye, an' his lor'ship do look wonnerful," replied Mr. Montog, his wrinkled face drawn up into a smile. "Only see how he holds his mama's hand."

"Short for a grown man," remarked Squire Pepperwhite. "Thought he would be a reg'lar giant of a gentleman. No taller than her ladyship, he be."

"But he has the most enormous heart," remarked Mrs. Pepperwhite. "He left his own home which he had just got back to, Gerald, so that he might come to Wyndhover to save the tyke."

Row upon row of the residents of Wynd poked and jostled one another and whispered behind raised hands, and all the while Rebecca smiled her quiet smile and kept her face forward.

"Mama, how come ever'one is whisperin'?" asked Lord Wraithstone, turning about in his pew to peer at the villagers.

"Shhhh, William. Turn back around, dearest. It is not at all acceptable to peer over the pews at the people behind us."

"But they is all peerin' at us, Mama."

"Yes, I know," murmured Rebecca. "They are happy to see you, William. You have not come to the church with me in ever so long, you know."

"Am I happy to see them, Mama?"

"Yes, my dear."

Before either she or Pope realized what he was about, William stood up on the seat of the pew and bowed quite properly to those in the church behind him. "I am very happy to see you," he announced loudly, secure with the knowledge that he could not possibly kill anyone in his magical tutor's presence. "An' me an' Mama an' our Mr. Archie wishes you all a happy Christmas!"

"They will all be upon us in mere moments," announced Pope as he arrived in the winter parlor, two brightly wrapped boxes in his hands and a line of kittens trailing at his heels. "And may I add, my lady, that there is something to be said for a silent child," he chuckled.

"Oh, do not say it," laughed Rebecca. "To stand up before the entire parish. And to think that only a short while ago he was afraid to speak to anyone. You are the finest of all gentlemen, you know."

"Me?"

"Indeed. To stand right up and bow beside William as you did so that he would not realize he had done the least thing exceptional. I thought I should die from laughing."

"I thought the entire parish would die from laughing. It will prove a Christmas service that lives in history."

Rebecca nodded as she took the presents from him and placed them beside the fireplace. "There was not the least need for you to. . . . Whenever did you?"

"Whenever did I what?"

"Manage to find presents and wrap them so delightfully."

"I brought them with me from home. One already wrapped and the other . . . well, Buzzerby helped me to wrap the other.

You do not think it presumptuous of me to give William and you a present?"

"You have already given William and me the best present of all. You have given us back each other, Archie."

"Yes, well, I said I would help the boy, did I not?"

"And you did precisely as you promised. I cannot thank you enough. You are—"

"We are comed!" announced his lordship gleefully as he raced into the parlor with Mrs. Oakwood and Archie the kitten upon his heels. He climbed immediately upon the portion of the Yule log that had not reached the fire and did an excited little jig. "Happy Christmas! Happy Christmas!"

"Happy Christmas to you," responded Pope. "And I do thank you, Lady Wraithstone, for allowing me to join in."

"Rebecca. You are to call me Rebecca. Have you forgotten? William, come, dearest, and give this present to Mr. Archie."

"A present? For me?" asked Pope as the boy skipped across the room to take the package from his mama and deliver it into Pope's hands.

"Uh-huh," acknowledged Lord Wraithstone, dancing happily beside Pope's chair. "Open it quick. I knows what it is."

"You do?"

"Uh-huh. I help-ded."

"You did?" asked Pope, unwrapping the silver paper and opening a small wooden box. "What on earth?"

"They is collars for Mrs. Oakwood an' the kit-tens!" William shouted excitedly. "The one with the red bow is for Mrs. Oakwood, an' this one with the bell is for Archie, and this pretty green one with the bits of gold is for Sapling, an'—"

"Sapling?" interrupted Pope. "Which is Sapling?"

"Why the little gray stripe with the gold eyes and without the mittens, who will grow up to look exceedingly like her mama," Rebecca offered, lifting that particular kitten from the floor. "And that red-striped rapscallion about to attack your shoe is Elm, and the triplets with the mittens are called—"

"Do not tell me," grinned Pope. "Yew, Pine and Willow."

"Actually, Blueberry, Strawberry and Shrub," smiled Rebecca, slipping the green knitted collar over Sapling's head.

"Though I do like your names for them quite as well. William, perhaps we ought to—"

"No, do not change their names on my account," Pope protested, placing one of three blue knitted collars around the first of the triplets. "I could grow very fond of a cat called Shrub. Now, William, you must fetch those two little boxes by the fire. Yes, those. This one," Pope said, weighing the two in his hands, "is for your mama, sir, and this for you."

Little Lord Wraithstone delivered his mama's present into her hands directly, but could not wait for her to open it, and began to unwrap his own present at once. "Mama!" he shouted, before Lady Wraithstone had so much as untied the riband Pope had fastened around hers. "Mama, Mama, look!"

Rebecca gazed at the pocket watch her son dangled before her eyes in wonder. "Archie," she began, "you cannot possibly afford to give William such a. . . ." And then the timepiece popped open and the watch began to chime a little tune.

"It is Throckmorton, Mama!" cried Lord Wraithstone, jumping about the room. "It is Mr. Archie's Throckmorton!" And then the boy ceased jumping and dashed to Pope, climbing up into his lap. "Am I truly to have Throckmorton?" he asked, his eyes aglow with happiness. "Is he really, truly mine? Forever and ever?"

"Throckmorton?" murmured Lady Wraithstone.

"Forever and ever. You must take the very best care of him. He was my grandfather's, you know, and he was a bit nervous to be called upon to leave me and go to you. But then, he is most fond of you and so he thought he would not mind to do it."

"I will take excellent cares of him."

"Yes, I know you will. William, there is something that I must say to you, and Throckmorton is telling me that now is likely the best time."

"He is? The best time to say what?"

Pope snapped the chiming watch closed and wrapped his arms around the child on his lap. "The best time to say that Archie and Mrs. Oakwood and the kittens are not truly magic."

Little Lord Wraithstone's blue eyes opened very wide as he

stared up at Pope. Little Lord Wraithstone's lower lip began to quiver. Across the room, Rebecca ceased to unwrap her present and watched and listened intently.

"I know that I said they were," Pope continued softly, "but I was mistaken. Mrs. Oakwood is merely an ordinary cat, William. And the kittens are ordinary kittens."

"N-no," murmured William in horror.

"Yes, and I am not magic either."

"You is," whispered William. "You gots to be."

"No, my dear, I am not."

Little Lord Wraithstone began then to struggle in Pope's arms. "Le' me go!" he cried. "I cannot be touchin' you!"

"Shhh, William, and listen to me. You do not need a magical Mr. Archie or a magical Mrs. Oakwood or a cache of magical kittens. Truly, you do not. Only think, my dear, how many times you have spoken to me and to your mama and to Cook and Buzzerby since first you began to speak again. Only think how often your mama has hugged and kissed you. How many times you have held my hand and sat upon my lap. It has been days and days, William, and you have done these things more times than you can count and yet, there is not one of us suffers for it."

"There mus' be magic," whispered the boy.

"Yes, there is magic, William. But it is not where you think . . . not in Mrs. Oakwood or the kittens or me. It is in you. In the glow of your eyes, in the sweetness of your smile, in the innocence of your heart."

"In m-me?"

"Your papa was very, very ill and already dying when you spoke to him and touched him last, my dear. You did not take his life away. He was already leaving this life when you went to him. What you did, William . . . what you did . . . you saw him off into heaven and you gave him the most magical and wondrous gifts just when he required them most. You gave him the joy of knowing that he would live on in you forever. You gave him the contentment of realizing that your mama would always have someone good and brave to protect her and cherish her for as long she lived. And you filled him up with pride so that he could meet his God with his chin held high. He could do that, William, because he knew when you touched him and spoke to him—he knew with a surety—that he had done the most marvelous of all things—together with your mama, William, he created you."

Pope waited in agony as the child upon his lap seriously considered his words—words with which he had struggled night after night until at last he thought he had got them right. "Well?" he asked anxiously, unable to wait another moment. "Do you understand, William? Do you see what I am trying to say?"

Little Lord Wraithstone nodded. "I did not killed my papa. I maked my papa happy even when he was most saddest an' dying."

"Just so," nodded Pope as Rebecca expelled a long-held breath. "Just so, William."

"An' I mus' always 'member him an' take care of Mama."

"Exactly."

"An' I is mag'cal."

"Yes, you are. Magical in the most extraordinary way," grinned Pope. "Now, go help your mama to unwrap her present, rascal. She has not so much as got the riband all the way off."

"Oh!" exclaimed Lady Wraithstone when together she and William opened her gift. "Oh, Archie, wherever. . . . I never thought to have . . . only look, William. This is your papa when he was a boy. And this is Mr. Archie, I think."

"Indeed," quipped Pope. "You can tell by the nose if nothing else. We were all of ten when Richard's father had that miniature painted by a gentleman passing through Wynd. Smart was his name. John Smart."

"That is Papa?" asked William, amazed. "He looks like me!"

"Indeed," nodded Pope as Rebecca fingered the glass that covered the oval surrounding two boyish faces side by side. "Very much like you."

Nine

Lord Wraithstone, with Pope's much-pleaded-for red muffler wrapped flamboyantly around his neck and trailing over his shoulder, took his mama's hand confidently into his own and led her onto the ice. Together they glided around the edge of the pond as Buzzerby and Dorothea, John Coachman and James the first footman and, in fact, all of the servants of Wyndhover stood upon the shore applauding. "Happy Christmas," they called in a cheery chorus, having taken time from a busy Christmas Day to catch a glimpse of the true pleasure, the extraordinary happiness that wrapped itself thoroughly about Lady Wraithstone. "Happy Christmas, my lady! Happy Christmas, my lord!"

Rebecca was so very thrilled to have her son beside her and to see him laughing and smiling up at her as he led her around the pond, that she barely heard the applause or the greetings, though she realized at once why her staff had been determined to require her aid every day between the hours of one and three for the past week.

They were all of them conspiring with Archie to keep this a surprise, she thought warmly. *They have each and every one of them contributed to this most marvelous of presents. What dears they are, the lot of them!*

And then she took a moment to look away from the golden-haired, smiling child beside her to wave at those upon the shore. They waved back, all of them, each in his or her own particular way. Buzzerby waved quite regally and with the utmost composure; Dorothea's was a tiny fluttering of her hand; John Coachman's wave proved a deal more enthusiastic and James and the other footmen and the grooms literally jumped up and down and waved with both hands; Cook had come hurrying with her ladle still in hand and saluted grandly with it; Mary, the little parlor maid, had a grin upon her face as wide as the pond itself and blew them a kiss.

They are all of them so very kind, so very wonderful, thought Rebecca. *I am blessed to have them. Not one of them ever thought to abandon us, not even when William was at his very worst. And only see how excited they are now. How proud for William. How joyous for me. And we all of us owe the happiness of this day to Archie.*

"Archie," she said aloud, looking down at William and then up at those who gathered upon the shore. "William, where is our Mr. Archie? I cannot see him anywhere."

C. Archibald Pope lifted Mrs. Oakwood out of his portmanteau and stuffed the last of the shirts he planned to take with him into it. He closed it and pulled the buckle tight.

"Mrrrrow mrrr mrrrow!" protested Mrs. Oakwood loudly, slapping at the handle of the traveling bag.

"You cannot possibly come," mumbled Pope. "You know that you cannot. You have a family to look after, my dear. They are not so grown that they can do without you as yet."

"Mrrrphgle!"

Pope stared at the cat upon the bed as she sat down stubbornly beside the portmanteau. The red bow on her collar made him smile a bit. "You have found a home, my dear. And a very fine home at that. Only think how much better off you are today than you were when first we discovered one another. It would be foolish of you to abandon an entire houseful of people willing to do your bidding just to traipse off into the unknown with me."

"Brrrrr phrggle fzsttt."

"Yes, well, I *am* going home, but I cannot remain there for any length of time. All of my brothers are married and on their own and I must be on my own as well, Mrs. Oakwood. A seventh son has few expectations, you know. I must discover my own way in the world—again. Only this time, I hope not to be accosted by a press-gang or anything else quite so dramatic. Perhaps I shall accept the position of secretary to Rutland since he was kind enough to offer it. Or perhaps I shall take up a life upon the stage. There are any number of peculiar characters written for the likes of me, you know."

"Mrrrrph," observed Mrs. Oakwood.

He could not say why that particular comment affected him so, but tears rose most abruptly to Pope's eyes at the sound of it. He sat down at once on the bed beside Mrs. Oakwood and stroked her thoroughly from head to tail. "I would remain here if I could," he said quietly. "It would be the finest thing in all the world to remain here. But I dare not."

"Archie!" cried Rebecca breathlessly from the doorway to the nursery. "Archie, are you ill? Why did you not remain at the pond? Why is your portmanteau upon the bed? Archie?"

He stood and turned to face her as she crossed the room. He forced the tears in his eyes not to fall, straightened his shoulders and arranged his face into a semblance of a smile. "I am afraid that I have been called away," he said over the lump of sadness in his throat. "It is . . . it is unavoidable. I left a note for you and for William in the foyer."

"On Christmas? Called away from us on Christmas Day? Oh, oh, it is your father or your mother. Something has happened."

"No." He could not let her think such a thing as that—that something dire had happened to one of his parents.

"What then? Not one of your brothers?"

"No, no, it is nothing bad happened."

"But—"

She stood so close before him that he need but raise his hand to touch one of those cherry-red cheeks the wind had kissed. But he would not allow himself to raise his hand. "It is . . . the most fortunate . . . opportunity. I have been . . . offered a position . . . as . . . as secretary to—"

"On Christmas Day?" Rebecca interrupted. "Not even the

Prince Regent himself would think to offer a gentleman a position that required him to leave his home on Christmas Day."

"N-no."

"We have done something, William and I, to offend you."

"Never."

"Then do not go. Whatever the position, do not take it. You are William's tutor. You cannot abandon him."

"I am his tutor and therefore must abandon him," murmured Pope, and unaccountably, totally against his will, one hand rose from his side and one finger touched Rebecca's wind-reddened cheek gently, tenderly. "I cannot remain here," he mumbled. "You are not at all the sort of female I expected and. . . ."

Rebecca did not move an inch, did not so much as allow a muscle to twitch while his long finger followed the line of her jaw, slowly, spellbindingly.

"I find myself falling in love with you, Rebecca," he whispered. "Somehow, I always imagined that Richard would marry a spoilt beauty with the sensitivity of an Amazon and the brain of a peacock. I thought that I could come and be a tutor without the least danger. And then you appeared before me and I knew—"

"What did you know, Archie?"

"That . . . that very soon my heart would break for wanting you. Very soon. It breaks this moment." His lips came near to brushing hers, very near, but he stepped back and turned away.

"Archie," she said, stepping up behind him, placing her hands upon his shoulders. "Archie," she whispered, his very name a caress upon her lips.

"No, do not, R-Rebecca. Do not you say my name so. I know who I am and I know what I am and—"

"Who are you, Archie? Turn around, sir, and tell me. Who are you? What are you?"

He spun to face her so hastily that she lost her balance and began to tumble back. He grabbed her elbows to keep her upright, releasing them the moment she had regained her balance. "I am an odd duck. An ugly little man with a nose the length of a billiard cue," he said, his hazel eyes flashing, daring her to contradict him. "A stubborn, opinionated, pushy elf. An elf without one great expectation to his name . . . with not even a tiny expectation to his name. I have nothing to offer the parlor maid, much less anything to offer the widow of Viscount Wraithstone."

"I do beg your pardon," Rebecca replied. "An ugly little man with a nose the length of a billiard cue?"

"Yes."

"Oh, Archie!" She grinned at him. It was the most endearing grin. His heart lurched at the sight of it. "How can you say such things? You have the most compelling eyes of any man I have ever known. One can never guess what color they will be. I have seen them mysteriously dark and bright as polished gold, tinged with green, then filled with flecks of honey. Ugly? How can any face that holds such fascinating eyes be ugly? And a nose as long as a billiard cue? It is prominent, your nose, I grant you that, but I could not stand here so close before you were it as long as you claim it to be. And were you any taller, sir, I could not do this," she added, taking his chin in her hand, tilting his head the least bit, and placing a breath of a kiss upon his lips. "Not without getting a kink in my neck, I could not. And our noses did not even touch," she said, as their lips parted. "Imagine that."

"R-Rebecca—"

"Be still, Archie. I have merely begun." And she placed her arms around him and kissed him once again, her fingers stroking the back of his neck and twisting into his dark curls.

"Mrrrrrrrrowmrph," Mrs. Oakwood observed as her kittens came tumbling into the room, the bell upon Archie's collar jingling.

"Mama?" asked little Lord Wraithstone, hopping into his tutor's chambers after the kittens. "What is you doing to Mr. Archie, Mama?"

"I am kissing him," replied Rebecca, ceasing that particular occupation to smile down at her son.

"But he did not open his really true present, Mama. Cannot you wait to kiss him until he opens his really true present?"

"Wh-what?" asked Pope, thoroughly discomposed.

"Your Christmas present, Archie. You did not think that all

you were to have were collars for Mrs. Oakwood and the kittens? Never. Take the box from William and open it at once."

"But—"

"Take it, Archie. Open it up. You may discover that it is filled with expectations."

"Expectations?" Pope sat down, cross-legged upon the floor. and opened the box William gave him.

"They are bedroom slippers!" William shouted, hopping about in a circle on one foot. "I thoughted of them an' Mama made-ded them! They are perfeck! Now you will not need to dance about ever' morning 'cause your feets is so cold! Now your feets willn't be cold at all no more!"

"And where do we expect him to keep them, William?" asked Lady Wraithstone.

"Right beside his bed!"

"And how long do we expect him to keep them there?"

"Forever an' ever!"

"And when he puts them on each morning, what do we expect Mr. Archie to do?"

"To 'member how much we loves him!"

"Precisely so. To remember how much we love him," said Rebecca, lowering herself to the floor beside Pope. "Those are our expectations, you stubborn, opinionated, pushy Mr. C. Archibald Pope, to keep you with us in this house forever and to know that you will always remember how much we love you. Those, I should think, are the sort of expectations that truly count. Oh, Archie," she whispered, her breath tickling at his ear, "do not leave us. Do not leave me. Not now. Not when I have just come out of the darkness and into the sunlight of your smile. Not when I have just begun to love anew."

"Are you going to kiss Mr. Archie again, Mama?" asked Lord Wraithstone, plopping down before the two of them upon the floor and scooping three of the kittens out of the slipper box and onto his lap.

"No, she is not," Pope replied. "I am going to kiss her this time, and you are not going to say a word while I do."

"I willn't not say not one single word while you do," agreed his lordship, his eyes large with expectation.

"You do not think it most unwise, a tutor and a viscountess?" Pope asked, rising from the floor and pulling Rebecca up into his arms.

"The seventh son of an earl and a *mere* viscountess."

"But still, I cannot possibly support you and William in the manner to which . . . and I will not live upon William's inheritance."

"You will think of something. You will write down all of your adventures and publish them in a book . . . from the headmaster's mattress on the ceiling all the way up to the day of our wedding. That will give Society something to read about."

"But—"

"Archie, *are* you going to kiss me or persist in worrying over insignificant nothings?"

C. Archibald Pope grinned. "I am going to kiss you," he said, and did precisely that for the longest time—until his heart thundered in his ears for lack of breath, until his arms ached with holding her and his brain threatened to turn to mush from the sheer ecstasy of her body pressed softly and confidently against his own, until Throckmorton began to chime his dingding diddle-de-diddle, and William giggled and Mrs. Oakwood and the kittens all mrrrred along with the timepiece in a rousing chorus of their own.

MISTLETOE KISSES

by
Jeanne Savery

The Cornish winter had been mild and Morgan St. Austell had forgotten Christmas was imminent until the invitation arrived for the house party at Kenway Castle. He had arrived several days earlier, enjoyed the company and Christmas Day, but *this* evening the annual Kenway Castle Boxing Day Revel was underway and he was *not* enjoying himself. Not at all.

Morgan stood above the party. He breathed in the scent of pine and fir and looked down upon the milling guests. Each spoke more loudly than the next in a futile attempt to be heard, the noise rising in a chaotic babble. He frowned. He should mingle but the notion did not appeal.

The Revel had been well underway when a cold draft blowing down his neck led to the discovery of an opening hidden behind a wall hanging. Circular stairs within the thick walls of the ancient keep in which the party was annually held led to his present vantage point. The keep's walls had survived intact down the centuries although now, in modern times, it was merely one corner of a much larger building. His present perch was *not,* he thought, an ancient minstrel's gallery, as he'd heard it called, but a balcony of relatively recent construction over beams which had once held flooring. Morgan peered into the shadows above and, just barely, made out dark beams which suggested that, originally, there had been a still higher floor.

Morgan leaned on the wide railing and envied the Kenways' guests' pleasure. Older couples chatted, hopeful youths and blushing chits eyed each other shyly, and the very young raced helter-skelter among their elders, crowing and chortling, playing a game only they understood. Observing the children's antics, Morgan's eyes narrowed and the corners of his lips tipped in what, for him, was a smile.

Then, a faint thump on the railing some feet to his left had Morgan tensing, turning, ready for defense . . .

. . . and relaxing. Morgan's teeth showed in a rare true smile. He chuckled softly, embarrassed by his reaction and held coaxing fingers toward the gangling, not quite adult kitten that eyed him curiously.

Last seen, the animal had curled bonelessly into Miss Grace Cheviot's lap. Morgan had wondered if he himself would ever again relax that fully. His life in the army had been nerve-wracking, and the constant awareness and attention to detail essential for survival was extremely exhausting. As careful as he was, he'd been wounded and barely escaped his last reconnaissance into French-held territory.

Morgan's features fell into brooding lines. He had promised himself he'd forget all that. The wound had healed and it was time to move on. Unfortunately, *moving on* meant choosing a wife. *Marriage,* damn it! A muscle in Morgan's jaw tensed.

The kitten purred under his caressing fingers and Morgan recalled a recent conversation with his mother. Once again Mrs. St. Austell had urged him to wed. "You are your uncle's heir, Morgan," she'd said, shaking her finger at him. "It is your *duty.*"

Morgan's expression cleared as he envisioned his tiny mother in one of her scolding moods. Small, dark and never still, that was his mother. Her scolds were always loving, but—

The muscle along his jaw rolled again.

—repetition made them wearing.

Worst of all, the morose thought passed through his mind, *she has the right of it.*

He tried to convince himself it was not so difficult a duty. One chose some chit, bedded her, and acquired the much-to-be-desired heir. Morgan winced at the cold-bloodedness of it and wondered how long he could he put off the inevitable. But, when he could not, how did one decide whom to court? Never the sort of man who made life-changing decisions easily, Morgan St. Austell gritted his teeth.

But the Christmas visit to Kenway Castle was a respite from those near arguments with his mother. Mrs. St. Austell always spent Christmas with her sister, whose cottage would accommodate no more than one guest. And Morgan's uncle, Baron St. Austell, had made it clear that although Morgan was his heir, his presence was unwanted and unwelcome.

Unwelcome. Morgan would come a stranger to his inheritance, to the estates and to the people. Untried, untrained and very likely unwanted, he would be forced to take up new duties instantly. There could be no excuses, no pondering.

Baron St. Austell's agent, sympathetic to Morgan's dilemma and likely looking to his own future, had written that the baron ailed. He suffered not only the aches and pains associated with the elderly but the unmistakable yellowing of skin and eyes that indicated a mortally ill man. And, for Morgan, there could be no postponing that momentous challenge—as he had and very likely would continue to do a decision concerning marriage. Worst of all, those new responsibilities would only underline the need for an heir and a spare.

Morgan's hand dropped to the railing when Miss Cheviot's kitten moved away. The long-legged, half-grown animal oozed down onto one of the massive beams and moved out over the room. The kitten stared down on one side and then the other at the noisy, glittering throng, occasionally leaping over the greenery looping the ancient support—until a holly leaf got in his way. The kitten batted at it. Obligingly, the stem broke and floated down to land on a gentleman's shoulder.

As Morgan watched the kitten's antics, his ears were assaulted by the nasty sound of a wicked snigger. It rose from below the balcony, and leaning forward, Morgan looked down. Two young men stood shoulder to shoulder before an enormous silver wassail bowl. Hidden from the guests by his friends, a third emptied a flask into the already heady drink, a second flask in his other hand. Morgan debated spoiling sport. But why? What the man added could do little additional damage to the already well-laced and spicy brew.

"Ha!" said one young man, a happier voice than that which had laughed cruelly. "Look at that." He pointed.

Following the pointing finger's direction, Morgan glanced along the beam. The kitten had crouched near a mature growth of mistletoe so large it nearly enveloped the age-blackened timber. It amused itself by batting the fragile stems, breaking them, sending them floating, and watching the downward progress of each brittle piece. Then it did it again. Then again . . . until a stem fell into the middle of the braid forming a crown atop a Kenway cousin's pale blonde hair.

Morgan eyed Miss Grace Cheviot. Pretty, in a pale sort of way. Or perhaps a trifle too pale with that ash-blonde hair and alabaster skin? Or was it the pale silvery color of her gown which washed any color from her complexion? Attractive, he thought, if a trifle lacking in decoration. Still the cut was good and the plainness suited Miss Cheviot . . .

The young man who had pointed toward the kitten interrupted Morgan's thoughts. "Miss Cheviot didn't even notice."

"Dare you, Jaimy," said the taller. "Grab her and kiss her."

The speaker was the snickerer. The man's sly tone fostered a strong dislike in Morgan.

"Kiss little Miss Ice and Snow? Not on your life. I'll not have my face nipped by hoarfrost! Plenty of girls'll stand beneath the mistletoe tonight. Won't need to steal kisses. Besides, there's my Amy to think on. Ain't you about done, Joel?" he asked the man with the flask.

Hoarfrost? Morgan frowned. Grace Cheviot might be withdrawn, an observer of life, and rather shy in a nice sort of way. Or so he'd found on those few occasions he'd attempted to converse with her. But cold? He didn't think so. He watched her weave through the crowd, slipping between and around couples and groups, no one paying her the least heed. And why would they? She was, he thought, no more than another example of that ubiquitous shadowy sort, the poor relation, who lived in so many prosperous homes.

Grace Cheviot. Graceful as her name, he thought, watching her. *Cheviot.* Why did the name tease the edges of his memory? He couldn't recall. Then he straightened as a child slipped and slid to her little rump just in front of the woman about whom he speculated. Morgan watched Miss Cheviot stoop, lift the girl and swing her high just as the child's face screwed up for a cry. She set the child on her feet before the girl loosed the first sob. The tears fled in laughter and a hug for her savior before running off.

Miss Cheviot stared after the child. Morgan caught, before she hid it, a yearning look. Then she presented her usual serene countenance to the world and continued toward the wall. Morgan observed her gradually approach a narrow door set partly behind an ancient hanging, saw her glance around . . . and slip through the door, closing it behind her.

Morgan's eyes narrowed into a thoughtful expression, his curiosity roused. There, just before she disappeared, he'd caught a mischief-look, an expression utterly out of character for self-contained, sober, self-effacing Grace Cheviot. Never in a hundred years would the lady he thought he knew adopt such an impish appearance.

Interesting!

Where had she gone? What did she intend? What, in fact, could be more important for a young unmarried woman than the Kenway family's Boxing Day gala?

A surge of movement at the hall's entrance indicated the arrival of more guests, more laughter and shouting, friend to friend, and still more chaos. Irritated, Morgan wondered why he'd accepted the Kenways' invitation.

The moody thought had Morgan scolding himself. This was one night of a fortnight. He had enjoyed strolling with other guests to church on Christmas Eve, joining his merely adequate baritone to the voices singing hymns. The midnight service was particularly moving after so many holidays when he'd hidden from the enemy or shivered in inadequate quarters in the Portuguese highlands with Wellington's army. Here he was warm and comfortable and tomorrow he'd again be at ease. It was only this crowd he did not, could not, enjoy. Miss Cheviot's kitten hopped onto the railing and nudged Morgan, nudged him a second time, recalling his attention.

". . . collect a few more of us," said the idiot who dared

Jaimy to kiss Miss Cheviot. "There were half a dozen berries on that sprig."

Still urging mistletoe kisses on Miss Cheviot, is he? thought Morgan, his fingers gently caressing the kitten.

"What if she's removed them before we find her?" asked the lad who had poured the rum or, more likely, gin into the punch.

The three held cups which, as Morgan watched, they refilled and downed. *How much have they drunk?* he wondered.

"Old icy eyes? Remove that sprig?" sneered the unnamed fellow. *"She'll* never notice."

"Where'd she go?" Stout Joel stood on tiptoe, staring over the crowd.

"I know where she went all right," said the leader. "I can find her." The peevish note returned. "Thing is, we need three more of us to make it a really good joke. There were six berries! At least six."

"But I don't want to kiss an icicle. I only want to kiss my Amy."

"Come on, Jaimy," urged the unknown. "It's only a kiss."

At that moment the kitten set his claws into the side of Morgan's hand. The prick sharpened his wits and he asked himself if it would *remain* just a kiss. Six healthy lads, all a trifle bosky or even well up in their altitudes? Perhaps utterly jug-bitten? And hidden away, alone with an attractive young woman?

Each lad egging on the next . . .

. . . And how far?

Even if these lads set off with no more than a stolen kiss in mind, such conduct could lead to worse. Far worse. Something terrible. And to find such horror here in Cornwall? In peaceful England? At Christmastime?

No. Never.

The lanky kitten climbed his coat and Morgan helped it to his shoulder. He turned, entering the Stygian darkness of the stairwell. He circled down, emerged from behind the tapestry, and eased between groups, nodding to anyone who spoke to him, but continuing on until he reached the far wall. There, as Miss Cheviot had done, he waited until no one watched before opening the door and, setting the kitten to the floor, slipped inside . . .

. . . where he was blinded by darkness. As he waited for his eyes to adjust, he heard, faintly, the kitten's outraged meow and hoped no one had stepped on it. There. The faintest of lighter patches. Arm stretched to the side, Morgan found a wall which took him to the arch where he discovered stairs leading upward.

Morgan climbed the worn steps carefully. The way grew brighter. Well around the first bend, he found a candle stuck into a rusty wall sconce. He climbed beyond first-floor height. Passing a second candle, he was soon above what had been the upper level as well.

Finally he faced a tightly closed door. A low door made of ancient planks crisscrossed with iron strapping. Which was barred. For a moment Morgan stared. No one could be beyond that age-darkened wood. Not with that bar on this side. He turned, stared downward to where the curve cut off his view.

Had he missed an opening? He was about to explore the notion when he heard the excited whisper of several voices rising from below. His mouth hardening, he edged down . . .

. . . and saw a young man turn sideways, slide through a narrow gap just where the light was dimmest. Quickly, silently, Morgan entered the passage built within the thick wall and at a height, he thought, level with what was originally the highest floor.

"Hey, don't bump me," hissed a voice.

"Can't help it," muttered another. "Gerald's pushing."

"Why didn't we think to bring a lantern?" whispered still another. "Should have plucked the candle and brought it—"

"You stepped on my heel, lout," snarled a fourth voice. "Brand-new slippers, too."

"I'm going back," said a voice Morgan recognized as Jaimy's.

There was some pushing, shoving, a grunt or two. "Missing your Amy?" sneered the leader. "She might get mad at you?"

Morgan added another dollop of dislike to what he felt for the man.

"Amy would have every reason to be angry with me and well you know it. I didn't want to come and I'm going back," insisted Jaimy on a stubborn note, his voice nearer than before.

Morgan raced back the way he'd come. He made it up the

steps and out of sight just before Jaimy appeared and clattered down the stairs, then Morgan retraced his steps.

Grace Cheviot strained to let down a long horizontal shutter. She put her hands on the stone and leaned forward slowly, knowing from experience that if she put her head too far over she would become dizzy from the excessive height. She fluttered her handkerchief, fluttered it again, and was rewarded. She chuckled softly as Dorcus Kenway waved her closed fan. Firmly. Twice.

It was time.

Grace raised the first crate's lid. She fished out two oddly shaped bundles and turned toward the opening . . . only to turn still again, sharply, her hands fisted about their tiny burdens.

"Ah! Barr." Tension drew her shoulders tight. "Did you come to help? Joel? What a lovely notion," she said coolly. "I have worried that one alone could not deliver the favors speedily enough."

The man called Barr instinctively lifted his hands as she extended hers. He found himself holding her offerings and stared at them. Joel, too, found his hands full, and behind the first two, the others milled about, uncertain.

"Gerald? Is that you? Would you tip down that other shutter? If we are all to toss these things we need more space."

In silence the shutter came down. "What do we do, Miss Cheviot?" asked Joel politely.

"Simply toss gently at different angles and nearer and farther as you wish." Miss Cheviot lobbed one and then another packet out into the great room. The objects arced out. As they fell, they unwrapped themselves. A square of brightly colored silk opened out and small boxes, attached by thread to the corners, floated down into the crowd.

"What an extraordinary thing!" said one lad. He grabbed a pair of the favors. The other young men emulated Miss Cheviot, grinning, happy . . . except Barr Kenway. His fists clenched and unclenched as he scowled, *glared,* at his friends.

Morgan, unnoticed, leaned against the entrance and waited. Kenway's heir, as he now perceived the sneerer to be, was not happy. Nor did he look the sort to allow a plot to fail so easily. Morgan's eyes narrowed. What did he know of Barr Kenway?

A cousin and, Morgan judged, about the same age as Miss Cheviot. And very angry. With her? Why? Had she, perhaps, rebuffed his attentions? The young fool was the sort to find rejection intolerable. Yes, very likely, he had revenge in mind. The question was how far Kenway would take his vindictiveness. The hard look in the man's eyes and line of mouth were not those of the merely disappointed, of someone who weighed the ruination of a mild jest.

People below noticed the favors floating into their midst and the noise level escalated. Childish trebles piped. Women's laughter shrilled. Men yelped in pretend disgust at a miss or shouted their success at retrieving a packet. Kenway's friends' tosses grew wilder, attempting to reach the far side of the hall. Impossible, of course. The favors were too light and the hall too wide, but they made a competition of it.

Miss Cheviot, smiling tightly, watched them. Smiling, yes. But Morgan saw the worried glance she flicked toward her angry cousin.

Finally, as the last favor floated gently down, Kenway straightened. He caught the eyes of some of his friends. "And now, if you are done playing the fool, perhaps you'll recall our reason for coming? Our real reason?"

One of the young men, looking sheepish, edged back. Morgan, obligingly, stepped out of his way. The lad cast a look toward Barr and hurried off. Joel did the same. Three men remained. Barr, Gerald and another, unknown to Morgan.

The odds, thought Morgan, would get no better. "Yes, Mr. Kenway?" he asked in a smoothly dangerous voice, "Why *did* you come?"

"Who the devil do you think you—"

Morgan interrupted. "I asked you to explain."

"What business is it of yours?"

"It is the business of any gentleman to protect the honor of a lady, is it not?" His eyes narrowed. "I presume you *do* wish your cousin's honor protected?"

The unknown lad's eyes widened in sudden foreboding. He

tugged on Gerald's sleeve, got his attention and tipped his head toward the passage. Not waiting to see if Gerald understood, he too made his escape. Gerald, a frown creasing his brow, looked after him, then back at the frozen tableau.

Morgan remained relaxed but watchful. Miss Cheviot stood at the end of the narrow room, her hands pressed against the wall and her breathing just a trifle fast. She stared with icy disdain at her cousin. Barr, his temper roused to the danger point, panted from frustrated emotion.

"Just a kiss," muttered Gerald. "Just a mistletoe kiss . . ." No one paid him the least heed. "Ain't that what you said, Barr?" he asked plaintively. "A mistletoe kiss?" The lad's confusion was obvious. He looked from one to another, heard Barr's teeth grit together and, finally alarmed, sidled to the exit. He too disappeared.

"Mistletoe?" muttered Miss Cheviot.

"In your hair." Morgan did not move his eyes from Barr's but caught a glimpse of Miss Cheviot's arms moving. "Ah. Have you all of it?" he said.

"I believe so. How did that get there?"

"I will explain later. Mr. Kenway, your excuse has vanished. And perhaps you might, er, vanish as well?"

"You'll regret this," snarled the younger man before he pushed by Morgan. The sound of his footsteps disappeared down the passage.

When certain Kenway was truly gone, Morgan turned. "Miss Cheviot? Are you all right?"

She ignored his question. "You knew they meant mischief?"

"I overheard part of a plot." He nodded toward the empty boxes. "I was impressed by your handling of them. You knew they meant trouble, did you not?"

"My cousin is not one to offer aid unasked. Nor does he engage in innocent jests. He is like an adder, Mr. St. Austell. There is always a bite to what he considers humor." She sighed. "I hoped I might move among them and, while they were occupied, might leave. Barr guessed." She shrugged. "He would not allow me by."

"What would you have done if he'd managed to renew his plot?"

She straightened, her chin rising. "What could I have done? Barr has the odd ability to coax others into doing his will. I fear that, without your aid, for which I thank you, he'd have seen me ruined."

"Ruined?"

"You would not have followed had you no notion what was in the wind, so do not pretend. Barr plotted my ruin. He cannot abide that anyone cross his will. My rejection of his offer of marriage did that. So, if *he* could not wed me, then *no one* would. Ever." She shrugged again, a frenchified gesture. "That is the way his mind works."

"I can think of happier gifts for Boxing Day giving," said Morgan. She shuddered. "Should not Oswin Kenway be told your plight?"

Miss Cheviot's withdrawn expression appeared, turning her alabaster features to marble. "Thank you for the excellent advice, Mr. St. Austell."

Morgan's eyes narrowed and his lips tipped the merest little bit. "Thank you, but no thank you?" He sobered. "Why do you *not* seek such obvious protection?" He saw a flicker of bitterness which disappeared instantly. "Ah! He supports Kenway's suit." Morgan frowned. *"Why* does he do so?"

Miss Cheviot's features softened and she tipped her head to stare thoughtfully, blankly, into a corner. "An excellent question. Why have I not asked it myself?"

"Forgive the impertinence, but I suspect you are not wealthy. So it cannot be the common reason, that you would bring his son a large dowry."

She chuckled. "It is *worse* than *not wealthy.* I must ask my cousin for every pence I spend! Yet"—she frowned—"my cousin *does* support Barr's suit. His nephew, not his son, you know. He adopted Barr as his heir." She frowned. "And Oswin *has* pressed me to change my mind."

Morgan's curiosity itched. It would require scratching until he solved the mystery. "You were quite young when your parents died, were you not?"

"Still in leading strings. I've no memory of them."

"Too young, then, to know your circumstances. Is it possible, Miss Cheviot, that your cousin lied about your situation? That he has always planned to gain a fortune for himself and his family? It would explain his behavior now, his insistence you wed your cousin."

"A Gothic plot?" Miss Cheviot smiled wanly. "Oswin hasn't the intelligence to contrive such a plan. Besides, from discussions I've had with people who knew them, I know that, although charming and fun-loving, my parents were spendthrifts. Cousin Oswin told me they had rowed so far up River Tick they jested they might move to debtor's prison and save the bailiffs the need to escort them there."

"I see." It was a lie. He did *not* see. "My dear, I cannot like your situation."

Her lips twitched. "Nor I, sir." The smile, if such it was, faded. "I hoped Barr would behave during the ten days of Christmas. The season of peace and good will! Besides, we've company and *usually* he is careful to keep others ignorant of his temper."

"This plot was, I think, the invention of the moment when he saw the mistletoe fall into your hair."

She looked at her hands which cradled the delicate piece of greenery and back up at Morgan. "You too saw it fall?"

"Yes." His eyes narrowed, his lips tipping a trifle. "We've a kitten loose among us. A mischievous, curious and active little beast."

"A young tabby? Mostly gray? On the beams?"

Morgan nodded.

"I wonder how Purrmew escaped my rooms." Her eyes widened. "Surely the silly creature will not jump from the beam. Oh dear! You don't suppose, do you, that Purrmew attempted to catch one of the favors as it floated by?"

"Be easy," soothed Morgan. "He was no longer perched up there when the favors were tossed."

Nodding, Miss Cheviot relaxed. "I must close the shutters. Such an odd device they are. I cannot understand their purpose."

"I suspect this is the last possible defense of an embattled castle. If an enemy achieved entry and fought their way up, bowmen here, aiming across at that stairwell"—he gestured to a dark opening in the wall opposite—"could hold them off as long as they had arrows."

"You appear to know a great deal about it."

He tipped a shutter into place. "It is my hobby, defensive architecture." He settled the second shutter and turned. "Perhaps we should return to the party before we are missed."

"I will not be missed."

"Barr Kenway might raise an alarm."

"He will not. Forcing me into a compromising situation where I'd be expected to wed another would do *his* suit no good."

Morgan's steady gaze reminded her of Barr's recent plans. Instantly, Miss Cheviot's brown eyes, which should never look cold, iced over and Morgan knew what Jaimy meant by being touched by hoarfrost.

"You may relax, Mr. St. Austell, and cease worrying you will be entrapped in such a way. It will not happen, but if you *were* forced by convention to ask for my hand, I would refuse you. You are safe."

The surprising thought flitted through Morgan's mind that he was less than certain he wished to be safe. Grace Cheviot neither fell into hysterics when confronting a situation which would send any other woman into a swoon, nor did she whine or cling. She spoke sensibly, remaining poised even when afraid. In fact, Grace Cheviot was an admirable woman.

And a woman who was not treated well by her family.

Morgan discovered in himself strong chivalrous feelings toward Miss Cheviot. He watched her tip down the lids to the crates. Her extended arms pulled her gown tight and Morgan recognized still other feelings in himself, less surprising feelings. *Feelings far from chivalrous.*

The mistletoe lay near to hand and he placed the sprig back into her hair. He reached for her shoulders. Very gently he turned up her face. Very slowly, he lowered his mouth to touch her lips. Touch them again.

When she did not withdraw, he pressed a quick hard kiss to her mouth and then looked into her bemused brown eyes. Cold?

Oh no. Definitely not. Not even particularly shy, he decided. But unused to gentleness, to affection? Yes, that, he feared, was true.

Morgan lifted the mistletoe from her hair and removed three of the berries, signifying the three touches of mouth to mouth. He dropped the sprig into her hand. Regretfully, he watched the remaining waxy white berries disappear, her fingers closing around them. There were four more. Seven in all. Not six, as Barr had guessed.

"Shall we go?" he asked softly.

"Yes." Her bemused expression cleared. "Yes, most definitely it is time to go." She paused only to remove the candle from the sconce.

Morgan, swearing a silent oath to protect her, followed after on silent feet. He'd not realized *how* silent until she turned and recoiled, startled, to find him on her heels. "You wished to say something?" he asked softly.

Miss Cheviot drew in a deep breath. "Yes. I truly doubt there would be a problem if we appeared together, but, it is the better part of valor, is it not, if we do not. You go as you came and I"—her eyes twinkled—"will achieve another manner of entrance."

Morgan, instantly alert, tipped his head. "There are other passages through these walls?"

"All the very best Gothic tales require secret passages," she said in an affectedly hushed voice. She smiled, impish lights dancing in her eyes. "If I admitted their existence, they would not remain secret. Assuming they exist, of course."

Her funning drew a smile, but it faded. "If you insist I will return as I came, but you go carefully. It is imperative you avoid your cousin."

"You may depend on it!"

"May I make a suggestion?"

"Of course."

"Will you carry this blade?"

She stared at the small knife in his hand. "Where did that come from?"

Morgan heard a touch of alarm and a sardonic smile tipped

his lips. "I have carried it for years. More than once, it saved my life. Will you"—he caught her gaze—"carry it now?"

She frowned. "How? A woman's clothing makes hiding such a thing difficult."

Morgan tipped back his cuff, revealing the sheath strapped around his arm. "I have noticed you favor long sleeves to your gowns, which is only sensible at this time of year. Might you contrive something if I give you the sheath as well?"

"It is very generous, but is it not important to you?"

"It is ridiculous for me to go armed here in England. It is merely habit. Will you take it?"

She hesitated. "Yes," she said with sudden decision. Carefully she took the short-bladed knife and stared at the well-worn carving on the ivory handle.

"It is the St. Austell crest," he said. He undid the sheath and extended the leather toward her.

She met his gaze with an intensity he found riveting. "Perhaps," she said, "you would add to your kindness by teaching me how best to use it. Tomorrow I deliver baskets to the Kenway tenants. Might we not—"

"Tell me where to meet you," he interrupted. "Somewhere beyond view of those who would gossip if we left the castle together. Lady Merryweather, for instance!"

"A prime gossip who should always be avoided. But I'd not have thought of, er, *gulling* our guests in that particular fashion!" Before slipping up the stairs she gave him directions for their meeting.

Morgan waited, fearing she might yet run into trouble, but there was no sound so he returned to the hall where he stumbled over the kitten. He picked up Purrmew, who seemed tense, butting his head urgently against Morgan's chin. As his senses were assaulted by the tangy resin smell of evergreens permeating the cat's fur, Morgan soothed him.

Evergreens.

Morgan blinked. Christmas. Once again he had forgotten Christmas. Putting the thought aside, he scanned the crowd, relieved to see Barr Kenway in the midst of a raucous group.

Cuddling Purrmew, he eased nearer. The men discussed a badger baiting. Bets were laid.

Just the entertainment to appeal to our Barr! thought Morgan, more than a trifle caustically.

Glad he'd already given the impression of liking his own company, Morgan left the castle early the following morning. He wandered west along the cliffs until well beyond view of anyone who might have watched his departure. Then he turned inland and, eventually, back east. His years scouting unknown territory while spying on French troop movements provided the skill so that he approached the lane at very nearly the exact point Miss Cheviot had suggested.

Five minutes later Miss Cheviot pulled a cart up beside him. "I was uncertain you would remember," she said and offered him the reins to the elderly gelding pulling the lowly cart.

He refused the reins and climbed onto the passenger side. "Do not look at me as if I had three heads," he said politely, but with a narrow-eyed smile.

She returned the smile, hers a trifle rueful. "You surprise me. Barr will never allow himself to be driven by a female. Nor will my cousin. I thought it a trait all men shared."

"I doubt I would back you in a curricle race, Miss Cheviot, which is the sort of prejudice you likely expect of a man. But we are merely making a few deliveries, are we not?" He glanced into the back of the cart and his brows arched. "Quite a few deliveries?"

She chuckled. "It bothers me that my cousin will not send out the baskets on Boxing Day. Still, when he orders the Revel's feast it includes a generous overestimate of what will be needed for the party."

"So that the kitchen need not prepare huge quantities of food twice?"

"I doubt he has in mind the convenience of the kitchen so much as his own. The family meals deteriorate when Cook must deal with anything so very out of the way."

Miss Cheviot clucked her tongue and the placid gelding

moved off. They drove inland between the ubiquitous low stone fences or winter-ragged hedges, passing through softly rolling countryside. Between stops they spoke of a number of things, none of which had any bearing on the preceding evening's contretemps. Morgan wondered how to introduce the subject, how to ask the questions he wished answered.

When only the smallest basket remained, Miss Cheviot turned down a narrow track toward the coast. She came to an abandoned field and asked Morgan to open a rickety gate. There they unharnessed the gelding.

"He'll be fine," she said when Morgan worried about the low wall. "Old Ivy hasn't an adventurous bone in his body!"

Miss Cheviot lifted the last basket from the cart which, after a brief struggle, Morgan removed from her hands. "I am unused to anyone helping me," she said and led the way to a path down the cliff face. "When the weather is good I occasionally have a little pick-nick here. You will share my basket, will you not?" Morgan hesitated. "You fear you'll be compromised?" The gamin expression he'd noted once before flitted across her features. "You need not. This is Smugglers' Cove, where no one *ever* goes. Not uninvited."

"You have an invitation?" he asked politely.

She chuckled. "No, but it is known I come here. I am careful to put the word about when I mean to do so."

"I cannot approve of smuggling," said Morgan sternly. "It was unwise to allow me to know about this place."

"Do you know where it is?"

"I could find it again."

She sobered. "Mr. St. Austell, we are far from London where profits might tempt a large trade. For the few men who cross the water and return with a keg or two, perhaps a little wine, the custom is so ancient its history is lost in time. Please do not allow modern legalities to make wretched their families, which truly would not understand why anyone wished to interfere."

"The problem, my dear, is not the law, but the gold. English gold pays for French weapons to kill English soldiers."

Miss Cheviot's eyes widened. "I will let that be known. The

men will be appalled at what they have done and will cease their trips immediately. Concern yourself no further."

"You have great faith in their loyalty."

Her chin rose. "I do indeed. Now, will you join me in one of my small rebellions to my guardian's strict rules?"

"His rules?" asked Morgan casually. *Finally,* he thought, *the subject I wish to discuss!*

Instead of the sad story he expected, Miss Cheviot made a joke of the way she'd been reared. Nevertheless, Morgan was shocked by how thoroughly she was fenced away from anyone who might become a danger to the Kenways' plans.

The cove was small and sheltered by arms of land curving into the water. The cliff face contained a few shallow caves. Miss Cheviot led the way to one in which a ledge at the back made a crude bench and a large block of stone before it an almost level table.

"This looks as if it had been arranged for pick-nicks," said Morgan.

"It is quite wonderful how nature occasionally anticipates our wishes, is it not?" She opened the basket. "We have wasted a great deal of time very pleasantly, but I suspect you've questions and, of course, I desire that you teach me to use this knife." She turned and lifted her sleeve, revealing how she had adapted the sheath to her slimmer arm. "I fear I've ruined the leather for any other use," she said, casting him a glance.

"You need not return it. I will ask questions while we eat and then teach you a trick or two when we are done."

"Ask away," she said cheerfully, concentrating on the plate she filled for him.

Morgan pondered how to begin. "Miss Cheviot, have you no relatives beyond your cousins? Your father's family perhaps?"

"My father's family?"

"Somewhere in my head I've knowledge of your name which predates our meeting."

Miss Cheviot chewed thoughtfully. "I wonder"—she waved the chicken leg—"why it never occurred to me to ask about my father's family. Perhaps because Cousin Oswin is not particularly forthcoming and Dorcus still more closemouthed, pokering up whenever I mentioned my parents, giving the impression my father was not quite the thing. Perhaps he *had* no family? At least"—she smiled that quick gamin smile—"none of which one may speak?"

Morgan chuckled, then sobered. "I have searched my mind, trying to recall why your name strikes sparks." He bit his lip, staring over the water, then shrugged. "I ask about relatives because I hoped someone might rescue you if they knew your plight. Tell me, if it will not upset you, of your parents' accident."

"I know no details. In fact"—her eyes widened—"now that you ask pointed questions, I find it surprising how little I know about anything! I was born at the castle and, once I was abandoned to the care of a wet nurse, my parents returned to the irresponsible way of life which had been theirs before I interfered in their pleasures. They made a habit of visiting friends, you see, always moving on just before they wore out their welcome."

"Why," asked Morgan, "do I hear Mrs. Dorcus Kenway speaking rather than you using words of *your* choosing?"

Miss Cheviot opened her mouth. Closed it. Then tried again. "I see exactly what you mean. Abandoned me. Irresponsible way of life. Wore out their welcome. I, as you guessed, parroted the story I was told."

"You cannot say exactly how they died?"

"An accident. Beyond that? No." She stared out over the water. "I have been surprisingly lacking in curiosity, have I not?"

"But not totally without interest." She cast him a look and he added, "Last night you said people who knew them told you they were charming."

"But I did not question it, did I? I simply accepted that spongers, living by their wits, must be charming. There was no contradiction."

"I see. Can you tell me the names of their particular friends?"

"You wish to talk to someone who knew them well?"

"Yes."

"It was so long ago. Now, who used to be kind to me for their sake?" Miss Cheviot gazed thoughtfully at a seagull which hovered hopefully. "Grampond . . . ? No. Lord *Grampound*."

"The Grampound to whom you must refer died some years ago. Who else?"

"It has been so long. There was a baronet who would tease me that I looked like my mother. Sir Owen. That was his name."

"I am fairly well-acquainted with Owen Tavistock but his home is too far for a morning call."

"What more can I tell you?"

"I would know why your cousin does everything possible to prevent your meeting men who might steal you from his control," said Morgan promptly. "But you have said you cannot answer that. Cheviot, *Cheviot,*" he repeated, trying to jog his memory. "Do you know where your mother met your father?"

"Now that I know. They met and married early in her first season. My mother's parents died not long after when my grandfather succumbed to scarlet fever and my grandmother, nursing him, took it from him."

"Then your father's will designated Cousin Kenway your guardian?"

Miss Cheviot got that mischievous look again. "My dear St. Austell! Do you truly believe anyone as irresponsible, as flighty as my parents are reputed to have been, would have done something so sensible as leave a will?"

Morgan frowned. "Are you certain?"

It was Miss Cheviot's turn to frown. "What can you mean?"

"It is all of a piece, is it not? There is no one to say your cousin nay in anything he tells you, to any plans he makes. But, my dear Miss Cheviot, when a man weds, a will is invariably drawn up, a part of the marriage settlements."

"How could one discover if such a thing ever existed?"

"They married in London?" She nodded and Morgan rubbed his chin. "If you do not object, I will write my London solicitor."

"If you think he can help, do so with my blessing."

"Perhaps Baker can discover the name of your father's solicitor, can ask if there was a will." Baker might also, thought Morgan, explain why the name Cheviot rang faint but interesting bells!

They put away the remnants of the pick-nick and, thinking, watched the waves roll up the rocky shore and out.

Morgan shook himself. "If we are to practice with that knife, we'd best begin. After I teach you the basic moves I will walk across the peninsula to St. Ives where I will hire a horse. A Kenway groom will return the beast and, if asked, can supply me with an alibi for my long absence."

She chuckled. "You are incorrigible."

"True, but it is also true, is it not, that you should not be absent much longer?"

"Yes. Although I do tend to procrastinate when sent on errands."

"I see Kenway has less control over you than he believes."

"I have managed to design a life for myself in and around the one he wishes me to lead," she admitted.

"I admire you for it. Most women would be governed by his authority and become mild little mice."

"I do not believe it is in me to scurry mouselike, forever looking fearfully over my shoulder." Her impish grin faded. "But I must not mislead you. My cousins were never unkind. I had excellent governesses and am not a drudge as was Cinderella in the old tale. Although it has been some years now, we traveled. But often I am alone, thrown onto my own devices. As a result, I am independent and deal with my problems by myself."

"Most problems, but not, perhaps, Barr Kenway in, hmm, a *venomous* mood. Let us see if we cannot do a little something toward defanging Cousin Barr."

Miss Cheviot was agile and quick to learn, and when they were ready to leave the cove almost an hour later she admitted to feeling easier in her mind where her cousin's machinations were concerned. "Barr is a coward," she explained. "Moreover, he hates the sight of his own blood. I've seen him green and woozy from nothing more than a drop of blood from a prick to his finger. One small cut with your knife will, as you jested, defang my snake of a cousin!"

On a wide place, halfway up the path, she turned, smiling. "Thank you, Mr. St. Austell. I am still in danger from my cousin, but that danger can now be faced with less fear. Last night I had no hope. Now I do. But I apologize! Dealing with my problems must make this one of the least pleasant Christmas seasons you have known."

"The least pleasant," he retorted, "was the year I was trapped behind French lines, enduring more than four and twenty hours lying in a shallow ditch with the French camped around me. I feared that, at any moment, one would stumble over me. *This* is"—his eyes smiled—"a far more pleasant Christmas!"

She chuckled. "I will apologize no more then, but only hope you continue to enjoy yourself."

"You are not the least bit shy, are you?" *How could I have blurted out such a thing!* he wondered.

She blinked. "Shy? Who has said I am shy?"

"I thought it," he admitted. "What I *heard* was that you are cold. I didn't believe it and I was correct in that, at least, was I not?" As he spoke he moved up the path toward her. He stopped a little below her and they faced each other, their eyes level.

"Cold." She stared beyond him, out over the waves. "Perhaps I have seemed so," she said slowly. "Dorcus insists that I not play the flirt. Besides, most of Barr's friends are not the sort I can like, so it is not difficult to treat them with a certain coolness."

"Of those I saw last night, the only one I felt might have a modicum of sense was called Jaimy. Perhaps that was merely because he is deeply enamored of someone and has no time for Barr Kenway's games?"

"James is a decent soul. Occasionally, he has gotten into difficulties following Barr about, but for the most part it is his good sense which keeps the boys from serious trouble. They are no longer boys, however. I fear his influence is less than formerly, which is too bad."

"They have reached an age where mischief of Barr's sort appears manly. They will rue it if he leads them into serious trouble. As he is likely to do from boredom if no other reason. My dear Miss Cheviot, I wish to thank you for a most pleasant morning." He held out his hand and she placed hers in it. He lifted it, turned it, and placed a kiss on her wrist above her glove. He looked up and his eyes gleamed at her rosy cheeks.

"You needn't flirt with me, Mr. St. Austell," she said, just a touch of chill to her tone."

"Perhaps I am not flirting," said Morgan and smiled a rare true smile.

Although he smiled, he felt stone cold sober. Because it was true. He was *not* flirting. Unexpectedly and without seeking her, he had found the woman he could face gladly across the breakfast cups. Morning after morning, year after year.

Now he must win her and wed her in the face of relatives who would deny him her hand. So, before furthering his plans, he must save her from her family! Morgan touched her chin with one finger and then her lips. For a moment he let his finger linger on her lower lip, fighting temptation.

We are alone, he scolded himself. *It would be unfair.*

"You sigh," she said. "Why?"

"My dear, you must go. I have a great longing to kiss you and that would never do. Not here and now. Not"—his eyes glinted with dark humor—"when you cannot scream bloody murder and know that rescue is near to hand."

The roses in her cheeks returned in a rush. Then, utterly unexpectedly, she raised her hand, curving it up over his head and lightly touching his hair. She leaned forward and, for a moment, pressed her lips to his. Before he could react, she rushed up the path away from him.

At the top she turned, smiling, and waved a small bit of greenery. "Just another mistletoe kiss, Mr. St. Austell. But this time *I* may keep the berry!" And then, on a delightfully contagious laugh, she disappeared. When he caught her up, she was already harnessing the horse.

Late that night, a hooded lantern in hand, St. Austell returned to the corner of the castle in which the ancient keep formed the walls. Miss Cheviot's kitten accompanied him, scurrying ahead, running back, disappearing into the dark only to reappear suddenly and pounce on a moving shadow provided by the lamp. Now and again he jumped straight up, only to twist around before landing on all four paws.

Morgan smiled at the animal's engaging antics and recalled how he was forced, that morning, to hand the creature to a groom when he went off to his tryst with Miss Cheviot. The kitten, it seemed, had adopted him. But now again Morgan felt he must prevent the creature from accompanying him and, with difficulty, he closed a door on Purrmew. Morgan was determined to discover the other secret passages and particularly wished to find the escape tunnel which must have existed at one time, although perhaps no longer.

Morgan began his search at the barred door at the top of the stairs. His careful inspection gradually returned him to Miss Cheviot's hidden room. He'd found nothing, but Miss Cheviot had reappeared from quite another direction than his own. There *must* be another passage.

Morgan set the lantern on one crate and himself on the other. Mentally, he traced through books he'd studied, recalling methods of secreting the entrances to escape routes. As he cogitated, his gaze drifted around the shadowy room . . . and caught on a faint crack around one slab. He rose, went to it and, stamped on it. It rang hollow.

And now, he thought, *we'll see if it tips . . . like this!*

Leading downward were dangerously narrow steps. Morgan lowered himself carefully as far as a wider step, there so one could replace the cover stone, which he did before moving on. For well over an hour he explored the passages. Twice he came to what seemed dead ends and twice discovered another stone which, when raised, revealed stairs.

Finally he reached a point where there seemed no way to go on. None of the flooring stones had cracks around them. None sounded hollow. Only by accident did he tilt his lantern in such a way he noticed half a footprint in the dust just next the wall.

Half a print!

Long minutes later Morgan breathed a soft, "Aha!"

The opening was less than a yard high and narrow. Bending double, Morgan twisted his shoulders and, with a grunt, passed through. Fearing he'd hit his head, he straightened slowly. And blinked. It was a storeroom. One in which newly installed shelves, the wood still raw looking, held an array of silks, delicate lace and other luxuries.

And *all were out of France.*

Someone was smuggling on a far grander scale than that Miss Cheviot had described. Had she led him up the primrose path? Surely not. Why should she protect Barr Kenway, his prime suspect, when she was in true danger thanks to her refusal to wed the man.

Did this have something to do with why the Kenway men wished for the wedding? But what? And if Kenway *had* managed to ruin Miss Cheviot that Boxing Day evening, would that have been an alternate solution to whatever problem the cousins' marriage would solve?

But *what* problem? Morgan stared at the smuggled goods, his thoughts roiling until it occurred to him that it would be safer to do his thinking elsewhere. He returned to his room where his mind continued to circle, going nowhere.

The next few days merely proved how difficult it was for a man to spend time with Grace Cheviot. It was improper to be alone with her, of course, but even when they found an innocent few moments in which they might converse, one of the Kenways soon joined them and some excuse was made to separate them. Miss Cheviot would be sent on an errand or Morgan invited to join a game of cards or billiards. Or plans would emerge involving the whole party. A ride to some point of local interest perhaps, or charades which isolated Miss Cheviot within the company. Before his interest in her became too obvious, Morgan ceased his attempts to approach her. She was too carefully guarded.

One afternoon Morgan sat in the library in a high-backed chair near the fireplace. He was hidden by it when Miss Cheviot entered with Dorcus.

". . . But," said Grace, continuing a conversation begun in the hall, "why can you *not* tell me more about my mother? Surely you knew her?"

"Oh yes. Skitterwitted chit who married to disoblige the family. You'll not follow in her footsteps I assure you. Better you know no more."

"It is unfair that you will tell me nothing about my family. I cannot understand why you are reluctant to do so."

Morgan smiled at the innocence, the touch of irritation he read in Miss Cheviot's voice, but he wondered if she had overdone it just a trifle. He also thought, but only briefly, of announcing his presence.

"Not reluctant," insisted Dorcus. "Just don't see that it will do you the least jot of good."

"Tell me how they died."

"But you know." The woman's exasperation was obvious. "Travelling in dangerous weather. Went despite it because they always had to have their way."

"But *where* were they going? Where did it happen?"

"Missy, you ask too many impertinent questions," said Dorcus Kenway. "I don't like it."

Silence followed this. Then, quietly, "Before I came of age I accepted that you and my cousin had the right to decide what was best for me. But now I am fully adult and I feel it my right to know more."

"Nonsense," blustered Dorcus. "What put such utter nonsense into your head?"

"Perhaps the fact that when asked kind questions about my family I am unable to respond as any other sensible adult could do!"

"Cut 'em."

"Why pretend a person does not exist when it makes far more sense to learn what I should know, enabling me to answer politely?"

Again silence stretched. Then, her tone one of baffled outrage, Dorcus exploded, "Missy, you will cease asking questions instantly!"

Morgan heard the click of one set of rapidly receding footsteps. The door slammed. Then he heard a sigh. He rose to his feet. "I didn't mean to eavesdrop, Miss Cheviot, but thought it better, perhaps, if your cousin was unaware anyone heard that."

"Mr. St. Austell!"

He noted the fluctuating color in her cheeks. "It is good to have a moment with you, my dear." She stared at him, a doubtful look in her eye. "I have avoided you, you know, so I'd rouse no curiosity in your family as to my intentions." He gave her a warm look.

Her eyes widened and an embarrassed laugh escaped her. "Is

that it? I thought you had lost interest in me. I mean, in my problems," she amended.

"If anything my interest is stronger than ever. In you *and* your problems. Still, until we know more, it is better that I not upset the Kenways by obviously pursuing you. Have you a moment to sit with me?" He led her toward a pair of chairs, sitting opposite her so he'd not be tempted to draw her into his arms, not be tempted to kiss her until she'd never again doubt his interest *in her*.

Purrmew appeared from somewhere and jumped into Miss Cheviot's lap. For a time they spoke of this, that and nothing in particular. He watched her play with an envelope made of bright silks, teasing the kitten with the trailing fringe. She would lift it just beyond a reaching claw, then let the young cat catch it, clutch it and paw at it with its hind feet.

Finally Morgan broke off what he was saying to ask what it was she held. He was surprised when she blushed rosily.

"A bit of nonsense," she admitted, at which he arched a brow in query.

"Which is no answer," he teased.

The blush deepened. "Merely the bit of mistletoe."

"It grew brittle?"

"Yes. It fell apart, but I wish to keep it. A memento of . . ." She halted, incapable of finishing the thought.

"Of mistletoe kisses shared with a . . . friend?" he suggested.

The blush returned and her eyes flickered up to meet his. He held her gaze for a long moment before hers dropped to the silken packet.

"Are you my friend?" she asked softly.

"I hope so. Miss Cheviot, will it distress you if I admit I hope to become *more* than your friend?"

This time when her gaze met his there was a touch of horror, perhaps fear, in it.

Hastily Morgan added, "My intentions are wholly honorable! Believe me, I would never insult you in the way you suspect."

That brought forth the impish expression he had come to love. "Am I so easily read that you must leap to reassure me?"

"Your expression spoke as clearly as words."

"Hmm. Perhaps it was my expression which roused suspicions in Cousin Dorcus when I questioned her."

"You've had little practice at deception. After all, it is not something one practices."

"Unless one is Cousin Barr. *He* is well-practiced in the art."

And so too are your other cousins. One only wonders exactly what particular deception is involved. Morgan didn't utter that thought. Instead he said, "I wrote my solicitor when I returned from our pick-nick. I hope I'll have an answer before I must leave."

"Do you truly think he can discover something? After so many years?"

"If he knows nothing himself, he will know how to find out. But if he must seek answers, it will take longer. Unfortunately my invitation ends in a little more than a week now."

"I will be sorry to see you go."

He sensed her sincerity, but not her reason. She had made no direct response to his assertion that his intentions were honorable. Did she see him as merely her knight in shining armor, protecting her from Barr Kenway? Was it even possible she felt the same liking, the rapport that comes before loving? Putting aside questions for which he'd no answers, Morgan said, "If, when I must go, we still know nothing, I will visit Tavistock, and discover what he can tell me."

She breathed in a deep breath and let it out slowly, her eyes closing. "Thank you," she said. "I feared that, once gone, you would forget my problems."

"Have I not said I harbor intentions toward you?" His tone was more caressing than quite proper.

"You tease me."

"No. Never."

"Intentions . . . may also be forgotten," she said, her chin rising.

"These intentions," he said softly, "cannot be easily forgotten. Believe me."

"I . . ." Her kitten batted her chin and her head shot around, her eyes widening in sudden fear. "I hear someone," she said and stood up. "Come!"

Morgan found himself crouched inside a cramped little cubby beside the fireplace, the kitten's tail caressing his nose. He hoped he'd not sneeze—from that or the dust! Not far from where he crouched he knew Miss Cheviot, who had taken a book from a shelf as she passed it, sat in a window seat.

"Ah! Your nose in a book, is it?" Morgan heard Barr Kenway's sneering tones. "When you *should* be helping our cousins entertain our guests. Come."

"Must I?" she asked plaintively.

"You must. Oswin decreed it. Old Ozzy grows distressed when you go off alone. You'll not wish our cousin to feel distress."

"He is never so much in need of my presence when there is no company. Besides, I have noticed that he is never particularly happy when I *do* entertain guests. Your words make no sense."

"There are *lady* guests. It is your duty to see to *their* pleasure."

"Surely it is Dorcus's duty!"

"You have grown exceedingly argumentative, my dear. I do not like that in a woman. When we are married—"

"Which," she interrupted, "will be never."

"When we wed"—Morgan heard a threat in Barr's voice— "you will learn your place. Put aside the book and come at once"—there was a brief pause—"before I must force you."

Morgan's temper caught fire and his hand tightened around the kitten who mewed softly. The sound recalled him to the dangers of the situation and, using the control he'd learned in the army, he remained silent and kept the cat from making another, possibly fatal, noise.

"Oh all right, then . . ."

There was an odd note to Miss Cheviot's voice and Morgan wondered if she merely pretended irritation or if she had heard her kitten's cry.

". . . I will come." He heard the rustle of her skirts. "But it is too bad of you, Barr, that I cannot have a minute to myself. What am I to do?"

The closing door shut off Barr's response and Morgan eased himself from the cubbyhole. The kitten hopped to the window seat where, between sour glances cast in Morgan's direction, he licked himself clean. Morgan, reminded by the kitten, brushed down his clothes and hoped no cobwebs remained to reveal where he'd been.

Neat again, he picked up Miss Cheviot's book. A glance at it set him to chuckling. *It is lucky,* he thought as he reshelved it, *that Cousin Barr did not take a closer look!* Not only was the tome in Italian, but, from the page he skimmed, Morgan deemed the subject totally unsuited to feminine perusal: The passage was warm enough it brought heat to his ears.

Two days passed frustratingly slowly. Then an ancient travelling coach pulled up before the castle. Morgan, who loitered nearby, was exceedingly surprised to see his solicitor hop down. He joined Baker just in time to help ease a heavy-set elderly gentleman to the ground.

"What a surprise, Baker," said Morgan.

"Nothing to the surprise in your letter, my old friend. I give you the honor of greeting Miss Cheviot's great uncle by marriage. Comte de Cheviot was informed his great niece died with his nephew and his wife. Sir!" he added, turning to the comte. "Another of my clients, Mr. Morgan St. Austell, who had the kindness to write us the news of Miss Cheviot's continued existence."

The old gentleman wheezed a greeting, the faintest of French accents giving his English an interesting intonation. Although he said all that was proper, including fervent gratitude for news of his niece, he barely looked at Morgan, his gaze glued to the huge doors which stood open to the surprisingly warm winter day.

". . . And my niece?" the old gentleman finished.

"She was picking flowers for the house not ten minutes ago. I doubt she is done. Shall we stroll around the corner to the cutting garden?"

The comte nodded regally. One hand clutching an ebony cane and the other Baker's wrist, he set off. The Frenchman saw Miss Cheviot just as she reached for a lovely rose which had survived the season's chill nights. He stopped and Morgan saw Baker wince as the mans's grip tightened.

"It is she." The comte's eyes devoured Miss Cheviot's features.

Miss Cheviot noticed the strangers. She glanced at Morgan as she approached. "Mr. St. Austell?"

"Miss Cheviot, allow me the happy duty of introducing to your notice your great uncle"—he smiled to see her color fluctuate at the news—"the Comte de Cheviot! Sir, be pleased to meet your niece, Miss Grace Cheviot."

"My dear child!" Tears ran down the Frenchman's cheeks. "You must know how very much you look like your lovely mother!"

"I did not know, but I am glad of it. Welcome to Kenway Castle." Miss Cheviot glanced up and all expression faded from her face. "Ah. My cousin."

She introduced Barr who, upon hearing the Cheviot name, made no attempt to hide a thundering bad temper.

"If you will come with me," said Grace, "we will find Oswin Kenway, whom you will wish to meet." She clutched her basket and stepped forward.

For a moment, Barr did not move. He glanced at the three men—the Frenchman, the second stranger introduced as Mr. Baker, and, lastly, at Morgan.

"This is your doing," he snarled before turning on his heel and rushing back the way he'd come.

"Barr will inform my cousin and his wife of your arrival," said Miss Cheviot. Her voice was light, her expression grim. "Ah! This is quite wonderful," she added. "That you would come so far."

"I could do no other. I believed you dead, my child. And then to discover you did *not* die with your parents! Why"—his voice took on a touch of petulance—"was I misinformed?"

"Since I knew nothing of your existence, I cannot explain it," said Miss Cheviot. Her tone soothed, but her frown did not smooth away. "I have only recently begun questioning my lack of knowledge concerning my parents. My cousins refuse to give me information so Mr. St. Austell was kind enough to write his solicitor to see what he could discover, and he, wonderful man that he is"—she flashed a smile toward Baker who flushed at the praise—"discovered *you*."

The Frenchman wheezed a chuckle. "Oh, he did not *discover*

me. He has known me since he was no more than a, what do you say?" The comte snapped his fingers once, a second time. "A whippersnapper?"

"Whippersnapper," said Baker softly.

"His grandfather was my solicitor when I first came to England and I have remained with the firm. As you see."

"That is where I've heard the name!" said Morgan. "You, Baker, have mentioned the comte."

"Very likely," said Baker. "Was Kenway as angry as he appeared?"

"Since the Kenways have done their best to isolate Miss Cheviot, I suspect he is indeed angry an unknown relative has appeared."

"If, my dear niece, you are not particularly fond of your relatives, why do you tolerate them?" asked the comte politely.

"They have given me a home since I was orphaned. I've nowhere to go."

"I did not mean that *you* should go, chère. I meant why do you not ask them to leave? It is your home, after all."

Miss Cheviot stopped, drawing the men to a halt. Her color faded to the point Morgan reached for her, but she gave herself a little shake and managed to control what had appeared an imminent swoon. *"My home?"* she asked.

"Of course. Your mother, at her father's death, became baroness in her own right. You, her only child, are Baroness Kenway now that she is dead. You did not know," finished her great uncle. It was not a question.

"I did not know."

"I wondered when you were introduced as a mere miss." The old man caught Baker's eye. He glared arrogantly. "I believe, Mr. Baker, that it is a nest of vipers with which we deal." He tapped Baker's leg with his cane. "You must do something."

"If Miss Chevi—" He started over. "If Baroness Kenway wishes me to act for her, of course I will be pleased to do her bidding."

"Yes, please." Grace drew in a deep breath. "I cannot take it all in. *My* home? The castle is *mine?"*

"We wondered why your cousin wished for you and Barr to wed," said Morgan. "Now we know, do we not?"

"A marriage to legitimize what they did illegally," suggested Baker. "Do you wish them removed from the castle while we sort out exactly what that is?" Baker looked beyond his new client. "Ah! We've no time to plan, my dear Baroness. At least, I assume these people approaching are your cousins?"

"My cousin, his wife, and Cousin Barr. All of them."

"Quickly. Do you want them removed from the castle?"

"Cousin Barr? *Definitely yes.*" She bit her lip. "Perhaps not the others?"

"What is this? What is Barr saying?" blustered Oswin as he bustled up.

"Merely that my great uncle has arrived for a visit," said Grace. Her arms crossed and her toe tapped. "A great uncle of whose existence I was unaware."

"Missy, you have been imposed upon," said her aunt in her dead-voice tone. "Surely you would know."

"I would know only if you had told me," said Grace. "And you refuse to discuss my parents. If I am imposed upon, my dear Dorcus, then who, I wonder, has been imposing?"

Oswin spluttered, cast a hunted look around, and then, his wife's fingers pinching him—hard, or so the twitch he gave in response indicated—he swallowed. "Nonsense. We reared you and cared for you and gave you everything—"

"Using what for money?" interrupted Baker, his voice stern.

"What?"

"You gave her everything," he said, "using what coin to pay for it?"

"You keep out of this."

"I cannot," said Baker blandly. "The Baroness"—the Kenways cast each other quick looks, but again Oswin alone revealed discomfort—"has asked that I act as her solicitor."

"Solicitor!" Oswin swallowed.

"As her solicitor, my first duty is to check her financial position. You, sir, will supply records going back to the death of her parents. Twenty odd years of records. I must determine any and all misuse of her income."

"You will discover nothing of the sort," said Barr smoothly, and Oswin cast him a grateful look. "The books will be in order."

"We have always had a care for Miss Cheviot's"—

"Baroness Kenway's," said Baker insistently.

—"income," said Dorcus Kenway in a flat voice. "We are not thieves."

"Merely greedy," wheezed the comte. "I have learned"—he and Morgan had had a quiet conversation while the others talked—"you wish my niece to wed this man whom she does not like and whom she wishes gone instantly."

"Gone!" Barr blinked rapidly several times. "But this is my home!"

"This," said Baker, his voice taking on the flavor of boredom, "is the baroness's home, into which she may invite whom she pleases. She is *not* pleased with you. You have two hours to collect your belongings and leave."

His expression thunderous, Barr faced Morgan. "This too is your doing. You will regret sticking your nose into what is none of your business!"

"It is everyone's business to see a woman is not harmed by villains."

"Bah!" Barr stalked off.

"Villains?" Oswin's color faded. He looked horrified. "Never. I'm no villain. Cousin! You cannot believe I would harm you."

"Perhaps not you, but Barr? He is capable of anything. And Dorcus?" Grace's eyes narrowed. "Frankly, I wonder if I trust your wife."

Oswin cast a quick worried look at Dorcus, whose expression changed not a jot. "Nonsense," he said, but without conviction. "Are we, too, to leave?"

"Not until you deal with Mr. Baker. And I've questions I wish answered now you've no particular reason to deny me information."

"Thought it best, you know," said Oswin confidingly.

"Who thought it best?"

Again Oswin cast a quick look toward his wife. "We did. You were too young. Didn't want you growing up immodestly. Didn't want you worrying about the estate. Didn't want you knowing what care-for-naughts your parents were." He shrugged. "Thought it all for the best."

"Care-for-naughts? I wonder. Are you certain you did not invent that tale, that my parents were improvident? Besides, how can you say all was for my good when that included marrying me to Barr?"

"Would never have *forced* you," insisted Oswin. But again he glanced quickly at his wife and away.

Morgan grew convinced Oswin was more weakling than villain, but that he was not unaware of his wife's self-serving machinations and was carried along by her.

Dorcus strode away. She paused, and with her back to the others, said, "At least this means I need no longer concern myself with the housekeeping. Our"—unexpected emotion, utter bitterness, rang through her voice—"*baroness* may see to her own work for a change."

"Now if that is not outside of enough," exclaimed Grace, outrage replacing her former pallor with too much color. "I have offered and offered to take some of the burden from her shoulders and she always told me to keep my nose out of things which did not concern me!"

Oswin seemed to grow smaller once his wife was no longer there to prop him up. "What do we do?" he asked no one in particular.

"We inspect the books," said Baker. Grimly, he added, "If you have absconded with funds which belong to the baroness, then you are in deep water indeed."

Baker took Oswin's arm and turned him toward the house. Morgan looked from Grace to her uncle. "I will leave you to become acquainted," he said bleakly. "You have many years of catching up to do." *And,* he thought bitterly as he bowed, *my Grace has years of lost freedom to make up for as well.*

He strolled off and Purrmew slid around a bush, into his path. The animal meowed plaintively until Morgan stooped and picked him up. He cradled the kitten in his arms, his mind travelling unhappy paths. The kitten's rumbling purr did little to ease his distress at the thought that Grace would go to London.

And why should she not? Not only had she been deprived of

proper society but, with her looks, title and estate, she'd be a plum on the marriage mart. She could have her choice from among the Eligibles and would feel no interest whatsoever in a moody ex-soldier who must face a new fight soon. One in which the enemy was in the form of hostile tenants rather than hostile French!

Morgan set the kitten down and, his head bowed and hands clasped behind him, strolled the garden paths thinking black thoughts and occasionally half tripping over the playful cat . . .

Then he tripped more seriously, nearly falling, just as a shot rang out. Blood burst from his previously wounded shoulder and Morgan fell to his knees. Pain and shock catching him unaware, blackness took him. He fell forward to lie half on the path and half on the grass.

A toe prodded him. "Bastard," said a softly vicious voice. "You *would* move. But one more shot . . ."

The sound of running footsteps prevented Barr Kenway from reloading, from placing a second bullet directly into Morgan's temple. Instead, the villain was forced to race away and disappear within the shrubbery before he was seen.

When Morgan roused, he was in a bed. A lamp's low flame cast barely enough light for him to see Grace Cheviot dozing in a chair. He frowned. She should not be there. It was not right that a young unmarried woman be in a man's room. Not, of course, that he wished her elsewhere, but *why* was she here? Incautiously, he attempted to raise himself and, with a grunt, dropped back to his pillow. Memory returned in a rush. The shot. Stabbing pain ripping into a shoulder already heavily scarred.

"You are awake," she said. "Thank God."

"I was shot." He breathed slowly, controlling the pain. "Who did it?"

"Barr, of course. Unfortunately, there is no proof. A gardener heard the shot. As he raced toward you he heard someone crashing through the shrubbery. There were boot prints in the path at your side." Grace spoke evenly, each word enunciated carefully. "It is believed my cousin meant to . . ." a sob broke through her iron control ". . . meant to—"

"To reload and finish the job," said Morgan, wincing at how close he'd come to lying dead. "I must remember to thank that gardener."

"I have rewarded him."

"I will repay you."

"No, it is my place to do it. If it were not for me you would never have been in such danger."

"Knowing your cousin, we'd have rubbed each other the wrong way over something. You once named him coward, did you not? I must agree. Shooting a man in the back goes against every tenet of the code of honor!"

She nodded. "I urged the servants to tell the tale. It will be all around the region in a trice." There was a note of satisfaction in her voice when she added, "No one will help Barr now."

"Most would suppress such a story. To save their family name."

Grace smiled that mischievous smile he loved. "But it is not my name. I am a Cheviot!"

Not for long, he thought, but dared not say. *Not for long,* ran through his mind a second time. *But will it be my name she takes when she decides to wed?* He sighed, jealous of the Corinthians and Swells she'd meet in London.

"Ah!" she said, misinterpreting the sound. "You are tired and in pain and I talk on and on." She felt his forehead and checked that his bandage did not bind. "The doctor left a dose he said you must take if you woke in the night." She poured it into a glass and turned to help him. She paused when he shook his head. "But the doctor said—"

He interrupted. "It is the merest scratch, Baroness! I want no laudanum unless the pain grows far worse. I prefer it to lying insensible."

She stared at him. "You fear Barr will return?" Morgan nodded. "I cannot think how he would get in, but I will put a guard at your door."

"Put the man *inside* the room. If Barr comes I'd as soon he be caught attempting to kill me. If he sees the guard and goes away we still have no proof."

She shook her head. "I will not put you in such danger. Not until you can defend yourself," she added when she saw his expression chill.

He compressed his lips. Staring at nothing in particular, he gave rapid thought to the problem. Then he nodded and wished he had not. Even that jarred his wound. "Very well. We will trap him later."

"The castle is locked at night, you know."

His expression didn't alter.

"You truly think Barr can come and go as he pleases?"

"I know he can."

"Nonsense."

"Grace." He glanced at her. "May I call you Grace?"

"Yes. Of course."

"Grace." He savored her name on his lips. "In your exploration of the secret passages, did you never come across one leading outdoors?"

"According to the records there was one, but it was blocked and even the knowledge of how to find it is gone."

"*Was* gone. Your cousin discovered the secret."

"Barr? He jeered at me, saying the secret passages were useless."

"*Someone* discovered a use for them," said Morgan and then wished he'd bitten his tongue. "Forget I said that. When I recover I will show you what *I* found." He caught her hand, holding it firmly. "Please. Do not enter the passages. Your cousin is the sort to lurk there hoping for just that chance of catching you alone. He is a man who will always feel the need for revenge. Nor will he care on whom he vents his rage."

Grace nodded. "I've no time to explore, even if I wished to. There is too much to do. At least, when you were brought in covered in blood, our other guests departed, tactful souls that they are." She smiled. "One older lady, hearing Mr. Baker calling me Baroness, told me she is pleased my cousins lifted the ban on the use of my title, that she always felt it was a bit much even if they did worry I might get above myself."

"Have you learned more of your mother and father?"

"My uncle is very kind. He tells me stories. As we guessed, Dorcus exaggerated or skewed things to make my parents appear as black as possible."

"And Oswin Kenway?"

"Oswin? He was closeted with Mr. Baker for hours and hours and came out for dinner this evening mopping his brow and looking exceedingly harassed."

Morgan gave startled thought to how long he'd been unconscious. All day and well into the night, it seemed.

"But Mr. Baker tells me that, so far as he can discover in a quick survey, the Kenways made no excessive inroads into my inheritance. He also suspects Oswin was innocent of the plot to coerce me into marriage with Barr. He believes it was Dorcus's idea in the first instance but enthusiastically adopted by Barr when he grew old enough to see the benefits."

"Have you made a decision concerning Mr. and Mrs. Kenway?"

Grace sighed. "I do not yet feel well enough balanced to do so," she admitted. "It has been too much."

"Especially your new status?"

"That is the least of it. I am who I am and adding the title and estate will not change that. Those only add responsibilities and leave little time to think of important things." She glared. "The important thing right now is for you to rest. Minnie will stay with you"—she nodded toward the end of the bed where an elderly maid curtsied, startling Morgan, who had thought they were alone—"and I will see about a guard. Minnie, have you a suggestion?"

"Henry."

"Henry?" Grace frowned. "Which footman is he?"

"Boot boy." Minnie spoke in the soft lilting tones of the Cornish. "Got on the wrong side of Mr. Barr, he did. He'll like a chance to do him one."

"But a boy?"

Minnie grinned, revealing snaggly teeth. "Not exactly a boy anymore."

Morgan chuckled and Grace smiled. "Very well. I will send

for him." Grace stared broodingly at Morgan. "It is irrational, I suppose," she said, "this feeling that if I do not watch over you, you will do something foolish."

"I promise I will do nothing foolish"—he grinned, a quick flash of white teeth in the dimly lit room—*"tonight."*

She sighed a theatrical sigh. "Ah. In that case I may sleep in peace." Her smile was both amused and tender. *"Tonight."*

Morgan drifted into sleep almost believing there might be hope for him after all. Grace Cheviot, baroness, harboring similar thoughts, scooped up her kitten. She went to her own room and slept peacefully—despite Purrmew who, curled up next her shoulder, lived up to his name.

For two days Morgan remained in his room although not in his bed as the doctor decreed. He never liked lying about when things needed doing and he had yet to tell anyone of the cache of smuggled goods. It fretted him, but he feared that, if he told, word would leak to the smugglers and precipitate the removal of the proof, a thing he dreaded. On the third day, swearing softly at the pain each incautious movement roused, he contrived a sling and appeared in the breakfast room.

Grace rose to her feet. "You should not be out of bed!"

"Nonsense. Are those deviled kidneys?" he asked the footman hovering near the sideboard. Asked if he wished a serving, he nodded. "And," he added, "a spoonful of eggs and two of those delightful-looking buns."

Coffee appeared at his elbow. He glanced up and blinked to see Dorcus staring down at him. There was a glitter in her eyes which convinced him he'd no desire for coffee.

"You drink it," he said, pushing it away. "I'm having tea." The woman glared, turned on her heel and left the room, the coffee remaining. Morgan touched the rim. His eyes lost focus, a dreamy look smoothing his features. Very slowly he moved his finger until it just dipped into the hot brew. Raising it to his nose, he sniffed. And winced.

"What is it?" asked Baker.

"Smell it."

Obligingly, Baker leaned nearer and sniffed. "Almonds? Odd, but not unpleasant." He straightened. "So?"

"I suspect tampering."

"Poison?" asked Grace, her tone sharp. "Oh, surely not!"

Morgan asked Baker to toss the coffee out the window. "... or a maid, thinking to have herself a treat, may suffer for it!"

Grace frowned. "I *cannot* believe Dorcus would . . . would . . ."

"Murder me?" suggested Morgan. "But what of Barr?" Grace looked troubled. More gently, he added, "He could, could he not, convince Mrs. Kenway that what was intended was harmless? A jest? Something to make me sick but do no permanent harm?"

Grace's shoulders tensed. "Unfortunately, I do not think that impossible."

She turned to her uncle and continued a conversation begun before Morgan's unexpected arrival. She was pelting the old gentleman with questions concerning her parents and growing happier with each response.

Morgan allowed his mind to drift. His suggestion that Dorcus was an unknowing dupe in a further attempt to rid the world of his presence *might* be true, but he doubted it. He was nearly certain Dorcus Kenway had a firm grip on the large spoon, stirring up the plots in and around the castle. Oswin was too bumbling to cook up a plan involving decades. Barr was too young when Grace's paternal uncle was deceived concerning her survival and also when the marriage between the cousins must have been first suggested, since she had been guarded long before reaching marriageable age.

But the current important question concerned the smuggling. Who planned it? Who found the secret room, the way into the keep from sea level? Today he would go to the storeroom and check that it still contained evidence.

As that thought ran through Morgan's mind he reached with the wrong hand for the salt bowl. He winced at the piercing pain and was reminded that he was in no condition to squirm through the tight opening to the hidden room.

There was a pause in the conversation and he took the opportunity to ask, "Baroness, does your cousin sail? Does he own a boat?"

"Is there," she asked, "anyone in Cornwall who *cannot* sail? Barr owns a neat little sloop designed for speed. It cuts the water like a knife." When Morgan merely nodded, she asked, "Why?"

"Just a thought . . ."

"I put about that word. As I said I would," she said, obliquely telling him that she remembered their discussion concerning smuggling.

"Very good. But what crew does Barr's boat demand?"

"I've seen my cousin handle it on his own," she admitted. "I don't know many who would care to attempt it, but Barr will."

Baker cast Morgan a thoughtful look before returning to his breakfast. He finished and rose to his feet. "Today will finish my preliminary work on the books. They must be gone over in greater detail, of course, but as a first approximation, things do not look bad. I've found little about which I'd complain. Only a very few withdrawals to which a body might object without argument."

"Describe the expenses you find suspect," ordered Grace.

"One large payment some years ago for which there is no explanation. Mr. Kenway just grows red about the ears and stalks off. I'd guess Barr Kenway had a gambling debt which could only be met by drawing on the estate. The past few years there is another regular expense which is unexplained."

Grace's lips tightened into a smile which resembled her uncle's. "Is it forty pounds twice a year?" she asked.

Baker cast her a surprised look. "You know?"

"Perhaps Dorcus is unaware, but my cousin has a son. The lad is in school and my cousin pays the fees." She colored slightly at the gentlemen's blank stares. "You feel I should know nothing of this or, if I do, that I should not mention it, but I have known about Timothy for years and have ceased to be shocked. I believe my cousin wished to discover if it were himself or Dorcus who was at fault that they had no children."

"A barren woman may be divorced," said Baker.

"My cousin is weak rather than cruel. Divorce would be cruel, would it not?"

"You are a sensitive, caring woman, Baroness," said Morgan. "And far more generous and forgiving than most. Do *not* underestimate Mrs. Kenway. And, because he is under her thumb, neither should you trust your cousin."

A look of deep sadness crossed Grace's face, then faded. "They are family."

"Yes," he said. "One forgives family a great deal, of course."

Her mischievous look appeared. "Except Cousin Barr, of course."

He met her look with one of his own. "Oh yes. Always excepting Cousin Barr!"

Baker excused himself and the comte soon followed. Grace and Morgan were left staring at each other across the breakfast table. "Have you time for a stroll in the gardens?" he asked.

"Not the gardens," she objected. Her gaze rested on his wounded shoulder, then flicked up to meet his. "The gallery?"

Morgan glanced out a window at the glorious day. "You fear your cousin lurks?"

Her color fluctuated from a deep rose to pale pink. "Is it a foolish thought?"

"We've no proof, of course, that Barr shot me."

"If there *were* evidence"—he smiled at the ice in her voice—"he would be incarcerated in the smelly cell which the magistrate constructed at the back of his pigsty. It is where villains await the assizes. I wish that *was* where Barr could be found! We'd know where he is."

"You do not know?"

"No," she admitted. She fiddled with her teaspoon. "It worries me."

Morgan thought of the secret passages. And of Dorcus, who had surely poisoned his coffee that morning. *Why,* he wondered, *does that woman support Barr's interests over Grace's?* He asked Grace.

"Barr is her twin sister's son. Her sister married still another Kenway, you see. He was eight when orphaned and Dorcus and Oswin took him in." Grace shrugged. "I don't wish to talk about Barr. Let us go to the gallery where you may walk off some excess energy and then you may take yourself back to your room for a nap."

"Thus removing myself from any need of your supervision. You would wash your hands of me!"

He pretended outrage and she chuckled. They bantered and talked of this and that, but of nothing stressful. Morgan, determined to ease her tensions as they paced below ancient portraits, managed very well.

"I must go," she said finally. "The washerwomen come today and will not know how to go on."

Morgan turned to her and reached for her hands. Extending one finger he checked she wore his knife but said nothing once assured she did. "Thank you for this hour, my dear. I have enjoyed it."

"I too." She freed one hand and removed the silken envelope from her pocket. "Morgan . . . ?" She looked up at him with that look he'd once considered meant she was shy. "A few berries remain." She glanced away, her words trailing off. And then, quickly, met his gaze again.

His heart raced that she would actually suggest they share a kiss. He carefully inserted the packet into the braid crowning her head, tucking it in so it could not fall out. Taking her chin in his good hand, he lifted it. For a long moment he stared into her eyes. Trusting eyes.

But was her expression perhaps a touch needy? Dare he kiss her as he wished to kiss her? Or should he do no more than touch her lips with his own?

Grace took the decision from him, putting her arms around his neck and drawing down his face. Her lips were soft and warm. Untutored. Oh, but very willing! A soft groan rose from deep within as Morgan put his good arm around her, pressing her close. His mouth hardened, slanted, took hers in a kiss so deep, so giving, she came out from it dazed and uncertain.

"Morgan?" she breathed, her eyes painfully wide open.

"I should ask your pardon," he said softly, "but I cannot. I will never forget our first true kiss."

"Nor I."

He smiled at her bemusement. "I think you are uncertain

whether to remember it with happiness, as will I, or if you should be utterly appalled."

"I think"—she frowned—"you are correct. I did not know a kiss could . . ." Shallow creases marred her brow as she searched for words.

"Could make one hungry for more?" Morgan suggested.

She looked surprised. "Yes. Exactly. I had not thought of it in just that way, but that is precisely how I feel."

"I as well. My dear, in future, we'd best spend little time alone. You may no longer trust me!"

She blinked, then colored up. "Nonsense. I am not so tempting you would"—she backed toward the door—"insult me so! I must go."

"A moment."

She paused. "Yes?"

"May I have my berry?" he asked in a wistful, little-boy voice.

Her hand went to her hair and the fading color returned. "I forgot."

She opened the envelope as he approached and held out his hand. She dropped a berry into it.

"Only two left," she said.

Morgan was pleased to read more than a trifling disappointment in her voice. "Only two. What shall we do when they are gone?" he asked with almost believable innocence.

For a moment she took his question seriously and then, realizing he teased her, she shrugged. "You will think of something," she said with an insouciance he believed she didn't truly feel.

"Oh yes." He spoke softly. "I will think of . . . something."

Either his words or his tone alarmed her and she hurried from the room. Still, she had participated fully in that kiss. In fact, one might say she'd participated enthusiastically. Something inside swelled, filling him with warmth and desire and every good thing.

She liked him. Morgan wished he dared think she loved him.

Purrmew wound around his legs. He picked up the kitten, slipping him inside his sling where the creature settled down, purring and kneading sharp little claws into his arm. The baroness's pet seemed as content with life as Morgan felt!

* * *

Grace did not go immediately to see to the work awaiting her but to her room where she poured tepid water into her basin. Leaning over it, she held a soaked cloth to her cheeks. *How,* she wondered, *could I have been so forward? How did I allow myself to beg for his kiss?*

Well, not beg . . . but only because she'd had no need to do so. *He was not the least little bit reluctant to oblige, was he?*

Grace rewet the cloth. *Of course he was not.* No man would resist what was offered so freely. Worse, a man would assume she wished for more. *Which I do! Oh, Lord help me, I do.*

Grace went to her window. *When,* she wondered, *did I fall in love with him? When did I give him my heart?*

Because, foolishly, she had done just that. Somewhere. Sometime. *How idiotic! What am I?* she wondered, *that a man like Morgan St. Austell would love me? Nothing. Nothing at all. For Heaven's sake, I don't even know how to flirt.*

Heat flooded her face again and she spoke aloud, softly. "No, I don't flirt. I simply *ask* for what I want." *And I want his kisses. I do!*

Grace talked herself into a calmer state of mind and decided she must never again throw herself at St. Austell's head. She would be cool when next they met, and would give him no further reason to think her willing to indulge in such unbecoming behavior.

Then, for a moment, she allowed herself to recall his claim that his intentions were honorable. She sighed. He might truly wish to wed her, but that did not mean he loved her.

So. Calm. Cool. Collected. And to work! The washerwomen first and then the menus.

While the baroness lectured herself, Morgan ran Baker to earth. He waited until the solicitor made a notation and turned the page, at which point he laid aside his pen and looked up from the ledger.

"Set that aside for a moment, will you?" Morgan asked.

Baker folded his hands. "Am I wearing my official hat or is it merely that you are bored and wish company?"

"Both?"

"Officially you are bored?"

Morgan grinned but sobered before speaking. "I need advice. Before you arrived I discovered the castle is being used by smugglers."

Baker's brows arched. "This is not a guess?"

"I saw proof but doubt it still exists. At least, *I'd* insist contraband never remain for long within the castle."

"Tell me."

Morgan described his explorations and finished, "It is possible, I suppose, that this is Barr's little game all on his own. Especially if Oswin is stingy with an allowance."

"There is no regular withdrawal which might be set down to an allowance for Barr Kenway, but perhaps Kenway gives his heir something from the fees he gives himself for acting as the property agent."

"Which wouldn't be much," mused Morgan. "Not when a frog like Barr Kenway wishes to make a large splash in his particular pond. Especially since we've reason to think he gambles, sometimes unsuccessfully." Morgan rose to his feet. "Talking to you has settled my mind. I'll send the information to an acquaintance I made in Portugal, an adventurer of sorts who hates smuggling."

"What can he do?"

"He owns a ship won from a Barbary pirate and he and his crew are under special orders from the war office. He'll put a stop to whatever Barr is doing."

Baker's brows arched. "A modern version of the Elizabethan privateer?"

Morgan smiled. "Now you mention it, Miles *was* born into the wrong century. He'd have fit smoothly into the Virgin Queen's reign and have given Sir Walter Raleigh a run for his money!"

"Miles?"

"Miles Seward. He obviously got an excellent education, but he told me once that every moment he'd spent in a classroom was a waste of time." Morgan grimaced. "The thing is, I've no notion how long it will take a message to reach him. He has no set schedule and hates anything that smells of discipline—unless self-imposed!"

"It is Christmas. Perhaps your friend is between adventures."

"I will hope."

Unwilling to trust just anyone with such an important missive, Morgan was pleased Baker meant to return to London. He would carry the letter with him. The comte, in no hurry to leave his new-found niece, remained. So too did Morgan, with no excuse whatsoever, as Dorcus caustically told Oswin when her quarry was within hearing. Morgan ignored her hint he'd overstayed his welcome, and waited, hoping Miles would reply.

In a surprisingly short time Miles Seward arrived in person. He closeted himself first with Morgan and then asked to speak with the baroness.

"My lady," he said, bowing. He looked her over with bold eyes and Grace turned her gaze toward Morgan, silently begging that he do something.

"Miles! Behave. Your hostess is unused to rogue adventurers."

Miles's teeth flashed in his sun-darkened face. "I ask pardon if I offend, but you, my lady, are well worth a look. Or two or three," he added, his eyes snapping sparks.

Grace turned cool. "You will be forgiven only if you cease teasing me. And, of course, Mr. St. Austell's friends are welcome."

Frowning, Miles asked, "Morgan, why do I think you've not informed the baroness?"

"I felt the fewer who knew the more likely the secret would be kept."

"Always true." He spun back to face Grace. "My dear lady, I am come only for permission to patrol the waters off your coastline and that I may explore the cliff below the castle."

"To what end?"

A muscle rolled in Miles's jaw. "The end of smuggling!"

Grace turned a horrified gaze on Morgan. She withdrew from him in some nearly imperceptible fashion. "You agreed I should pass along word to the local men. I did. They swore an oath they will no longer cross the waters. *What more can you want?*"

"This is more than a keg or two," said Morgan stiffly, realizing his secrecy had harmed his hopes of her. "And it is the *castle*, not the *cove*, which is used for something far beyond what you described."

Grace rose to her feet. "Nonsense. We've no traitors here!"

"Not even Barr Kenway?" asked Morgan.

Grace sank back into a chair. "Oh dear."

Miles chuckled. "I see you feel there might possibly be *one* traitor?"

Grace ignored him, her eyes locked onto Morgan. "What do you know that I do not?"

"I explored the passages to find the escape route." He shrugged.

"I told you, it was blocked."

"It has been opened."

"I tell you it was blocked."

"How?" asked Miles.

She turned a quick look his way. "The records do not say," she responded slowly. "Merely that the passage was unsafe and the way blocked."

"So perhaps the blockage was no more than a wooden barrier or, at best, stone stacked in the entrance?"

Grace's lips compressed and her eyelids drooped slightly. "I suppose that might be it. I pictured a collapse of the tunnel." She sighed. "Explain why you believe Barr uses the castle for smuggling purposes."

"Because I saw a storeroom full of silks and laces and elegant trifles which could only have come from France."

"You *saw* them!" She glared. "And only *now* inform me?"

"My dear, I did not wish to add to your danger by giving you information for which you've no need."

"This is my castle and my responsibility!"

"But was *not*," Morgan growled, "at the time I discovered the cache!"

"Children!" said Miles in a penetrating voice, "we must discuss what to do *now* rather than what was *not* done."

"I wish to see this cache!" insisted Grace, rising.

"No," said Morgan, standing to face her.

"There is no place in the castle where such could be hidden!"

"Only another secret room. One you didn't find!"

"I will not believe it."

"Children, children." This time Miles sounded weary.

"I am not a child!" stormed Grace, turning on him.

"Then cease to act like one," retorted Miles unkindly. "Morgan, there is one point where the baroness and I agree. I too need to see the goods."

"Frankly, I doubt anything remains. It will have been moved."

"Nevertheless, I should have a notion what is involved, passage and all. I also wish to see this Barr Kenway's boat. He designed it himself?"

"For speed," said Grace, nodding.

"Implying a stripped-down, functional design," said Miles. "Where, then, could he hide contraband?"

"There is a cabin of sorts," she said, obviously unhappy that Barr might, along with all else, be a smuggler.

"Of sorts?"

She sighed. "When it was new, he showed me over it. Even I cannot stand up in the cabin, but there is a bunk and cupboards."

"The bunk. Is it enclosed around the base?" She nodded and Miles frowned. "I must see for myself," he repeated. "And now, Morgan, m'lad, we will discover if your secret room has been stripped bare."

"I too will come," said Grace.

Her chin rose when the men seemed about to deny her. They exchanged a glance. Miles shrugged. "No one is likely to be there."

"True."

"And, possibly, she will know how to discover the passage to the shore."

Morgan's lips compressed. "Very well," he said. "Come if you will, but remain behind us. If there is trouble, you run, do you hear?"

"Why?"

"Because, my dear, I do not want to have to worry about *your* safety while saving my own skin!"

"How noble!"

"How *sensible,*" interrupted Miles sternly and firmly changed the subject to a more practical matter. "We," he said, "need lanterns." Standing, he bowed in a flamboyant manner and gestured toward the door. One could almost see a swirling cape and a sword at his hip!

They traversed the passages and Morgan explained the mechanism for opening the storeroom door. Miles managed it easily and, smaller and more wiry than Morgan, slipped into the room beyond. Morgan restrained Grace from following.

"Let me go," she whispered.

"Wait."

"No one is here. She may come," said Miles from within.

Grace slid through the entrance and Morgan, his wound healing but not completely back to normal, grimaced as he too wormed his way in.

"Well, Baroness? What do you say to this?"

Grace stared at the lamp-lit shelves on which lay several bales of fine lace and one of jewel-toned silk. "I did not believe it possible." She touched the silk with one finger.

"This is not as you found it?" Miles asked Morgan.

"Previously the shelves were pretty well filled with silks and laces, a keg or two of brandy. There were also a few china figurines and a box of fancy ladies' watches, of all things. I did not take an inventory."

"So the previous cargo is gone and this is a new one?"

"There is so little left I suspect this is the remnants of the other."

"Why leave anything behind?"

"Gifts for his whores?"

His ears heating, Morgan glanced at Grace but she ignored his ill-considered comment, watching him tap the blocks of stone flooring the room. "Try the one in the corner," she said, as he moved to the next row.

"It is under the shelf."

"Try it."

Morgan did. "By all that's . . ."

They discovered the shelf was hinged. "Ingenious," said Miles, tipping it against the wall.

"You think that stone will open on stairs?" asked Grace.

"We can soon find out."

"But not now," said Morgan. "We must return to the castle before we are missed and suspicion is roused."

Miles nodded reluctant agreement. "My lady, will you object to an extra houseguest for a day or two?"

"Of course not. This must be stopped!" She frowned. "Why do I feel guilty? I had no part in it."

"Perhaps because it is your home," soothed Morgan.

Upon their return to the main part of the castle, the men left the baroness to go about her business and went to Morgan's room. On the way, Morgan detoured into the dining room to pick up a decanter and glasses to assuage their thirst.

Grace finished her work and did what she often did when she felt the need of time to herself. She took a book to the keep's anteroom which connected it to the more modern portion of the castle and had a door to the central courtyard. A smallish room, it required only a small fire to warm it.

Reading usually soothed her, but today Grace could not concentrate. She laid the book aside and stared over the water, her thoughts roiling. Some time passed before a noise startled her and she twisted around. Dorcus stood in the arch into the keep, the heavy curtain pushed aside.

"Cousin?"

Dorcus hesitated, then joined Grace. "You been here long?"

In turn, Grace hesitated. She discovered she'd no wish to tell Dorcus exactly how much time she'd wasted in dreaming and musing. "No," she said.

Dorcus's tense shoulders relaxed. "You know we did our best for you." For once there was no snideness in the woman's tone. "You understand that what we did was for you?"

"Until you insisted I wed Barr, I would agree you did well by me."

"Barr is . . . has become . . ." Dorcus bit her lip. "I worry about him," she admitted. "I thought you would steady him . . ." Her mouth formed a hard line. She stared at Grace and then, her cape swinging around her, stalked from the room.

Has Dorcus begun to see through her precious Barr?

Another thought smothered that one as Grace stared at the drapery-covered entrance to the keep, its only entrance if one discounted the escape route. Dorcus had worn a cloak, as good as admitting she'd been outside. Something icy cold settled inside Grace as the only possible solution to the riddle occurred to her. Dorcus had entered the keep through the supposedly blocked passage. Which meant Dorcus knew about the smuggling.

And Cousin Oswin, as well?

Grace concluded, as had Morgan, that Oswin would not be trusted with knowledge of illegal activities. But Morgan and Miles must be told that Dorcus knew. Now. Before it occurred to the woman she had given herself away. Grace hurried off to find one of the men. She failed to do so.

Morgan noticed Grace was troubled the moment she entered the salon where the family met before dinner. Discovering she was the last to arrive, she said something under her breath. If he were not mistaken, she'd allowed a few well-chosen swear words to escape, which was unlike the Grace Cheviot he thought he knew. Morgan vowed to discover what bothered her as soon as possible.

The party returned to the salon after dinner and Oswin suggested cards. Miles and Dorcus joined him and, requiring a three-handed game, they chose ombre. As the trio drew lots to determine who would play the solo hand, the comte settled by the fire with a recent newspaper.

Morgan joined Grace, who stared into the dark courtyard. "What is it?"

She turned a surprised look up at him. "How did you guess?"

"I knew the instant I saw you this evening. Tell me."

Grace was more interested in discovering how he read her. Besides, the opportunity to be alone with him could not be ignored. "I will send for a shawl so we can walk in the courtyard."

The shawl arrived and he helped her over the low windowsill. Once they were well along the graveled path, he again asked what troubled her.

She described Dorcus's arrival from inside the keep. "I'm certain she was outside and returned by way of the passage. She wore a cloak, not a shawl, which is what she'd have wrapped herself in if she'd merely gone to inspect the keep as, at dinner, she said she'd done."

"Did she carry a lantern or candle?"

"She had nothing in her hands."

"Then she did not inspect the keep. How could she have seen anything if she'd no way of lighting the room?"

"I'd not thought of that . . ."

"And if it occurs to her you are likely to have thought of it?" Morgan put his hand on her shoulder. "I wonder how safe you would be."

Grace, perforce, stopped. She shivered. "It is the Christmas season. It should be a time of joy. But *this* Christmas"—light streaming from the salon revealed her scowl—"is the worst I've ever known. Horrid thoughts should be impossible!"

"They *would* be impossible if horrid people did not exist," he said softly. They stared at each other. "Christmas was never before my favorite holiday," he added, equally quietly. "I sympathize with your distress, but I wish you to know that, for me, Christmas will, in the future, be a very special time indeed."

She blinked. "Why?"

"Because I met you," he said. "Because I have come to know you. Because I hope you will . . ." No. He could not use the word love, could not yet ask that she wed him. ". . . be my friend." It was far too soon and she must have her chance to see her world.

"Friendship is important," she said after a moment.

"Not something to be undertaken lightly," he agreed.

Again they were silent. "I feel sure," she finally said, "that we will remain friends." But, in her heart, Grace cried bloody tears. Friendship was not what she wanted from this man. She shivered again.

"I've been thoughtless and you have become chilled. Let us go in."

They did and Grace excused herself, going to her room where, for reasons she didn't try to explain, she locked her door. She wanted no one coming in to her unexpectedly. Not her maid. Not Dorcus. Not . . . anyone.

Not that he *would* come. He was far too much the gentleman.

Morgan, unsure what had happened, was nevertheless unhappy. The kitten climbed into his lap, purring loudly, bumping his head against Morgan's chin whenever Morgan's fingers ceased moving. He had the odd fancy the kitten was insisting that all would be well, that he must only persevere, and have faith. He laughed at the odd fancy, but to his surprise, he felt soothed.

Morgan and Miles met in the small hours of the morning. They wore dark clothing and carried lanterns when they entered the half-natural, half-manmade passage from the keep down through the cliff and then a cave to the shore. They peered out. The entrance was hidden behind a tall column of freestanding stone, which meant it would be unseen by anyone sailing by.

"Voices carry over water." It was a bare thread of sound.

"Yes," agreed Morgan, equally softly. "I hear nothing."

"I must see the moorage available. Stay next to the rock and move slowly."

After their foray onto the beach they went again to Morgan's room for a glass of good brandy to warm them. "So," Morgan asked. "What is next?"

"My crew and I will hide along the coast and the next time Kenway goes out we'll know. I've a man watching Kenway's boat. He'll have company on his return." Miles frowned. "It is unfortunate that the cove below the castle is so open. If it were the old smuggler's cove which you showed me, the exit could be covered by no more than a dory and two men with loaded guns."

"Miles, are there enough of you for this job?"

"Feeling bored with life, Morgan?" Miles grinned, his teeth flashing white in his dark face. "Sorry. My crew knows its work and you would upset the balance."

Morgan, disappointed, nodded understanding. "Very well. Would you, at the least, let me know when you act? I could watch at this end."

"And discover if either or both the elder Kenways reveal involvement." Miles nodded approval. "I'll send a message. I'd guess our man is addicted to the excitement, needing it as an opium eater needs opium, so I doubt we've a long wait." He grinned. "In three days there is a dark of the moon."

Three peaceful days followed and Morgan spent as much of the time as he could manage with Grace Cheviot, quietly courting his love. When she was where he could not go, he sat with her uncle. On the fourth day, they, all three, sat together when a footman entered and requested the baroness's presence in the kitchen. The same footman held forward a salver bearing a note for Morgan.

Morgan read it as Grace left the room. His lips compressed.

"Some difficulty with which I may help?" asked the comte with exquisite politeness.

"Hmm? Not a difficulty. Merely information for which I've waited."

The Frenchman smiled a tight little smile which tipped his lips into a V shape, a smile Morgan had occasionally seen on Grace's face. "My dear niece's cousin eyes you with something which seems very like a wish to throw you out. If I had not come and if Grace were not in charge, I believe you would be waiting elsewhere for this news?"

"Quite likely, but I will not bother Dorcus Kenway much longer."

"That would be too bad."

The comte spoke so blandly Morgan almost missed the implication. "You have guessed I court your niece?"

The Frenchman smiled again. "It is rather obvious, is it not? If it is of any importance, I approve."

"Your approval of the man she weds will be important to Grace, but it may not be me. I must not approach her formally until she has had an opportunity to see something of the world and . . ." Morgan's eyes narrowed. "You shake your head."

"My niece has not confided in me, Mr. St. Austell, but I watch her. When she thinks herself unobserved, she reveals her, um, affection for you. I fear she will be devastated if you leave without speaking." Again the Frenchman smiled his characteristic smile. "Of course I am merely an elderly gentleman who has, perhaps, become something of a romantic in his old age."

Morgan eyed him. "A compromise, perhaps? I could ask her

if I might follow her to London. You do mean to invite her there, do you not?"

"Yes, but I do not count on her company." Again that knowing smile. "I believe my niece will like London in small doses only. I have seen many like her."

"You, on the other hand, prefer the country in equally small doses?" asked Morgan politely.

"You read me well," admitted the comte. "Once you have won my Grace, I pray you and she will visit several times a year. I am, I fear, likely to find it difficult to come all this way for the brief visits I'd prefer."

Morgan's brows arched. "I have no knowledge of what Baker told you of my circumstances."

"Enough. He says you will inherit a barony."

"Did he say my uncle's primary estate is in east Sussex? *He* prefers the manor here in Cornwall and resides there year round, but I will do no more than visit it occasionally."

"I see. *Perhaps* I could manage the relatively short journey into Sussex. Once in a while." Again that odd smile. The smile faded. "And perhaps," he said, "it would be proper for me to discuss with you my niece's prospects."

"I fell in love with her when I thought she had nothing. I would take her in her shift," said Morgan sharply.

"I believe you. I have, you see, watched you watching her as well as observed her watching you."

Morgan felt his ears warm. This cultivated and elegant Frenchman was far too knowing!

"Mr. St. Austell, I am elderly. My remaining years on earth are limited, although perhaps a trifle longer than if my niece had not been restored to me! Boredom alone can kill, you know." The comte outlined what his great niece would receive on her marriage and what she would gain at his death. "I beseech you, my friend, do not be so nice in your notions you make Grace unhappy."

"There is no necessity to bribe me," said Morgan a trifle crossly. He realized he glowered and smoothed out his expression.

"I am aware," said the comte soothingly. "But it is also true that I've no desire to see Grace courted by fortune hunters. The fact you do *not* care is important to me."

Morgan drew in a deep breath. "I see. I will think about it." He glanced up at the sound of a throat clearing. "Yes?"

The footman stood in the doorway looking bewildered. "Miss Cheviot—my lady, I should say—is truly needed in the kitchen. Cook is sorry to send a second message, but . . ." His gaze danced around the room. "Her ladyship is not here?"

"She left immediately when you came for her." Morgan rose abruptly.

The footman nodded. "I will seek her elsewhere." He bowed and backed from the room. The door closed.

"You are concerned," said the comte sharply. "Why?"

"Something has begun . . ." Morgan's fist tightened around the note.

"Tell me." The suave gentleman suddenly turned into a hard-edged aristocrat. His features sharpened and his whole bearing changed.

Morgan was not intimidated. Nevertheless the Frenchman deserved an explanation. "Barr Kenway has left port and, we believe, sails for France. Smuggling. One or both of the elder Kenways may also be involved."

"What do you fear?"

"Very likely I am making mountains from molehills but—"

"Tell me," insisted the comte.

"If they have twigged my suspicions they may take the baroness hostage against trouble." A muscle jumped in Morgan's jaw. "I must find her."

"Find her, my boy," said the old man. He suddenly looked every year of his age. "Find her for me. Keep her safe."

"I will find her for the both of us," said Morgan, dropping a hand on the elderly gentleman's shoulder as he passed the man's chair. He turned before opening the door. "Perhaps it would be wise for you to go to your room?"

"Yes." A hint of his old smile touched the man's lips. "I am too old for these games and would not wish to give away our fears by my expression or too hasty a word."

"I do not fear *that*, Comte."

"Thank you. Nevertheless, I fear I have a . . ." His brow quirked. "A quinsy perhaps?"

Morgan flashed a quick smile. "Better sciatica. There would be no reason to change your diet as you must if you suffer from a sore throat."

Oswin dozed in the library and Morgan did not disturb him. He searched further, finding no trace of either Grace *or* Dorcus, and his concern deepened. Then a maid said she'd seen the two turn into the hall leading to the keep.

Morgan's heart raced and his footsteps didn't slow until a glance into the central courtyard revealed the women walking side by side. He felt the blood rush from his head and leaned on the wall between two windows. As soon as he steadied he continued on into the antechamber.

As he reached the room, the door to the inner garden opened and Dorcus gestured toward the keep, her voice low. Then she saw Morgan. She stopped short. "You."

"Yes. The baroness is desperately needed in the kitchen. The footman returned to discover why she had not arrived. It must be something serious."

"Oh, dear, I forgot. Dorcus, I must delay seeing whatever it is you've discovered. Mr. St. Austell, thank you for reminding me. Excuse me," she finished and, moving quickly, passed into the corridor.

Dorcus swore softly.

"Is there something with which I may help?" asked Morgan politely.

"You?"

If, as some believed, looks could cause injury, Morgan would have been permanently scarred! Still glaring, Dorcus shoved aside the hanging over the keep's entrance and disappeared.

Morgan was tempted to follow but decided it was more important to discover Grace's whereabouts and remain as close to her as her shift for the remainder of the day. He must also, he reminded himself, send a message up to her uncle. The old man need worry no longer about his niece.

Grace examined the damaged chimney, which, upon its collapse, had ruined a half-cooked roast and dented the heavy pots nestled into the coals. She turned to find Morgan leaning against a work table, a half-eaten tart in his hand.

"I don't believe it is as bad as it looked at first glance," she said.

"No, but it must be fixed," he said. "In the meantime is there somewhere Cook may attend to her business?"

Grace chuckled. "You fear for your dinner, perhaps?"

One of Morgan's brows arched. "Will I appear entirely too crass if I admit it?" He popped the remainder of the tart into his mouth.

Smiles appeared on rosy faces shiny with sweat from working in the overly warm kitchen. "Cook must use the new closed stove"—Grace spoke firmly—"which she has resisted. She must learn everything new and says she will ruin everything, but she has no choice."

Cook, shamelessly listening, grew red with embarrassment.

Morgan lifted Cook's work-roughened hand to his mouth. "You will do very well. Even with no knowledge of the stove, you are too excellent a cook to possibly fail to serve up an entirely delicious meal."

Cook's expression became exceedingly coy. "I will try not to disappoint you, my lord."

"You will not," he said, ignoring the undeserved honorific.

Grace, afraid he would overdo his all-too-blatant flattery, tugged at his sleeve. "Since Cook must deal with the unexpected, perhaps we should leave her to get on with it. Contrive something simple, please. Anything. We do not expect you to do the impossible."

Suggesting she simplify the menu obviously did not set well with the woman. Morgan suspected their dinner would be as elaborate and just as delicious as any he'd eaten at the castle. "You," he said, "are a minx."

"Me? How can you say so?" She turned wide eyes up toward him. Eyes filled with laughter.

"Shameless. How dare you tell that poor woman we would be satisfied with something simple! As well dare a boy to walk a roof tree!"

Grace nodded. "Yes, I thought it would put her on her mettle.

She will find the closed stove far easier to use and will grumble about how long it takes to fix her fireplace, and in the end will ignore it! Now," she said, changing the subject, "I wonder what it was that Dorcus wished to show me."

That reminded Morgan and he caught a boy scurrying toward the kitchen. "A minute lad." He scribbled a note on a portion of an old letter. "Take that to a footman to take up to the comte's room," he ordered and then turned to Grace. "Tell me. Of what did Dorcus speak while you walked in the garden?"

Grace shrugged. "It was ridiculous. First a diatribe against you. Then a long, involved, and not exactly logical apology for never feeling the time was right to inform me of my great uncle's existence. And then"—Grace's frown ran several creases across her brow—"suddenly, actually breaking off in the middle of a sentence, she claimed to have discovered something in the keep she wished me to explain."

"The middle of a sentence!" Morgan frowned. "Blast. I had not thought of *that* possibility. Likely we are too late." He took her arm and hurried her back through the kitchens and out the door into the yard where he rushed across the paving and through a wicket gate. They navigated a kitchen garden protected by a low wall over which one could look down into the castle's widely curving bay. Ignoring the odor from rotting kitchen oddments thrown over daily, Morgan leaned far out. When he felt Grace tugging at his coattails, he stood back. As there was no boat near the shore he scanned the horizon.

Far out, a mere smudge of white near the skyline, was a sail.

"You frown," said Grace when he turned, sightlessly, toward her.

"Just a thought. I may be wrong, but I thank the Lord you did *not* follow Dorcus into the keep."

"Why?"

"I'd thought of the possibility Dorcus might take you hostage in case something went wrong, but now I suspect Barr awaited you there. I believe he signaled her to bring you in and I think he would have forced you onto his boat. What he'd have done with you then . . ." His thoughts raced.

She paled. "Drowned me?"

"More likely he meant to elope with you."

"Worse," she said.

Morgan chuckled. "Not *worse,* but certainly not good." Again he frowned. "Still I've no reason for more than suspicion."

"You are too cautious!"

"No. I learned long ago one must not jump to conclusions."

"You think Barr has gone to France again?"

"Yes."

She bit her lip. "Morgan, can we do nothing?"

"Not a thing," he said promptly.

Her eyes narrowed. "That, I think, is unlike you."

He grinned, the unusual expression giving him a piratical look. "That is exactly what I said to Miles when he told me there was nothing I could do. He will take care of everything, Grace."

"Mr. Seward told you . . . ?" She frowned. "The man acts very like a rogue adventurer. How can he do what we cannot?"

"He is commissioned by the war office to intervene in the smuggling going on up and down this coast."

"And if he catches Barr?" She raised worried eyes to meet Morgan's. "Will my cousin hang? Or be sent to prison? To Botany Bay, perhaps?"

Morgan frowned. "Would you be unhappy if he were?"

"Dorcus would be miserable."

"Dorcus is up to her ears in this."

Grace swallowed. "I had not thought. Yes, of course she must be if she was guiding me to him." She bit her lip. "The scandal will be terrible."

It was a problem of which Morgan had not thought. "Miles is not *officially* official. Perhaps we may arrange everything in such a way you need not suffer for their sins. Perhaps send them away. To India. Or to our remaining colonies in America perhaps?"

"The Canadian provinces may be the rougher, but I would prefer they go there than to face the heat and sickness in India."

"Whatever you think best."

"My cousin. Oswin. I cannot believe he knows about this."

"I too doubt it, but by law, as Dorcus's husband, he is responsible for her misdeeds."

Grace turned an ashen color and Morgan kicked himself for

causing her new pain. She rallied and he refrained from further discussion, drawing her thoughts to happier things.

The day passed. Slowly. It wasn't until the family gathered for the evening meal that anyone realized Dorcus had not been seen since Grace and Morgan left her. Oswin, fearing she'd hurt herself, asked the servants to search. They did but found no trace of her.

Nor did she appear the next morning for breakfast. Oswin looked as if he had not slept, haggard, his eyes deep-set, and the skin below them dark and baggy.

"Cousin, have you no notion where she might be?" asked Grace gently.

"I don't understand it," said Oswin. "She would go nowhere without telling me. Something has happened. We must search again."

"I have organized search parties, Cousin, and sent messengers to see if she visits elsewhere."

Morgan quietly excused himself. He went to the stables and had a horse saddled. Very soon he was in Porthleven where he searched out the man Miles had told him remained ashore at such times.

"No word from Miles?" he asked with no preliminaries.

"No sir," said the man, all innocence. "Was you expecting word?"

"Cut line. Does he often disappear like this?"

"Should be back soon." The man picked his teeth with the point of a wicked-looking knife. "Morning, after all."

"Does he follow his prey or does he wait in hiding on this side?"

"Depends," was the laconic response.

"Blast it, man, I need information. Where can I find him?"

"Can't say."

"Cannot or will not?" Morgan received another bland look, growled, and gave it up. "Tell him Dorcus Kenway has disappeared." He spun on his heel and strode out of the low tavern.

Miles's man was on his heels. "Here now," he said, his hand on Morgan's bridle. "Can't leave me with no more 'n *that.*"

"It is more than you gave me."

The fellow had the audacity to grin. "But that's different, ain't it?"

"I *have* no more than that. Dorcus has disappeared. Tell Miles."

Morgan raced back to the castle. Something was wrong. Very wrong. Had Dorcus merely gone with Barr? Or did she say or do something which led to Barr losing his temper? His vicious and uncontrolled temper . . . *Would* Barr harm his aunt?

Oswin met him as he entered the castle, his whole manner that of a man suffering from strong emotion.

"She would not wait."

"She? Dorcus?"

"Grace. She said she must explore the passage. What passage?"

Morgan, already rushing off, called over his shoulder, "Was she alone?"

"Two footmen," he called. Puffing, he followed in Morgan's distant wake. Too distant to learn how to enter the passages. All he gained for his effort were several new and interesting swear words which floated back to him.

And a kitten who yowled when denied entrance to the keep's passages.

Wishing she'd awaited Morgan's return, Grace picked her way down the awkward tunnel leading to the shore. One footman led, carefully directing the lantern's light toward her feet. The one following, impatient, offered, with all due respect, to carry the baroness.

"That will not be necessary, Jeffrey. I know you could manage more quickly alone, but I must come in case my cousin is hurt."

They reached the rock-strewn cavern at the bottom. High tides, storms and wind had filled the bare spots between boulders, the fine sand making walking easier. They approached the opening, lit on one side by the morning sun, and Jeffrey caught the baroness's arm. "Please allow us to go first," he said. "You do not know what we will find. It is better if we see first."

He didn't await her agreement, but pushed by her and shoved

the other footman through the narrow opening. A few minutes later Jeffrey returned.

Grace frowned. "What is it. Why do you look like that?" She backed, uncertain, and then, when he reached for her, turned to run. She was too late. Jeffrey caught her and bound her arms to her sides with her own sash. Only then, when it was too late, did Grace remember she wore Morgan's knife!

"Why?" she asked.

"Can't have you poking your nose in where it ain't wanted," he told her. "Barr'll decide what to do with you. In fact, thought he had plans for you earlier." He frowned. "Missus Kenway was ordered to help him."

"Ah." Grace settled her shoulders against the cavern wall. "You mean yesterday when she tried to show me something in the keep. I suppose Barr was there," she mused. "What did he mean to do? Kill me?"

Jeffrey grinned wickedly. "Barr only meant what was meant from the first. Marriage, o'course."

"You appear to know my cousin very well, Jeffrey," said Grace, remarking on Jeffrey's references to Kenway's first name. "How is that?"

"Half brother," admitted Jeffrey. He scowled. "Not fair he should be rich and me poor."

"No, very likely not. But then, life is often unfair. For instance, I was kept in ignorance of my true place in life, was I not?" she asked.

"Guess you were at that," muttered Jeffrey, looking confused.

"What would you do if you had a true stake with which to work?"

"Take a ship to the colonies," said Jeffrey promptly. "That's what I'll do when Barr pays me what he owes me."

"You believe Barr will *pay* you?" asked Grace politely.

Jeffrey steadied himself against the wall. "What are you saying?"

"That once you are no longer needed, you will be discarded."

"I'm his brother."

"Bastard half brother," said Grace softly.

Jeffrey swallowed.

"I am not like Barr," she continued. "I can be trusted." When Jeffrey turned his eyes toward hers, she caught his gaze and held it. "I will give you a good stake and your passage on a ship leaving for the United States of America. If you release me."

"Too late," whispered Jeffrey. "He was sailing into a mooring as I came back."

"Far too late, coz," sneered Barr, entering from the shore. "Not very nice, subverting my brother. Not nice at all. Don't you agree, Dorcus?"

"Now what do we do?" asked the exasperated woman.

"What we intended earlier. I marry the wench. Jeff, bring her out and put her into the boat."

"I want paid," said Jeffrey, crossing his arms.

"See what you have done, Grace?" asked Barr. "I pay him and he takes off. Then where am I?"

"Perhaps doing some of the work yourself, Barr. Like unloading your own contraband. Jeffrey, remember I will give you a stake and see you away from here. You should not trust that Barr and Dorcus will allow you to live. Accidents happen when a ship crosses the Atlantic!"

"You keep your mouth shut, Grace Cheviot. Jeffrey can trust me to see to his interests!"

"His or *yours?*" retorted Grace.

Barr lashed out viciously, backhanding her, pushing her head into contact with rough stone.

Grace felt blood ooze down her neck. She glared. "I thought I knew the worst of you, Barr Kenway. Now I find you not only use your fists to win arguments, but you do so against bound women!" She had heard Jeffrey gasp and Dorcus make a mild objection, but doubted either would come to her aid.

"Bring her," ordered Barr. He ducked out the entrance.

Feeling more and more desperate although she was too proud to allow Barr to see it, Grace found herself dumped into Barr's yacht. "Where's Dorcus?"

"You don't need her. We'll be married and home before nightfall. Jeff," he said to his half brother, who was moving contraband from yacht to dory, "do that later when I return."

"You get caught with that stuff and you're sunk," objected Jeffrey.

"Who's going to catch me?" asked Barr.

Jeffrey laughed. "Right you are, Barr, but when you get back, you and me"—he grinned a mirthless grin—"we're going to have a little talk."

"Just as you wish, Jeff," said Barr, grinning back. But the instant he'd raised sail and turned the yacht into the wind, his grin faded and he swore fluently. "Damn you, Grace. You've spoiled everything."

"Oh no. You and Dorcus did that to yourselves. You roused the curiosity of the wrong man and you did it by your own behavior."

"Blast St. Austell. Should have kept his nose clean. He'll learn." A muscle jumped in Barr's jaw. "Not that it'll do him any good once he's dead."

At that threat Grace's panic rose to impossible heights and it took some time to control it. *She had to do something.* She tried to free her knife but, when she found it impossible the way she was bound, asked, "Now we are well away from shore. Do you think you might untie this sash? I cannot catch myself when the boat rolls. I'll be black and blue."

Barr snarled. "Maybe I should just let you roll." But he lashed the tiller and moved to her side.

Freed, Grace rubbed her arms where the sash had cut into them. Her spirits, raised by Barr's willingness to release her, dipped when she looked around for some means of saving herself. Barr, who depended on servants to do everything for him, appeared to have a different attitude aboard ship. *Here* all was neat as a pin and nothing lay near to hand which she might use to beat him over the head.

If worst came to worst she had the knife, but, she discovered to her dismay, the worst would be pretty bad before she found the courage to use it.

Arriving too late to stop Barr, Morgan had knocked Jeffrey out, tied him and Dorcus up, and eased the wounded footman.

Then Morgan signaled Miles who approached the cove just then and was taken aboard.

"Damn it, Miles, why don't you close with him?"

"He has Lady Kenway. We have to be careful. Relax. He must put in to shore at some point."

"You will lose him."

"As I did when he picked his way through that damn reef that wasn't on my charts? Mea culpa, Morgan. If we hadn't been delayed, we would have cut him off before he sailed with her. Quite a tongue on that Dorcus woman," he finished, trying to turn Morgan's thoughts.

"Natural born fishwife," said Morgan absently. "You are too far from him," he added, his fists pounding the railing.

"Patience, Morgan. There is a right time and a wrong time. We won't lose him again."

"You will if night falls before you come up with him."

"That footman said Barr claimed they would be married and home before dark. He cannot wed without a priest."

"Or a sea captain," said Morgan through his teeth.

"Or a captain," agreed Miles. "In either case he must put to."

Silence followed this exchange, Morgan never taking his eyes from the speck which was Barr Kenway's yacht. *Finally!* "He turned landward," he said.

"As I suspected," responded Miles calmly.

"Where?"

"Falmouth. It is the first good-sized town. He likely has a special license in his pocket, but he wants anonymity."

"Get closer. If he gets ashore he could lose himself in the alleys."

"Stop worrying," soothed Miles. "Remember, the footman said he hadn't unloaded. He weds her, she'll be widowed before you know it!"

Morgan practically shook with anger. "That is the woman I love, you dolt. She must be terror-stricken, either because she doesn't know what he intends, or because she *does*. Damnation, Miles, don't jest!"

"I was out of line," said Miles, apologizing.

He ordered a bit more sail and they began, too slowly to suit

Morgan, to close with Barr's boat. Morgan, climbing atop the cabin, trained a telescope on their quarry but it was some time before he discerned details.

"She's not tied," he told Miles, who was at the tiller.

"Good," said Miles, ordering a trifle more sail. "I mean to come up to him just as he enters the harbor."

"Bloody hell."

"What?" Miles turned the tiller over to a crewman and joined Morgan. He took the scope. "Blast the woman! Doesn't she know better than to wave at us? Once you marry her, train her to be more discreet, will you?" he said bitingly.

"She cannot know it is us, Miles." It was Morgan's turn to soothe. "She merely hopes for help."

"He's twigged us! More sail, boys," he ordered, returning to the helm. "We're closing. Now."

The added canvas brought them up more quickly, but Barr also raised more sail. Still the larger ship slowly closed the gap. It carried far more sail and, although much larger, was built for piracy. It too was constructed for speed.

Morgan watched the water separating the two ships narrow. He never took his gaze from Grace's tense features as she huddled as far from Barr as possible. From time to time, Barr turned to glare at them.

"He can't escape. There is no way he can escape," muttered Miles, frowning.

"There is. Assuming he thinks of it," said Morgan, his mouth clamped into a hard line. He took off his boots and unbuttoned his coat. "Miles, be prepared to come about instantly if I yell."

"He wouldn't!" insisted Miles, guessing at Morgan's meaning.

The distance between the boats quickly narrowed. Morgan was back on his feet, watching their quarry.

"He just did. Come about."

Morgan stripped off his coat and dove over the side, striking out to where Grace bobbed up for a moment. Once again she fought her way to the surface. The third time she went down she was caught in a strong embrace which, frightened out of her wits, she fought. Morgan, sending her a silent apology, hit her, knocking her out, and brought them to the surface.

A dory approached. Farther off, legs straddled and arms akimbo, Miles stood at the rail of his ship, glaring after Barr's boat, which would soon disappear and would be impossible to find. Grace was lifted over the dory's gunwales. Then Morgan clambered aboard. When they reached the ship, Miles helped them aboard and a sailor brought rough blankets. Morgan cuddled Grace. Settled on a padded seat in the stern, he awaited her return to consciousness.

"Had to knock her out?"

"Yes," said Morgan shortly.

"It was necessary, so stop kicking yourself. See? She stirs."

They were escorted below to the privacy of cabins where each stripped and their clothing was dried by a seaman. While it dried, the ship returned to where Miles was moored while awaiting his chance to catch Barr.

His business here, thought Miles, was nearly done. The footman would be put away where he'd do no more damage, but, Miles decided, he'd leave her Kenway cousins to the baroness. Not a totally satisfactory ending, but better than nothing. And he could return to his own affairs. Miles grinned at the thought of a certain intrepid Frenchwoman who thought herself so clever. She'd soon discover there were others still more resourceful!

Once on land again, Grace huddled in her corner of the carriage returning them to the castle. She seemed extraordinarily subdued. Morgan kept a concerned eye on her. What, he wondered, went through her mind? He asked, "What is it?"

"Barr. I never thought he would try to kill me."

"He knew we'd rescue you. He merely wished to escape. Which he did."

"What will happen to him?"

"Nothing at all. He has contraband on board and will sell it, use what he gets as a stake for his next, er, business effort."

"He'll remain in England?"

"I doubt he is so foolish. The Rhine has any number of small principalities bordering it. I suspect he will transfer operations there."

"Dorcus will be miserable," she said after a moment's silence.

"Dorcus helped Barr," said Morgan. He felt the brute, but was convinced Grace must see clearly. "Do you care if she is miserable?"

Grace sighed. "What am I to do?"

"I"—

Lord, how he wanted to tell her to send her cousins from the castle instantly. And far away.

—"cannot advise you, my dear."

How sad she looks, he thought. He wanted to take her into his arms, wanted to console her, keep her safe from worry and care. But he could not. They should not be alone in the closed carriage. It would be *worse* if he took advantage of their isolation.

"You saved my life today," she said abruptly, disrupting his thoughts.

"Did you think I would not?"

"I didn't think one way or the other simply because I'd no *time* to think. It was a horrid shock when Barr threw me overboard."

"But you knew we followed?"

"It was only when you got near that I recognized you," she said. "You cannot know how pleased I was to see you."

To keep his hands off her, Morgan leaned sideways into his corner. "Had Barr explained what he meant to do? I mean before he saw us?"

"He meant to marry me." Grace's lips compressed. "Perhaps"—she frowned—"I could have convinced the vicar I'd no wish to wed Barr."

"Very likely your cousin knew of one who could be bribed."

"A *vicar?*" The thought obviously appalled her.

"It didn't happen. You are safe."

"Safe? Yes, but I *must* decide what to do about my cousins."

They remained silent until they reached the castle where they were met by a flustered housekeeper rather than the butler.

"What is it?" asked Grace sharply.

"Missus Kenway . . ."

"Yes?"

"She threw herself over the cliff," wailed the woman. She threw her apron over her head.

Grace drew in a deep breath, darted a quick look toward Morgan and then asked, "And my cousin? Mr. Kenway?"

"In the library with that Frenchy."

"Thank you." Grace shivered, wishing she could rid herself of her still damp clothing. "Bring a tray for Mr. St. Austell and myself," she ordered, giving the poor woman a task which would help her gain control of herself.

They found Oswin and the comte seated together near the fireplace, the baroness's kitten on the comte's lap. Oswin turned a horrified gaze on Grace when she entered. Then peered beyond her.

"Barr?" he asked in a strangled tone. He"—Oswin pointed at the comte—"says Barr is smuggling! Why would he go smuggling? Where is he?"

"Barr escaped," said Grace. "Cousin, did you know of the smuggling?"

"No! No and no and no. I told your uncle again and again I know nothing of it." Oswin's voice rose, a whiny tenor which grated on the ear. "He won't leave me alone. He won't let me grieve! Dorcus couldn't . . . wouldn't . . . She . . ."

Under Grace's steady look he ran down and, silent, bit his lip. "Cousin," said Grace steadily, "your wife *helped* Barr. She was guilty of aiding and abetting a smuggler, if nothing worse."

"But *suicide!*" His eyes were stark with horror. "No. Surely not? It must have been an accident."

"What would be your response, knowing you were revealed to be a smuggler?" asked Morgan.

Oswin blanched. "I cannot believe it. I will not believe it!" He rose to his feet. With some return of dignity, he added, "But you, at least, are safe. I thank God for that."

"You wished me wed to Barr."

"Yes. We wished all kept in the family. It would be best that way."

"Best for whom, Cousin?"

He winced. "For *all* of us, Grace. All of us."

"Except me."

"Nonsense. Even you. Everything would have gone on as it always had. Now everything is spoiled. Everything." He turned and left the room.

"In his way," said the comte, "he loved that terrible woman."

"Yes." Grace, standing with her back to the fire, lifted her arms. She shook her fists. "And I still do not know if he had a notion of what went on!" Finally warm, she slumped into a chair. "Not for certain."

"I think he did not," said her great-uncle. "His shock was real when he learned his wife was guilty of smuggling. Eventually he will accept that she jumped rather than be taken up by the law."

Grace was reminded of earlier. "There were two footmen with me when I foolishly went looking for her," she said.

"Yes. One has a concussion, but will recover. The other, Kenway's half brother, is under lock and key, an unhappy and bitter man."

"I promised him money and a ship to the new world."

"Assuming, surely, that he did something to deserve a reward," said Morgan sharply.

His tone drew her mouth up into a slight smile, her first since her rescue. "Oh yes. And he did not, but if he had had time I believe he might have done so. I'd convinced him Barr would double-cross him, you see."

"With reason. Barr's temper is unbalanced. He will come to ruin merely because he never learned to control it."

"I have long predicted he'd come to a bad end. I *know* him. There were good reasons why I'd no wish to wed him." She brightened when the housekeeper entered with a tray. "Excellent," she said. "Adventure must rouse the appetite because I find I am exceedingly hungry."

"Perhaps it is merely the passage of time since you last ate," said her uncle, rising. He waited until the food was laid out on a small table and two chairs placed near it before excusing himself, saying he was an old man and the excitement had tired him.

"Or perhaps," said Morgan, with a gesture to a clock that read nearly midnight, thanks to all their toing-and-froing, *"it is merely the passage of time* since you last rose from your bed."

The old gentleman chuckled softly at Morgan's mimicry and left the room, the half-grown kitten nestled on one arm.

"Should I too depart, Grace?" asked Morgan. "I should not be here with you. Not alone."

"Sit and eat," she said. "You too must be starved."

"You have decisions to make, my dear."

"Yes. Mr. St. Austell, I have known Jeffrey practically all my life. I know he is not a bad man. I just don't know what to do."

"Jeffrey is the least of your problems, Grace."

"You refer to Cousin Oswin. He loves the castle, you know."

"Yes."

"And he has done well by it over the years."

"Yes."

She sighed. "Why must life be so complicated?"

He made no attempt to answer that. Instead, he asked, "What would you do if you could do anything you wished?"

"Go away." She forked up another mouthful, chewed, swallowed. "I'd go right away and leave all my problems behind."

"Then do so."

Her hand halfway to her mouth, she froze, then lowered her fork to her plate. "What do you mean?"

"You were cheated of the life you should have lived, Grace. Your uncle would introduce you to it."

"Would he?" She looked blankly out the night-dark window. "Strangers. No friends. A strange place. Perhaps I do not wish to leave my home after all."

"Grace, I am . . . your friend. I too would come to London and help introduce you to the world which is yours."

Grace eyed him as she finished eating. When satiated she rose to her feet and wandered to the window. Morgan followed her.

"Morgan, you once told me your intentions were honorable. Was that simply an unguarded comment made to make me feel more the thing?"

"My intentions, my dear, are honorable in every sense. And the honorable role just now is to allow you time to discover who and what you are. To meet men better suited to you. To fall in love with—"

She turned a stormy countenance toward him. *"You,* Morgan St. Austell, are honorable to the point of foolishness." Grace reached up and grabbed his ears, pulling him down. She kissed him, a hard kiss, right on his unready lips. Pushing by him, she crossed the room, pausing with her hand on the door. "You may count that another mistletoe kiss, Morgan, and a thank you for saving my life."

On the words, she disappeared into the dark hall beyond. Morgan stared after her. But not for long. She would, he thought, have gone to her suite. Following, he found the door to her sitting room open.

Dare he? He dared.

She stood by the mantel, silhouetted by the red embers of a dying fire. He moved to her and took her shoulders, turning her. "Grace." Tipping her chin, he took her lips in a kiss so loving, so giving, she'd no choice but to lean into him, prolong it, yield to it, savor it . . .

. . . and to discover that, as all good things ended, so did this.

"I love you," he said, and smiled tightly at the shock he read in her shadowed features. He went on soberly. "You thought I did not? But Grace, you must understand me! I love you far too well to take advantage of your ignorance, your lack of experience. You must meet men who did not spend their youth in the rough life of the army. Men who know music and theater. Who can dance with greater facility than I will ever have. Men other than a simple country gentleman who does not love city life. A life where you would sparkle and shine and have all the attention you deserve."

"Even if I do not want such attention? Are you, too, going to force me into a life I do not want?" She compressed her lips and glared. *"As my cousins would have done?"*

He stared down at her, slightly baffled by her retort.

"For my own good?" she added, pressing the point.

"I suppose I had something of the sort in mind," he admitted.

"Am I so stupid I cannot know what is good for me?"

"Not stupid," he retorted, on surer ground. *"Ignorant.* How do you know you'd not like life in London with the ton?"

"Morgan, under close supervision I visited Bristol and Bath. I spent two weeks in Brighton when the prince was in residence. I found the society false and the pleasures shallow. I enjoyed concerts and one visit to the theater but a second play was badly acted. I could never go out alone. There was nowhere to walk freely. And towns stink, Morgan." She wrinkled her nose. "I hate the smell."

He stared at her. She met his gaze freely, her eyes steady on his own.

"Morgan," she said urgently, when he neither moved nor spoke, "what are we to do? We are out of mistletoe kisses!"

Her words brought a smile to his eyes and tipped just the corners of his mouth. "Minx."

She tried not to smile.

"A terrible fate," he added. "I must think of something, must I not?"

He tipped her chin with his thumb, his mouth descending for a far more passionate kiss then they'd yet exchanged.

Later Grace snuggled into his arms before a rebuilt fire. She stared down to where a satisfied-looking kitten curled up on the hearth rug, its slowly blinking golden eyes staring at them.

Did you plan this, Purrmew? she wondered.

The cat seemed to smile lazily which, she decided, must be her imagination. Her eyes still on the animal, she murmured, "I have decided I like non-mistletoe kisses the best."

"Good," he said. He too stared at the cat. "Because," he added, "I mean for you to experience a lot of them." He heard the kitten purr. "Once we are married, of course." The purring stopped abruptly.

"We are to wed?"

"Are we not?" he asked, startled into forgetting Purrmew's odd behavior.

"Oh, I think so." Her eyes smiled into his. Wistfully, she asked, "Now you've taught me to kiss properly, is there not more you might teach me?"

He grinned. "You, my beloved baggage, must wait until we are man and wife before you get an answer to that!" His arm tightened and, despite her squirming and her hinting—Morgan was honorable to the end—he refused to indulge her in anything more than kisses. Non-mistletoe kisses, of course.

The kitten's purring resumed.

NOËL'S CHRISTMAS WISH

by

Donna Simpson

One

Mignon Heloise Montrose . . . such a long name for the tiny, forlorn figure that was curled up in the window seat in the third floor nursery of Russetshire Manor. Perhaps that was why everyone in the household, down to the lowest scullery maid and boot boy, called her "Mossy." She was six going on seven, elfin of feature, blonde, with hazel eyes that normally radiated cheery happiness.

Jade green eyes winked up at her, glowing in the pale moonlight that streamed into the window. Her thin, sensitive fingers threaded through the silky fur of the kitten that curled purring in the nest of her nightgown.

"Papa's going away again, Noël, right after Christmas."

The diminutive kitten kneaded ecstatically as Mossy scrubbed behind shell-pink ears and under a tiny pointed chin.

"He just came back a week ago, an' already he's talking about going away again." She sniffed and blinked back the tear that puddled in her eye and threatened to drip down her cheek. "At least he brought me you," she whispered, lifting the gray and white kitten up to her eye level. She kissed his nose and cuddled him back in her lap.

As she gazed out over the stretch of frosted lawn that rolled down toward the big main gate, a flash of light in the heavens caught her eye. "Oh, Noël, that's a shooting star! Papa told me once that if you see a shooting star and make a wish, it will come true!"

The kitten reached up with one delicate paw and touched her cheek.

"I know; I have to wish quickly. But for what? I already have everything I could wish for now that Papa's here and has brought me you. OH!" She bounced up and down and Noël let out a squawk of protest and clung to her leg with pin-sharp claws. "Ouch! Sorry." She resettled the tiny animal on her lap. "It's just that I know what to wish for, and you have to wish too. Close your eyes."

The kitten blinked and mewed.

"Oh, all right. I'll close mine and you can do what you want. But you have to wish what I do." She squeezed her eyes tightly shut and grimaced. "I wish . . . I wish that something would happen that would keep Papa home forever an' ever! Something that would make him want to stay with me and not go away again after Christmas."

She opened one eye and looked down at the little kitten. It was curled into a tight ball, one tiny paw over its eyes. "You *did* close your eyes! Clever kitten! Now our wish is sure to come true. Papa said so."

A hare shot from the hedgerow at the side of the Bath road, and the carriage driver, who was trundling along almost asleep, had no time to control the spirited but weary team. One horse shied, the other balked, and in a moment the air was filled with screams and imprecations as the carriage toppled down the slight grade into the ditch by the roadside.

Lady Ann Beecham-Brooke had allowed herself just the one ladylike scream as the carriage toppled sideways, but her lady's maid, Ellen, felt no such compunction and rent the night with her high-pitched wailing. The air filled with the smell of lamp oil, but as the carriage lantern had gone out there was no danger of fire to the straw that had covered the floor and now was scattered around the carriage, nor to the blankets that held bricks long gone cold.

"Oh, do shut up, Ellen," Lady Ann muttered, trying, in the darkness of the carriage, to figure out which way they were oriented. She didn't want to move precipitately in case it caused the carriage to tumble farther down whatever incline they were on.

Ellen's screams calmed to a moaning, eerie in the darkness but preferable to ear-splitting screeches. The carriage rocked, then slid a few more feet and steadied.

"Milady, are you all right?"

Ann's driver, Jacob Lesley, was already unlatching the door—now that the carriage was on its side, the door was above her head—and opening it. She could see stars above her. Warily she stood, finding she could just see over the top. Jacob's anxious face appeared.

"Milady, are you—"

"I am in one piece, but Ellen seems vastly more upset. Help me out, Jacob."

The grizzled coachman, well into his sixth decade of life, put out a gnarled hand as he said, "I believe, milady, that the carriage has settled firmly agin' a rock. Mayhap it will move no more. 'Tis worth the attempt, methinks, for you canna stay in the carriage all night."

Confounded by long skirts and a heavy velvet cloak, climbing out into the frosty December air proved a difficult chore. Lady Ann's voice, when she finally touched ground, was as frigid as the night.

"I assume, Jacob, that you have an explanation for this?" She brushed her cloak down and straightened, glaring at her driver in the pale moonlight.

"Aye, my lady, that I do, an' it has to do with the folly of night driving with a tired team and an even more weary driver. I'd best get Miss Ellen out o' the carriage, afore she swoons."

The maid's moans still shuddered through the air. It took all of Jacob's coaxing and Lady Ann's demands before Ellen would think of moving, and then it was a matter of twenty minutes before they could get her out. She promptly sat down at the roadside and wept.

"Now what shall we do?" Lady Ann demanded, scowling at her driver.

Jacob peered up and down the dark road. "Feller at the last inn we stopped at to water the horses—the inn I suggested we stay the night at, if you 'member, milady—he were a talkative sort. Said as how there was a manor house along this road—big iron gates he said. I believe as how we passed them gates not too long ago, mayhap a half mile back."

Ann raised her thinly arched eyebrows. "And what do you propose we do?" She had not missed the veiled criticism in her driver's words, but decided to ignore it . . . for now.

Jacob glanced at her and grimaced, catching the angry glint in his mistress's eye. She was a feisty one, was Lady Ann. He would catch it for sure later, but right now it was his duty to find them aid, despite his own bruises, sustained in the fall. "Feller said as how the lord o' the manor, by the name o' Montrose, Viscount Ruston, he's one o' them world traveler fellas. Never home. But the place is always open and staffed, as 'tis a busy road and they be used to travelers in trouble. Bound to be a place to stay for the night and some help to get the carriage righted agin."

"I dislike intensely imposing our presence on a household, especially at this time of year." Ann frowned down at the road, but could come up with no alternative suggestion. "All right, Jacob, we shall stay here. Take one of the horses and go to that house. But hear me well. If the lord of the manor is home, I would prefer that we borrow a carriage and go on to the next village or roadside inn. I . . . I would not like to intrude on family at this time of year."

Jacob glanced at her, understanding in his keen gaze. He had first seen her as the young bride of his master, Baron Reginald Beecham-Brooke. All of the household had felt sorry for the eighteen-year-old beauty with the huge violet eyes who had been bartered by her parents to the thirty-seven-year-old, clutch-fisted, heartless baron.

As the years passed, though, and Lady Ann hardened before their eyes into an icy, frigid woman, their sympathy wore away. It was not that she abused the help; she was fair-minded and generous enough with food and pay. But never did anyone see the softer side of her, the youthful optimism with which she had arrived at the baron's seat.

Jacob alone, of all of the staff, still defended her, believing that her frostiness was a cloak she donned to protect herself. Grooms in the stable crudely suggested that she needed bedding by a man capable of warming her frigidity, and Jacob, as old as he was, had challenged more than one young buck to a wrestling match over such remarks.

He had his own theories about Lady Ann, but he never shared them. In this case he simply responded to her demand with a grunt, neither assent nor dissent implied, he thought. He disliked leaving his mistress alone like this, but saw no alternative, and limped away to mount one of the carriage horses.

As he rode off, Ann turned to her maid, who still sat huddled at the roadside. The young woman was holding her arm at an awkward angle.

"Ellen? Have you been hurt?"

Sniffing back tears, the maid said, her voice quivering, "It . . . it's nothing, milady."

Ann strode over to the roadside, crouched by her and examined the young woman's arm, noting the wince as she moved the limb. "You have hurt it! Why did you not say anything?"

"I-I-I did not like to cause trouble, milady."

The moonlight was beginning to fade, but Ann could see the apprehension in her maid's face. Was the girl afraid of her? Good heavens! Had she become one of *those* women, whose servants trembled at their anger? She sat down beside Ellen, undid her cloak and wrapped half of it around the shivering maid, keeping half for herself. They huddled together in the frosty night, their breath coming out in steamy puffs.

"We'll have help soon, Ellen, and then we can look after your arm properly. I dare not move it, for fear it is broken."

Suddenly the road seemed very dark and lonely to Ann, and she did not deny even to herself that the closeness of another human was reassuring. A chill wind swept down the road and she shivered, pulling the cloak closer. Together, the two women settled down to wait for help to arrive.

"My lord?"

Charles Philip Montrose, Viscount Ruston, looked up from

an exceedingly dull book on agriculture, glad to be interrupted at such a pastime. "What is it, Stoddart?"

"There is a man, a carriage driver, at the back door, my lord. He says he is Lady Beecham-Brooke's driver, and they have had an accident just down the road from here. He was wondering if we could render him assistance, and offer his mistress and her maid a place to stay for the night."

"Good Lord!" Ruston leaped to his feet. "What would anyone be doing driving in the middle of the night? Is he mad?"

"He seems to be in full possession of his wits, my lord," Stoddart said, with the merest hint of a wry smile. "What may I tell him?"

"What would you do if I were not here?"

"Take them in, sir."

"And there is no difference just because I am in residence! Of course, we shall offer any assistance we can."

The butler turned to leave.

"Oh, Stoddart?"

"Yes, sir?"

"Have . . . oh, the green room made up for Lady Beecham-Brooke, and a fire laid."

"Very good, sir." Stoddart started for the door.

"And have a room set aside for the maid, and space for the driver, of course."

"Yes, sir." This time he made it all the way, and was about to close the door behind him.

"And Stoddart?"

The butler opened the door again and bowed.

"Have the gold saloon fire laid, and a light collation prepared, in case Lady Beecham-Brooke is hungry. I would have a place to greet her."

"Certainly, sir." He bowed and closed the door.

"Stoddart!"

The butler opened the door again and stood stiffly, waiting.

Ruston grinned. "Just testing, old man, just testing."

A smile flickered over the butler's somber features. He bowed and exited.

Lady Beecham-Brooke. Why did that name tease his brain

so? He had heard it recently, if he was not mistaken, on his stop in London as he returned from his most recent jaunt to the Continent. Ruston, who much preferred to be called Charley by friends, took up his book again, shelving it as he contemplated. Who had he met in London who would have mentioned her name? If he was correct, this must be the widow of Baron Beecham-Brooke, a dry stick many years his senior. So an older lady?

No. That didn't seem right.

He poured himself a brandy and went over the few days he spent in London, searching for the connection his brain insisted was there. The first day he had arrived he had gone to his town house and looked through all the gifts he had sent back for Mossy, his daughter, in the several months he had spent traveling through Italy and France. His next trip after Christmas, he decided, would take him through the Balkans and down into Greece.

After looking through the treasure trove of French dolls, Italian silver brush sets, lace, ribbons, every kind of frippery thing a little girl could care for, he had gone to greet his sometime-mistress, Lady Callander. They had spent the evening and much of the night making love. He had had a few amorous adventures in Italy, and one memorable night in Paris with a songbird of extraordinary beauty, but there was nothing like a woman whose ardent murmurings he understood! Not that he believed half of what Lydia said.

The next day he had gone to Rundell and Bridges for a trinket for her, to make up for not being with her at Christmas, and had spent the afternoon at White's. Then he had gone back to Lydia's, presented her with the emerald bracelet, and had spent the evening and night again in her arms as she thanked him exhaustively for the emeralds. In the early morning light she had started softly hinting that she would be very glad to wake up with him on a permanent basis if his next gift should happen to be a ring, and he had taken fright and quickly departed.

Lydia was very well in her way, but he could not imagine being tied to her for life. He knew she was not faithful to him while he was gone on his jaunts to Europe, and he did not expect her to be, but a wife . . . that would be different. If ever he married again, and he saw no reason to think he would, he wanted a woman of a much different stamp than a Lydia, who could take a lover casually, entertaining other men as the mood took her. He had been faithful to his wife, and she to him; it was the only way to conduct a marriage.

And so the next day he had sent a note around, telling her he would be going to the country immediately; he hoped she had a very nice Christmas. He subtly suggested he was freeing her from any imagined connection between them, implying that the emerald bracelet was a farewell present. He would not be seeing Lydia again.

He had been at loose ends that day, so he had gone to his friends, Sir Peregrine Haunton and his very gravid wife, Sylvia. Perry was an old friend of his from school, and they spent the day reminiscing and gossiping; he had dinner there, then went to a gambling hall for the evening. That was where he found his first gift for Mossy, oddly enough. He drank too much and then stumbled out the back door for a breath of fresh air, knowing it was even odds he would cast up his accounts. There he heard a low snarl, and as his eyes adjusted to the semidarkness of the alley, he spied a brindled stable hound. It was stalking down the alley and growling as it paced toward its prey, a tiny, dirty kitten.

But the little thing was not going to go down without a fight. Though it was cornered against some wooden crates, it had its back up and was hissing and spitting with all the courage in its small frame. He just couldn't let nature take its course. He had scooped up the kitten, getting a scratch for his efforts, and had taken the little thing home in his pocket, not sure what he was going to do with it, but determined not to let it die.

In the light of morning, after the scullery maid at his town house had given it a bath, it turned out to be an enchanting, fluffy ball of fur with a precocious attitude that reminded him of his daughter. Impulsively, he had decided that would be her first Christmas gift, and so he found a red ribbon and tied it around the little devil's neck, which was no easy chore since it never stopped wriggling and batting at the ribbon.

But back to the mystery of Lady Beecham-Brooke. It had only been a week ago that he was in London. Surely he could remember all the gossip he had heard just that long ago?

A stirring in the great hall made him put his glass down on a table and leave the library. Two women stood blinking in the chandelier-lit great hall, one with her arm over the other's shoulders in an oddly protective gesture. Ruston's housekeeper, Mrs. Bowles, greeted them with Stoddart, and she led away the shorter of the two women, by her dress likely a lady's maid.

Ruston stepped forward. "Good evening, my lady. I trust your accident left you unharmed?"

The woman left behind whirled, her velvet cloak swirling around her and settling in folds. She was tall for a woman, and slim, with a regal air. She lifted her chin and said, her voice brittle and as cold as the night air. "My lord, I had no idea you were in residence. We would not have imposed had we known that was the case."

Staring into her eyes—violet eyes; how rare!—he thought how cold and penetrating her glare was. And then it came to him.

"Of course!" he blurted out, jabbing the air with his forefinger. "You are Lady Ice!"

Two

Her glare turned to an expression of disdain.

Ruston froze. Had he actually said that out loud? He had remembered quite suddenly where he had heard her name; Perry and Sylvia had been full of the latest *on dits* about her. He had not expected the subject of London's favorite tittle-tattle to be quite so beautiful, though, and his shock had caused him to blurt out that savage sobriquet.

A maid descended the wide staircase from the second floor. While the girl helped divest Lady Beecham-Brooke of her cloak, he stared at the woman before him.

She was absolutely lovely—flawless, creamy skin, raven hair dressed high, with bunches of curls near her exquisite face, and with a figure that, though slim, was curvaceous, too. When she turned, she pierced him with those amethyst eyes, but stood composed and wordless. Lady Ice.

He bowed. "Please, warm yourself in the gold saloon while your room is being prepared, my lady." Only after he said it did he realize how that sounded. He grimaced.

Up in the gallery, above the great hall, a pair of hazel eyes and a pair of green eyes gazed down at the scene. Mossy stared. "I wonder who she is, Noël?"

The kitten dug his claws in and wriggled in her arms.

"You aren't going anywhere," she whispered, tightening her hold. "Look, she's taking off her cloak and turning back to

Papa, but he's just standing there with his mouth open." She giggled, but stifled it with her hand. The woman glanced up, as if she heard something, and Mossy stared at the lady's face.

She was beautiful—the most beautiful lady Mossy had ever seen—but there was something else. Furrowing her blonde brows and squeezing her kitten to her, though he squawked in protest, Mossy thought she had never seen a lady whose eyes looked so sad.

Lost in her thoughts, she let Noël leap from her arms and scamper down the hall.

Ann raised her eyebrows, but followed the viscount's direction. She thought for a moment she had heard a ghostly laugh in the gallery, above the hall, but that was superstitious nonsense. She was furious; she was as angry as she had ever been in her life. She had left London to escape that ridiculous epithet, only to be taunted with it in the middle of nowhere!

She had thought by accepting her old schoolfriend Verity's invitation to spend the Christmas season in Bath with her and her husband, she would let the furor of her appellation, and how she had earned it, die down, but it appeared that it had infiltrated even this far into the countryside.

Outwardly she maintained her air of calm disdain. Who was this Viscount Rustic, or whatever Jacob had called him? He was well enough looking, she supposed. Under her dark lashes she studied him as she waited to see where he planned to sit in the warm, golden room, so she could sit a distance away from him.

He was tall and broad-shouldered. Reggie had been tall, but thin and dark, whereas this fellow seemed to glow with health and vitality. His hair was a dark auburn, his skin tanned, golden in the light from the fire. He moved with an easy grace, whereas her husband had always had a rigidity about him, as though he was a puppet.

"Please, you must be cold, er . . ." The viscount colored, his cheeks mantling with a brick red color. "What I mean to say is, the fire is warm, and the night has been exceptionally frosty. Why don't you come closer to the fire?" he coaxed. "You must have been frightened out there on the Bath road alone with just your maid. I can't imagine what your driver was thinking!"

"Jacob knows me well enough to be aware that I am never frightened," she said. It wasn't the truth, but it sounded well. "I am quite happy here, my lord." Knowing he would not sit until she did, she sat on a sofa between two big, gold-draped windows.

The butler entered, followed by two footmen with trays, one of tea and one of food. They set the trays on a low table near Ann and she glanced at the viscount. "Shall I pour, my lord?" She was pleased with herself. She was in a towering rage, and yet no one would have known it by her voice, which was calm and even, unlike during that little incident in London, the one that had cemented her reputation.

"Certainly."

He was prowling closer to her, and to her annoyance her hand on the silver handle of the teapot trembled slightly as he joined her on the brocade sofa. He loomed so . . . so large and warm; he radiated heat like one of the great beasts she had seen at the Tower menagerie.

What was wrong with her? She was tired and overwrought, that was all; it had been an eventful night. She handed him a cup and served herself, gratefully sipping the steaming brew. It was certainly nothing to do with being sorry he knew the gossip about her. Nothing at all.

Ruston, too, sipped his tea. He had taken the opportunity to sit next to her because he had not believed it possible that any woman could be as beautiful as she appeared. Surely there was some flaw. He gazed at her steadily, pleased beyond reason to see her hand tremble, then castigating himself the next second. She had been through a horrendous experience and then waited by the roadside with just her maid for company in the frigid darkness. Despite her brave words she must have been cold and just a little afraid. How unchivalrous of him to take pleasure from any discomfort she might feel.

She was, indeed, flawless. Her skin had the pale beauty of cream, her full lips the color of pink roses. Her hair was black and glossy, and even after tumbling in a carriage accident was still coiffed and neat. But it was those violet eyes, clear and large, fringed in coal-black lashes, that had taken his breath away from the first moment. She would not look up at him. He cursed himself again for the ill-timed blunder of calling her Lady Ice, but the wicked appellation being bandied about London had come to him just at that moment, and had been out before he thought.

Lady Ice.

She was proud—no, haughty was more the word—with a cold, piercing glare and a supercilious tilt to her small nose. It was said that she took pleasure in crushing the pretensions of love-struck young men who were wont to throw themselves at her feet. Perry declared that she had seen the woman refuse an invitation to dance, made by a young cub who stared adoringly at her, saying loud enough for all to hear, "Sir, if I should ever feel the need to stumble about the floor and humiliate myself with an inept partner, I shall know upon whom to call." It was said that after that crushing embarrassment the young man had dejectedly departed from the ball, setting out immediately on the Grand Tour to recover from the humiliation.

Aware that the silence had been too long and that he was still staring at her, he rushed into speech. "I hope you may be convinced to stay more than just one night here, my lady."

She gazed at him in frank astonishment, as if he had just asked her to disrobe in front of him. "Why would I do that, sir?"

"I-I . . ." Damn, but she made him feel like a tongue-tied schoolboy!

He took a deep breath and gathered all of his considerable experience around him like armament. He was *not* one of those love-struck cubs, to immolate himself on the pyre of her disdain; he would seize control of the conversation and prevail. He moved closer to her on the sofa. She put her cup down on the tray, using the motion to move slightly away.

"It is often lonely in the country. Surely you must realize how welcome is the diversion of a beauty like yourself?"

She glanced at him once, impaling him with her icy stare. "You mock me, sir."

"Mock you? By calling you beautiful? I only concur with common feeling, I believe." Enthralled once again by those amazing eyes, he wished she would look at him—really *look* at him—for longer than that brief moment. What would it be like to be the man who lit those icy orbs into violet fire? Ah, but he was falling into the same trap those other poor sots—the ones she demolished with a well-placed *bon mot*—fell into, the desire to warm the ice-maiden.

"I have no wish to pander to 'common' feeling," she replied.

"Let us move away from what is evidently a sensitive area. Where are you headed, my lady, so late on a December night?"

They made desultory conversation as she told him of her friend Verity, and then Ruston, mindful that Lady Ann must be exhausted, rang for a footman to show her to her room.

Ann was relieved to be led up the stairs and down a wide hallway, grateful to be away from Ruston's warm brown regard. She glanced around her room with pleasure. It was done in shades of softest moss green, like a leafy bower. Sage draperies and bed hangings figured in a muted leaf pattern continued the verdant motif, and the heavy Turkish carpet underfoot was pale green with a pattern of wood violets and emerald green ivy wending around the perimeter. It was an exquisite room, planned by a person of exceptional taste.

The vicountess, Lady Ruston perhaps, if there was such a person?

A scratch at the door was followed by a young woman who curtsied and said, "Mrs. Bowles said as how I was to be your lady's maid while your abigail recovers, milady. My name is Sarah."

"I will appreciate your help, Sarah. First, will you tell me where Ellen is?"

"She is in the servants' quarters, ma'am. Mrs. Bowles said not to worry yourself about Ellen; her arm is just twisted, not broke, and she is in bed with a mite of laudanum, and sleeping like a babe."

Satisfied, Ann said, "Good. I will see her in the morning, before we leave. I will get ready for bed now." She glanced over at the bed, so inviting. The covers were turned down to expose snow-white sheets trimmed in lace. The counterpane was heavy emerald brocade. It looked inviting and soft, if a little lumpy just in the middle. Perhaps this room was not used much, and they had an old mattress in it. Oh well, she thought. She would be able to sleep on a bed of nails, she was so tired.

Sarah helped her into her nightrail and then brushed her long hair out.

"Shall I braid it for you, milady? Such beautiful hair!"

"I prefer it loose. Braids give me the headache."

Sarah snuffed all the candles but one, and put that at the bedside, curtsied and then left, closing the door softly behind her as Ann climbed into bed.

The chill was off the sheets where a warming pan had been, and she slid her bare feet down into the delicious heat. Her toes encountered something warm and furry and she gasped, kicking at it. Needle-sharp teeth sank into her toe and she stumbled out from under the heavy covers and stood staring at the bed and shrieking.

"A rat! A rat!"

In moments the door was flung open and Ruston raced into the room, holding a branch of tapers high. "What in God's name is going on!" he shouted, his voice a commanding bark.

Ann had the strangest impulse to throw herself at the broad chest, bare beneath an open shirt, but she resisted and pointed one trembling hand at her bed.

"Th-there . . . a r-r-rat! It *bit* me!"

Ruston squeezed her arm with one strong, long-fingered hand. "Hold the candles, my lady, and I will dispatch the creature, and then we will see that you get another room."

Ann took the candelabra in her trembling hand and watched the viscount grab a hairbrush from the vanity table and approach the bed. Sarah, her temporary lady's maid, stood in the doorway with horror writ over her young features. Ruston prowled to the bed, grasped the bedclothes in one hand and glanced over his shoulder at Ann.

"If it escapes do not worry about me, just get yourself away."

Sarah gave a squeak of alarm, but Ann nodded and said fervently, "You can believe I will, my lord."

Ruston jerked the bedclothes back with one mighty yank and held the brush high, ready to swing down doom on the rodent. Instead he was faced with a spitting, growling, hissing little ball of erect fur and glaring green eyes.

He dropped the covers and erupted into huge gusts of laughter.

A kitten! Ann stared at the tiny gray and white ball of fluff and slumped with relief, her heart thudding a sick tattoo in her breast. A kitten! Finally, though, it registered on her that Ruston was having his huge laugh at her expense.

"I do not see what is so funny!"

"If you could have seen your face!" Ruston tossed the brush back on the vanity table and took the branch of tapers from her. In a falsetto voice he said, "A r-r-rat!" He broke into laughter again and set the tapers on the table by the bed, then moved to pick up the kitten.

Anger boiled over in Ann's heart and, her hands balled into fists, she flew at Ruston, buffeting his arms, then his chest as he turned toward her, with the hardest blows she could manage. "You brute!" she screeched. "You wretched, wretched . . ."

Ruston caught her hands in his and held them easily away. His dark brown eyes held a dangerous glint, and Ann gazed up into them thinking that never had she been so angry in her life, and yet . . .

He was devastatingly handsome. Warm, big, strong, and with his shirt open to the waist, though it was still tucked into his breeches. The expression in his dark eyes changed, subtly, as he gazed down at her. She felt his gaze like a touch over her brow, her eyes, her cheeks and finally her lips.

Time slowed to the beat of her pounding heart as his eyes dropped lower, lower to the ties of her nightrail where they had come loose, exposing her white skin to his caressing scrutiny. The intimacy of the surroundings did not escape her. Never had she been in a bedchamber with a man other than her husband, Reggie, and truth to tell, never had her heart pounded like this in the presence of her husband.

She jerked her hands away, breaking the spell that had bound them both.

Ruston swallowed and stepped away from her. He paced to the bed and scooped up the kitten that was unconcernedly washing its face, licking its paw and scrubbing it over one ear, and then leisurely doing the other.

"My daughter's first Christmas gift this year. May I introduce you to Noël, Lady Ann?"

"D-daughter?" Ann faltered over the word. She glanced toward the door. "I . . . is there a Lady Ruston I should have met, or . . ."

Ruston shook his head, ruffling the kitten's fur under its chin. The tiny animal's rumbling purr could be heard through the room. "My wife died many years ago. Mossy is my only child."

"I . . . I am sorry." Finally Ann thought to cross her arms over her bosom. She could not meet Ruston's eyes and she stood, silent and uncertain.

The viscount stirred. "I shall leave you to your sleep, my lady. I will see you in the morning."

He exited, and Ann was left alone in the big room. She paced around it, touching the brush Ruston had used to defend her, remembering his booming laugh and masculine presence with feelings she could not decipher. It was good that she would be leaving in the morning. Very good.

Three

The door opened silently on well-oiled hinges. The figure in the bed did not stir at the incursion into her room. A small figure crept in, but an even tinier one darted ahead, leaped at the dangling bedclothes and clambered up the dark green counterpane.

"Noël," Mossy hissed. "You bad boy! You've caused enough trouble tonight."

The figure on the bed stirred.

Mossy crept closer and peeped up over the edge of the bed, appalled to see her madcap kitten chasing its gray-ringed tail in whirling circles. "Noël!"

He scampered up the bed and stood, right by the lady's face, gazing at one exposed earlobe with an arrested expression in his glittering green eyes.

"Oh, no," Mossy moaned, knowing, after only a week, of her pet's penchant for sinking his pin-sharp teeth into soft human flesh.

She had come to apologize to the beautiful lady, but it wouldn't make a very good start if he assaulted her again. Sarah, her nurse, who was also looking after the lady, had told her all about it in her stern, you-are-in-such-trouble tone of voice. And so, with Sarah sound asleep in the adjoining room, Mossy had crept out to apologize and Noël—naughty kitten—had followed.

She could hardly see in the dimness of the room, but it seemed to her that the kitten had much better night vision and took advantage of it sometimes to tackle wriggling toes or fingers at the most surprising times. Noël gathered himself to leap and Mossy yelped, throwing herself up on the bed and grasping at her pet, though he squirmed and slipped out of her fingers.

"Augh!" the lady yelled as Mossy tumbled over her and finally got hold of the kitten. The lady sat bolt upright, her dark hair hanging loose around her shoulders like a silk scarf.

"I'm sorry!" Mossy cried, scrambling to the other side of her.

"Wha'? What? Who . . . ?"

"I-I-I am Mossy and this is my kitten, Noël, and we came to apologize, but then he was going to bite you again and I couldn't let him, so I jumped on the bed, and . . ."

Ann scrubbed the sleep from her eyes and gazed at the elfin child, gowned in a white nightrail, who crouched on her bed with the gray and white kitten securely held in both hands. Her first response was anger and she frowned, ready to severely reprimand this hoydenish child who disrupted her sleep.

But then, in the dim light that filtered into the room, she saw a tear glimmer in large hazel eyes. No matter how angry she was, she would not make a child cry.

"Noël and I have met already," she said dryly, sitting up properly in her bed. It seemed she was not destined for much peaceful sleep that night.

"I'm sorry," sobbed the little creature, clutching her cat to her. He protested and leaped from her arms, found a spot on the counterpane, and promptly curled up and went to sleep.

A sudden gust of wind rattled the window and the child jumped.

"You must be frozen," Ann said, lifting the covers. "Come under, for a moment."

A tremulous smile hovered on the child's lips. "You . . . you mean I can?"

"Why ever not?"

"Sarah says I'm too old to sleep with someone."

"Sarah . . . the girl who acted as my lady's maid?"

"Yes," Mossy nodded, scrambling under the covers and pulling them up to her pointed little chin. "She's my nurse."

"Ah. Is that how you know what your kitten did to my toe?"

She nodded, twisting her head to look up at Ann. "Are you married?"

"I . . . I am a widow. Like your father, I lost my spouse."

"Do you have any children?"

"You are rather impertinent, did you know that? It is not polite to pry. But no, I have no children."

"Do you want children?"

"Young lady! You do *not* ask questions like that! Ever!"

"Oh." Her voice was small and chastened.

Ann felt she had been overly harsh. It was just so strange to be questioned like this, in her bed, by a strange child. It was all of a piece, she supposed, with this bizarre night.

No, she had never had children. At first that had been a sadness to her, but over the years she had learned to be grateful. There was no room in her serene city life for a child. She had her town house, her embroidery, the theater, her pianoforte. It was enough. All she sought was tranquillity, which was why the gossip and speculation whirling around her after the imbroglio with that young pup, Madison, was anathema to her and why she had finally succumbed to Verity's annual invitation to come to Bath for Christmas.

But how could one say to a child that children only complicated one's life? Children were emotional ties that would never go away and that made constant demands on one, demands that could not be ignored. If friends became too clinging or importunate, one could put a little distance between oneself and them, and they soon found others to plague, but children! That was a lifelong obligation of love and care and involvement that neither time nor distance could weaken.

It was much, much too taxing.

No, she was glad she had never had children.

But still . . . she gazed down at the tiny creature beside her, who squinted into the darkness, trying, unsuccessfully as it turned out, to stifle a yawn. Another gust of wind rattled the windowpane, and a tap-tap-tap of rain started. Mossy's eyes were heavy with sleep.

Ann slipped from the bed. If it weren't for the fact that if she were missing from her bed it would raise a panic, Ann would have let Mossy stay the night. But the child must return to the nursery.

"Mossy, you must go back to your own bed, dear, or your nurse will be worried."

"All right." The child yawned and stretched and slipped from the bed, scooping up her sleeping kitten and padding to the door after Ann.

"I will go up with you and tuck you in," Ann found herself saying. Surely that was not necessary, but she found that even so, it was something she wanted to do.

The nursery on the third floor was a blue and white haven with slanted walls and lovely patterned draperies. Had Lady Ruston done this for her child? Most mothers that Ann knew could barely find their way up to the nursery, much less worry about what it looked like. She remembered the nursery from her youth as a grim place with ugly draperies and lumpy furniture discarded years before from the main living areas. Somebody had loved and wanted this child very much to make her room so pretty.

Mossy climbed into her low bed, child scaled and with a blue and white counterpane. Ann pulled the covers up over the little girl, who still clutched her kitten, and then sat on the edge of the bed. Her toes were freezing on the cold floor, but she tried to disregard that as she gazed down at the pale, piquant face.

"I really am sorry Noël bit you. Does it hurt?" Mossy asked.

"Only a little." Ann gazed down at the sleepy child. Time to leave, but still she lingered. "Are you looking forward to Christmas?"

"I guess." Mossy sounded doubtful.

"What an answer! Are you not looking forward to roast goose and playing snapdragon, and presents from Father Christmas?" Ann reached out and smoothed the blond curls away from the tiny child's forehead. How frail she seemed under the heavy covers, and how sad! Why was she so sad? Ann twined a satiny blond curl around her finger.

"I guess."

Closing her eyes, the child moved her face until it was resting against Ann's lingering hand. Ann felt an unaccustomed warmth spiral through her heart.

"What do you want for Christmas?" she found herself asking, though she knew she should leave the child to sleep. She stroked the soft cheek with her thumb.

Mossy opened her eyes and gazed up into Ann's in the dimness. "I already made a Christmas wish," she answered obliquely. "I hope it comes true."

"What did you wish?"

"I can't tell, or it won't happen." Mossy stared up at her.

Ann stood. It was time to go back to bed and leave this child to sleep. The little girl was gazing at her intently, and the sadness was gone from her eyes.

"Are you a friend of Papa's? Is that why you're visiting?"

"No," Ann said. "No, I am on my way to Bath to visit an old school friend over Christmas. My carriage was just a little way past your house when something scared the horses, and we were tossed into the ditch. We'll be leaving in the morning."

Mossy's face pinched. "Do you have to go? Can't you stay . . ."

"No, my dear," Ann said. She leaned over and patted Mossy's head awkwardly.

"Can you kiss me good night?"

Ann stopped in the act of straightening. "Well, I . . ." What could she say? She leaned over and laid a cool kiss on the child's high forehead, inhaling deeply the sweet scent of childhood. For one brief moment she wondered how mothers—or fathers, for that matter—could send their children off to be put to bed by their nurse every night without a little ritual like this. It was so precious, so utterly heartwarming.

"Good night, Mossy," she whispered. "Sleep well, little one."

She slipped from the room.

Mossy opened her eyes and gazed at the door that was shutting quietly behind the beautiful lady. "Noël," she whispered to the sleeping kitten. "She's a nice lady. I hope she stays for Christmas."

With a smile on her face, she closed her eyes and was soon sleeping as deeply as her pet.

* * *

The morning was dull and rainy, but Ruston whistled cheerfully as he strode down the hallway from his room, dressed in sturdy riding boots and a heavy coat he used only for his infrequent inspections of his land. He turned the corner of the hallway and stopped dead, his tuneless whistle dying on his lips.

The door to the green bedroom was ajar and he could see in to the bed. Lady Ann Beecham-Brooke, the little spitfire who had brought a definite spice to his dull country holiday, was sitting on the bed, her slim figure clad in her white nightrail still, but with a dressing gown over it now. She held out one shapely foot and frowned down at it, twisting it this way and that.

She put the foot up on her knee and inspected it closer, causing her nightgown and dressing gown to fall away, revealing a lovely length of white, shapely limb. Ruston licked his dry lips, and then grinned. He was never one to miss an opportunity like this.

He pushed open the door and strolled in.

"Do you have the witch hazel, Sarah?" Lady Ann said, not looking up.

Ruston moved toward the bed, knelt in front of her and had her foot in his hand before she was even aware who he was.

"Oh!" she exclaimed. "I-I-I thought you were Sarah; she is b-bringing me . . ."

"I heard you, my lady. Is that ferocious kitten's bite hurting?" He looked down at her delectable foot and saw the evidence with his own eyes. Two red puncture wounds were visible on her big toe.

She pulled at her foot. "Please unhand me, sir." Her clear voice was almost panicked.

He retained his hold. He looked up and was once again entranced by her violet eyes. She really was the most enchanting creature, if only she wasn't so provokingly icy! Watching her face, he began, with deliberate motions, to rub her foot. Instead of relaxing, he could feel her stiffen.

Sarah came into the room, but stood gawking when she saw the master knelt in front of Lady Ann with her foot in his hands.

"Bring it here," Ruston said to Sarah, indicating the bowl of witch hazel alcohol and soft strips of cloth in her hands.

She did as he commanded, setting it down by him on the floor.

"You can go to Mossy now, Sarah," he said casually.

She curtsied and exited quickly, leaving the door open.

"What do you think you are doing?" Lady Ann fumed, trying again to pull her foot away.

"I am taking the very best care of an accidental visitor. I would not have it bandied about that I did not do my best as a host to take care of you, my lady. In fact, I believe I will take great pleasure in taking care of you."

He spoke casually, but when he glanced up at her lovely face, flushed in embarrassment, he did not doubt that she had caught his double meanings. And it was true. He would take the greatest pleasure in taking care of her, if she would let him. Just touching her satin skin was proving to be enough to send his pulse hammering in his temples. This lovely widow would make a delectable mistress, if she were so inclined.

Her reputation spoke against that, of course.

Lady Ice. Her skin certainly felt warm under his hands. He soaked a cloth in the witch hazel and patted at the bite marks. They were fiery red, and must be sore, he thought. He glanced up to find Lady Ann staring at him with wide eyes. Her foot trembled.

Perhaps she had been so cold in the past because she was being approached by boys, not men. She was not a child just out of the schoolroom; maybe she would prove susceptible to his own brand of charm, which had been tested successfully on a decent number of women. He bent to his work again, soaking a strip of soft cloth in the witch hazel, binding the toe and wrapping it in a strip of dry cloth.

Some devil prompted him, and when he was done he raised her limb, letting one hand slide up the inviting curve of her calf, and laid a warm kiss on the palm of her foot, then on the toe.

She jerked her foot away.

"Have you gone mad?" she said, pulling her gown down over her bare leg.

He gathered up the bowl and extra cloths and put them on the vanity table near the door. "Not at all. That is how I treat my little girl when she has a hurt. I kiss it better."

"When you are here," she said with a sniff.

His expression darkened. "What do you mean by that?"

"I have heard that you spend most of your time away from home on trips abroad. I cannot imagine you take Mossy with you, ergo, you must not see her all that much." This was said with a haughty lift to her chin, as she slipped off the bed. "We will be leaving this morning, my lord. Thank you for your gracious . . . hospitality."

The sarcasm in her voice was evident. He quirked a smile. "I rather doubt that you will be going anywhere, my lady," he returned, his voice heavy with exaggerated courtesy.

"What do you mean?"

"Have you not heard the rain all night? And how it rains still?"

"A little rain will not stop me!" she declared.

"A *little* rain would not, but it has been raining for almost ten hours, steady. Even if your carriage is repaired, which I am not convinced—it was well after midnight before my men could get it into the stable due to a cracked axle—the roads could be washed out, or even the bridge. I am on my way out now to check conditions, and I shall give you a report at luncheon, if you would be good enough to join me for that meal?"

Ann had raced to the window, and what she saw there did not please her eye. The countryside looked drowned. At the bottom of the rolling lawn a pond had formed that had not been there the day before, she would wager.

Ungraciously she said, "All right. I guess I have no choice." Even as she said it she was shocked at her discourtesy to her host, who, even if he had been unforgivably cheeky, was still her host.

He crossed his arms over his chest and she was reminded of how . . . *big* he was. He dominated the feminine room.

"I shall hold you to that, my lady." He bowed. "Until luncheon." He looked down at her feet and smiled. "You may wish to come to the table unshod, my lady, to give your toe a chance to heal. I assure you, I will not stand on ceremony. I might even be convinced to . . . re-dress your wound." He grinned and exited.

Ann picked up a cushion from the chair by the window and threw it at the door as he closed it behind himself. "Insufferable, conceited popinjay!" she cried, not caring if he heard her or not. He needed a lesson. Badly. He needed to learn that not every woman was susceptible to a good-looking, well-bred, magnetic man. And she was just the woman to deliver that salutary instruction.

Four

It was still raining. Ann paced away from the window in the rose morning parlor and sighed deeply. A flustered maid hurried into the room, examined every corner, looked under the furniture and exited, curtsying deeply before she did so.

What was going on?

Ah, well. Remembering her mother's lecture on idle hands, and being rather desperate for something to do, Ann went up to her room and found her embroidery bag. It felt unaccustomedly heavy, but she thought little of that until she felt it jerk and pull in her hand.

She dropped it with a startled exclamation, and heard a squawk. The bag started moving, the soft cloth sides bulging and rippling while an "errrr" sound vibrated from it.

Ann was just ready to call a footman when her experience of the previous night came back to her. Noël! She glanced around the room, then went down on her knees on the carpet and gingerly opened one end of the bag. A screech, and a gray and white streak erupted from the bag and whizzed around the room, under the bed, over the vanity table bench, past the door and into the open wardrobe.

A tremor shook Ann, and before she knew it she was laughing, holding her stomach with both hands and submitting to gales of laughter that shook her whole body. The kitten shot from the wardrobe and stood before her, gazing up at her with head cocked to one side and quizzical green eyes that sent Ann into fresh gusts of hilarity.

"What on earth . . . ?"

She whirled around on her knees to find herself being observed by Ruston, dirty and tired-looking, bootless and coatless, and with his auburn curls plastered down on his forehead. He was staring at her with much the same quizzical expression as the kitten, and a fresh bout of giggles claimed her.

"Y-y-you look like a drowned rat!" she laughed, scooping up the kitten and standing. She had not felt so light and carefree since she was a girl, and it thawed all the frost from her demeanor.

He grinned, and passed one big, ungloved hand over his wet hair. "I feel like one! I was up to my knees in mud, helping a daft traveler get his curricle out of the ditch. Seems to be a favored pastime in the last twenty-four hours."

Noël settled into her arms and started purring. "Is it that bad out there?" she asked with concern, glancing over at the rain-slicked window.

"Awful! There is an irrigation cut just west of here that has flooded and washed out the road. I'm sorry. It looks like you're going to be here at least another night."

It was the worst possible news, and yet it was not so crushing as it would have been just a short while ago. Her heart felt lighter, as if she had laughed away some weighty worries. She gazed into the viscount's warm brown eyes. "I . . . it's all right. It will give Ellen another night to recover. Her arm injury is merely a strain, but she is still in bed and I was concerned about moving her."

"Well, that's settled then. Mossy will be delighted. I had breakfast with her this morning and all she could do was talk about you and her midnight visit to your room."

Ann felt the flush rise to her cheeks. She stroked the kitten's soft fur and glanced down at it, suddenly shy.

"Right, then," said Ruston after an awkward moment. "I shall take myself off and see if my poor valet can make me respectable again."

And he was gone. She heard voices in the hall, and a moment later Mossy danced into her room.

"There he is," she squealed. "The maids have all been looking for him," she explained, reaching up and taking the kitten from Ann.

Ann gave the soft head one last pat. "He had crawled into my embroidery bag," she said, retrieving the brocade bag from the floor and putting back the folded piece of work that had spilled out of it.

Mossy stared at the bag and then looked up at Ann with hopeful eyes. "You do 'broidery?" she whispered, her hazel eyes huge and round.

"I am an indifferent embroiderer, but I still do it."

"May I see?"

Ann motioned to the chairs near the window. "Come and sit."

Mossy put her now sleepy kitten down on the bed, and knelt on the seat of the chair across from hers. Ann pulled out the piece she was working on, a tropical forest alive with macaws and parrots, and a leopard that prowled on the jungle floor, its green eyes picked out in glittering spangles. No doubt an ornithologist or explorer would resent the wild profusion of animals that likely didn't even belong on the same continent, but she loved the color of her invention. It was almost done. She glanced up and was surprised by the expression of utter awe on the little girl's face.

Mossy reached out and reverently touched the piece with one tiny hand. "It's bee-yooo-tiful," she said, drawing out the second syllable on a sigh.

Touched, Ann was speechless.

"Would you . . . ?" Mossy hesitated.

"Would I what?"

"I . . . I'm making a present for Papa, but it isn't . . . I don't know what to do." Her thin voice quavered. "I want him to like it so bad! Sarah has been trying to teach me 'broidery, but she's only good at straight sewing."

Impulsively, Ann said, "You bring it here and we'll see what can be done."

Mossy leaped from her chair and raced away, returning in minutes. She stood before Ann, her hands behind her back. "It . . . it's not very good," she said.

"Let me be the judge of that!"

They spread the stitched sampler out on the table and Ann's

first instinct was to chuckle, but she stifled that. The piece was haphazard at best, and the alphabet scrawled on an angle over the cloth. It was wrinkled and grubby, with a sticky smear that looked suspiciously like a jam handprint.

Ann gazed steadily at it, lost for a moment in her own past. She remembered so clearly the birthday party the family had held for her father when she was about Mossy's age. Father had been a tall, stately man. Ann saw little of him, and what she did see frightened her; but she desperately wanted his approval. She was plain, not like Fanny, her oldest sister, who was blonde and pretty. And she wasn't clever like Judith, who was only a year and a half older than her, but already could speak French. And she wasn't a boy, like Bert.

To honor their father on his birthday, Judith was reciting a French poem, Fanny was going to play a piece on the piano, and Bert was going to recite an epic story by heart. There was nothing that little Annie could do. And so she had painstakingly embroidered her father a set of pen wipes, emblazoned with her approximation of the family crest.

She had presented it to him just before the special birthday luncheon. Heart pounding with nervousness, she had watched while he unwrapped her crudely tied package. He had looked at the pen wipes for a moment, then asked what they were.

She told him, her voice quavering. He had pointed to the crest and asked her what in blazes that was supposed to be. In the silence of the parlor, she had explained. Coal black eyebrows lifted, he had examined them, and then tossed them onto the table.

"Nonsense," he had boomed. "Doesn't look anything like the family crest."

He had turned then and led the way in to luncheon, which Ann was judged too young to join. Later a maid threw the wipes away, mistaking them for trash. She had been crushed.

She glanced over at the little girl opposite her, whose hazel eyes held all the suspense and fear she remembered from her own childhood. Ann glanced down at the sampler again.

"It's not very good, is it?" the child asked in a small voice.

"Of course it is!" Ann said stoutly. She beckoned for Mossy

to join her and the little girl climbed on her lap. "Look," Ann said, pointing to the last line. "You can see that you're getting better and better. This part," she said, and placed her finger on the line that said 'Wrought by Mignon Montrose, December 1816—for Papa.' Look at the lovely flourishes you've put on the M's! Very good."

"Is it good enough for Papa? I want to give him something special for Christmas."

"This *is* special, sweetheart," Ann said, conviction ringing in her words. "If I had a little girl and she gave me something like this, I would treasure it my whole life."

And to her own surprise, Ann found that not a word of that was false.

Ruston had bathed and changed in a bemused state, thinking of the subtle changes in Lady Ann's demeanor when he surprised her with the kitten. Laughter had turned the straight slash of her mouth into a soft bow, and her firm chin had not been raised in defiant anger. Lovely in any circumstances, she was enchanting when she smiled.

He had invited her to join him for lunch, and wondered if she would remember. He was about to walk past her room when he heard laughter. He peeked in, curiosity overcoming his scruples, to find Mossy sitting on Ann's lap, the woman's arms snugly around his child. Mossy was gazing up at her with such a smile of delight on her face it tightened a band of pain around Ruston's heart. He backed away from the door.

It was like a scene of mother and daughter, a scene he had never witnessed, since Celia had died just hours after giving birth to Mossy. Alone he had placed his babe in the cradle in the nursery his wife had decorated so lavishly. Alone he had drunk himself into a stupor that same night, crushed by the unexpected pain of losing Celia.

She had been more friend than wife. He had been just twenty-three when his father had died, leaving him a young and unprepared viscount. Overwhelmed by the burden of his new role, he had decided that he must marry and ensure the succession.

He turned to his childhood friend. Celia had been affianced at seventeen to a devil-may-care younger son of an earl, but the young man had died when he overturned in a curricle race. Celia went into a decline, lost her blooming looks, and years later at twenty-four, just a little older than Ruston, had seemed destined for the shelf.

He proposed, she accepted gratefully, and they had married, even though his year of mourning was not even half over. They had set up housekeeping at Russetshire Manor. Theirs was a marriage of comfort, not blazing passion, and he had tried to keep from being too demanding of her in the marriage bed, as she clearly did not enjoy that aspect of marriage. It had taken her three years to conceive, but she had been glowingly happy about the coming child.

They had hoped for a male, for the succession, but in the seventh month Celia had become ill, the birth had been unexpectedly early and hard on her, and she had died within hours. Ruston's grief had surprised even himself, but then he had gotten over it, accepted his child, and moved on, finding solace in travel.

He peeked back into the room. Mossy was leaning back against Ann as she pointed to something they had spread out in front of them on the table. Gazing up at her, Mossy had an expression of adoration on her face.

Ruston felt a spurt of unaccustomed anger. What did Lady Ann Beecham-Brooke think she was doing? Mossy would be crushed when she rushed off the minute the road was better. He had to break up this cozy little scene. He strode into the room.

"Mossy, Nurse will be looking for you. You should have had your luncheon an hour ago."

Ann glanced over at him, her brow furrowed.

Mossy slid off Lady Ann's lap and gazed at her father. "Can't I have lunch with you and Lady Ann?"

"No!" He realized how harsh that sounded. His daughter's tiny face was pinched and sad. "No, you're going to have dinner with me, remember?" He had gentled his voice. "Go to Sarah and wash your face and hands for lunch. And don't forget Noël."

Obediently she picked up her sleeping kitten from the bed and left the room. He watched her go and then turned back to

Lady Ann. She was back to her poker-stiff posture again, her expression grim. Well that was fine. Better she should show her true colors than deceive everybody by pretending she was no Lady Ice. The softer side she pretended to was beguiling in the extreme, and dangerous for that reason.

"Did you have to yell at the child?" she demanded.

He strode over to the table, and she hastily hid something under a piece of embroidery. "How did my methods of raising Mossy become your concern, my lady?" Guilt tugged at him. He *had* been unduly harsh, but the picture they made, the idyllic mother and daughter tableau, had been too much. He didn't need to explain that to a woman who was anxious to be out of his house, though.

"It is none of my business, as you point out," she said icily. She stood and busied herself with putting away her embroidery. "You could have the decency of being courteous, though."

"So speaks the woman who owes me appreciation for my generosity, my *courtesy,* in offering her a place to stay in the worst rainstorm this part of England has seen in twenty years. I haven't seen you weary yourself with any notion of gratitude toward me."

Two spots of high color flagged her cheeks. She glared at him, her movements arrested by her obvious anger. "You . . . you are utterly unchivalrous, sir! That was rude and . . . and . . ."

He stalked toward her. Unfortunately it seemed that the angry spitfire enchanted him as much as the smiling, laughing beauty. "Unchivalrous? Perhaps. I'm sure Lady Ice must think so."

She slapped him, leaving a stinging imprint on his cheek.

"A little dramatic, don't you think?" he said. "I would save such desperate reactions for despicable acts that truly deserve them, like this."

He stepped forward and grasped her in his arms, lowered his face and kissed her. He had intended it to be a rebuke, punishment for her willful spite, but in a single second he felt his anger slip away and the velvet softness of her lips seduced him wholly. She had gone still and he lingered, feeling the sweet curve of her mouth an enchanting place to tarry.

He moved away, his hands still on her shoulders, shaken by the swiftness with which anger can turn to something warmer and sweeter. "You enchant me, my l . . ."

He trailed off as he gazed at her. She was absolutely rigid, her eyes starting out from their sockets.

"Get your hands off of me," she muttered through gritted teeth.

He dropped his hands. "My deepest apologies, my lady, but I was overcome . . ."

She shook herself, and took in a deep trembling breath. An expression of deepest distaste marred her lovely face, and she said, "Overcome! Men are not overcome; they like to keep control of a situation, and if they cannot do that with brutality, they will do it with sexual conquest. Please close the door on your way out."

Her voice was frigid and her lip curled in disgust as though she had smelled something bad. Again he was shaken, but this time by the loathing on her face as she viewed him. "I will assume that Cook should send something up for your luncheon, my lady." He bowed and left the room quickly.

Ann, alone, started to tremble. Memories had flooded her of the way Reggie always ended an argument with her. It had taken *that* to trigger his lust, and it made her afraid. Were all men like that? Or was it just the way she affected them? She sat down on the bed. She had to leave, and leave soon. What had scared her most was that after the jolt of the first second, the feel of Ruston's lips on hers had been pleasant . . . no, more than pleasant. She had liked it, and that shocked her more deeply than anything else.

She had to leave.

Five

"Sorry I be, milady, but I can no see any way around it. The road is washed out, and we can no go for'ard." Jacob Lesley stood in the rose parlor, twisting his cap around in his hands.

Ann paced, her wan face showing clearly her agitation. "Then can we go back to London?"

Jacob considered that. "Well, the trouble, ma'am, is that we ha' no report o' the road back to London. But if the road ahead be washed out, mayhap the road back is bad, too. Why can we no sit tight an' enjoy his lordship's generosity?" He squinted at her in the dull light from the fire.

Ignoring his suggestion, she said, "Find out what the road back to London is like. I would rather go back and face that pack of society hounds than stay here another night."

"Aye, milady." Jacob bowed and started out of the room.

"Jacob!"

He stopped.

"What . . . how are they treating you? I will not have my servants abused or shuffled aside." She stood straight and tall, her nose in the air.

Allowing himself a smile, Jacob said, "A decent household this is, milady. You've no need for concern. My stable loft room is a sight more comfortable than the one in London, beg parding, milady, and the cook here is a rare treat! A right plump beauty wi' a hand as light as a feather wi' bread! And all belowstairs worship yon gentleman, Viscount Ruston. Say he is the best of masters." With that he bowed and edged out of the room.

When her driver was gone, Ann grimaced. She had heard the same song of gratitude from Ellen, who had been cared for like a part of the extended family of Manor servants, she said. Well, she was not one to seek faults where there apparently were none, and so she must admit that Ruston was accounted a good master by one and all.

Perhaps he was a better master than father.

Feeling peevish and out of sorts, Ann climbed the stairs. All this emotional turmoil was precisely why she had left London. She was used to going her own serene, unruffled way in life, but after the Madison fiasco she had felt the need to play least-in-sight for a while. Verity's annual invitation, which she normally turned down in favor of a staid, lonely Christmas in London, had come as a godsend.

She entered her lovely green bower room with unseeing eyes. Most of London was busy this time of year, going off to family and friends, planning parties and balls and extended country visits, but Lady Ann invariably stayed in London. Her sister had invited her this year as she always did, but the invitation held no allure for Ann. Fanny was on her perpetual sickbed in Wales, peevishly forecasting her own death or that of one of her three children. Her letters were infrequent and complaining, envying Ann her freedom from children and husband.

Judith, the sister closest to her in age, lived alone in London. One would think they would spend Christmas together but the older sister had, in her discriminating snobbery, gathered about her a group of "artistic" types who dressed in a great deal of black and put their noses up at anyone who had not read the Iliad in the original Greek, or who did not write pretentious little poems, obscurely insulting those who did not understand them. Ann and Judith occasionally crossed paths in London and were polite to each other, but not even Christmas could bring them together for dinner.

And Bert! Ann shuddered as she sat down on the bed and smoothed the lovely counterpane. Bert had grown into the very image of their father, only worse. He invited her to their ancestral home every year, and had always done so since the death, by cholera, of their parents within months of each other, nine years ago now. She had never accepted and never would.

What a sad family tale. Agitated for some unfathomable reason, Ann stood and paced over to the table by the window. Was Mossy destined to spend her childhood desperately trying to please her father, only to be sold to some aging roué with a need for a family when she turned seventeen? She shuddered. Taking a seat at the table, she leaned her cheek on her hand and stared at the rain-covered window, watching the droplets gather and run in rivulets down the glass.

Ann had been full of hope when she married Sir Reginald Boccham-Brooke. Perhaps he was not the stuff of her childhood fantasies, a strong, handsome gentleman come to rescue her from her hateful life in the Pelham family, but he evidently wanted her. Ann had been given to understand that he had seen her in church one Sunday and decided there and then to take her to wife.

It seemed so romantic! Love at first sight, and a man desperate to wed her!

When she met him, her agreement to the marriage already secured—though as she knew, her agreement was just a formality to her father—she had been disappointed. Reginald was tall, thin and grim, and twice her age or more. But she had beaten down her unsuitable chagrin, preferring to go into marriage with an optimistic outlook.

What a fool she had been!

Her wedding day was a dream. For the first time in her life she felt pretty. She had never been allowed to wear her hair up, and the heavy dark locks had always seemed to overshadow her narrow face, but that day, with her black hair up in glossy ringlets and dressed in lavender silk with violets and diamonds in her hair, she had been beautiful. Even Bates, her mother's dresser, had said so, and she was not given to praise.

After the wedding breakfast, she and her new husband had started off immediately for Reginald's family estate, a three-day journey. Indiscreet whispering among the maids had led her to a basic understanding of what would be expected of her on her wedding night, and though scared, she was prepared to be brave. The first night, in her small but comfortable room at an inn, she had awaited her husband in frightened anticipation, her stomach doing a nervous little dance. Finally, around two in the morning she fell asleep.

When she timidly brought it up at breakfast the next morning, her new husband had grunted that he hated travel; it made him sick. She felt for him, filling in all the words of apology in her heart that he never uttered. She knew not to expect him that night.

So their first night at the Beeches, his country home, would be their first as man and wife. It was fitting, she thought. She waited again. Reginald would know how scared she was, she assured herself. He would take her in his arms and tell her he would give her all the time she needed to get used to accommodating a man's desires.

He had entered her room at about midnight and crossed to the bed, wearing just a nightshirt. He smelled heavily of brandy. Staring down at her briefly, he had blown out the candle and climbed into bed, and in a moment he was on top of her, spreading her legs with his bony knees. He was already aroused. She had felt a tearing pain as he entered her, stretching her young, fresh body for the first time with no preparation, and then came a flood of warmth, and that was it. No words were said, no tenderness expressed.

He had patted her on the head, after, and left the room.

That became the routine of their couplings for the first year. Ann learned after a month or so that Reginald had a mistress in London, a woman who was married to another man, but who lived in a house Reginald provided. She had borne him two boys, but as they were not legitimate he still needed an heir, which was why he had married Ann. Her dreams crumbled and the pain became self-loathing for the silly widgeon she had been, to expect love in marriage when she had never seen any evidence of it in her parents' marriage.

Occasionally she railed at Reginald, but she found that the fighting aroused him, the only time he took her to bed outside of the dutiful nightly couplings. She hated that more than anything, to know that she had aroused him with her anger, and so she schooled herself to an icy composure at all times. After about a year, with no sign of a child on the way, Reginald had sneeringly referred to her as a barren ice block. He never came to her again.

A tear trickled down her cheek, and Ann impatiently wiped it away, drying her hand on the tablecloth. She took a deep, if shaky, breath and stood. She had made a new life for herself, one that was serene and tranquil. Importuned occasionally, since Reggie died, for her hand in marriage, she always turned the men down, telling them that nothing could ever tempt her to give up her precious independence.

She would return to London now. She could ride through this latest annoyance if she refused to surrender ground. It was what she should have done from the first, but she had let the gossips drive her from her city.

She supposed it was the shock, after so many years, of finding that her social circle could take so much delight in pillorying her. Thomas Madison had seemed an unexceptional young man, and at first had shown no signs of infatuation. But eventually he haunted her, following her to every gathering, and glowering angrily at any man with whom she danced or to whom she spoke.

She had had to speak sharply to him on a couple of occasions. And then he had trespassed unforgivably on her person, and she had had to publicly humiliate him.

Society had condemned her as frigid for that. If only they knew how restrained she had been!

But there was worse to come. Just days before she had left London it had been whispered in her ear that she was on all the betting books in all the clubs, or all the less reputable ones, anyway. It was called the "Madison" bet. Who could bed her first? Who could seduce Lady Ice and warm her frigid blood, to gain revenge for poor Madison?

Humiliated, she had grasped at Verity's invitation and hurried from London, hoping the chatter would all have died by the time she got back. But evidently even a traveler like Ruston had heard the gossip. Ann balled her fists and struck the table. Maybe that was the explanation for the kiss. Men relished a challenge! Well, she would be no man's game, and so he would discover.

* * *

Ruston stared at his figure in the cheval mirror and adjusted his neckcloth a fraction of an inch. "Okay Cobb, you may go. I am as presentable as I am going to get."

His man left the room and Ruston frowned at his reflection once more and headed for the door. He wondered if Lady Ann would come down to dinner. He had issued an invitation through Sarah, her temporary lady's maid, but he did not know if she would have gotten over her resentment enough to descend.

He had been an ass, he decided, and deserved her anger. What was wrong with him? Why did Lady Ann inspire such a swirling confusion of emotions in him? And what on earth had possessed him to be so despicable as to kiss a woman who clearly did not want him to?

He remembered her laughing eyes and open expression when he had caught her playing with the kitten. She had looked at him with lighthearted delight, and it had . . . yes, his feelings had frightened him. He had wanted to freeze that moment in time, to pull her to him and see her eyes close and lips part in sweet submission. Was that why he was so harsh when he came back down the hall and found her cuddling his little girl? Was that why he had kissed her, not with gentleness, but with anger? Was the anger at himself, for allowing his heart to wish?

He jammed a ruby stickpin into his neckcloth and stabbed his finger. Cursing, he sucked the blood from his finger and strode from the room. It was enormously uncomfortable to feel himself in the wrong, but he had been deliberately cruel to her, and he was not deliberately cruel to anyone, ever! He had killed the soft, gentle light in her eyes on purpose, and he felt utterly reprehensible. Could he make it up to her? Or would she have retreated for good into her Lady Ice persona?

And was that maybe the best thing that could happen for both of them?

Nervously, Ann patted down the rose silk dress. It was one of her favorites, the one she had brought to wear on Christmas Day at Verity's. Its snug bodice was encrusted with a diamond pattern of pearls, as were the tiny puff sleeves, and the skirt was deep rose with an overskirt that was gathered with tiny silk roses. Long rose satin gloves finished the ensemble. Her hair was done up simply in a Psyche knot with curls dripping from it, since Sarah was not experienced with hair as her own Ellen was. A tortoise-shell comb with pearls held her heavy hair in place.

She needed every bit of her self-confidence to face Ruston again at dinner after that shattering kiss. Her anger had burned off quickly, like morning fog, leaving her feeling curiously vulnerable and longing for the armor of her fury. All she had left was her cloak of icy composure, and that would have to carry her through. When the invitation to dine had come her first thought had been to reject it, but her pride would not allow Ruston to think he had bested her. She would prevail, and win back her serenity.

She descended. The viscount was speaking to the butler, but at the sound of her footsteps, as quiet as they were in her satin slippers, he turned with a calm expression and looked up at her. Then his eyes widened. His voice was husky when he spoke. "My lady, you look absolutely lovely. Of course I cannot imagine you looking otherwise."

Despite herself, Ann flushed. Ruston, himself, was breathtaking. Tall and sturdy, he wore his evening clothes of unrelieved black handsomely. His white evening gloves stretched over broad hands and he held one out to her as she descended the last step. He bowed and placed a kiss a polite inch above her hand, in the air. His demeanor was faultless.

"I am delighted you decided to honor us with your presence at dinner. Mossy will be especially pleased," he said.

"I thank you for asking me."

"And me!"

The small voice from above made them both look up. With the instincts of a debutante, Mossy paused at the top of the stairs to display her lovely white dress tied with a sash of moss green. Her blonde hair was tied back with a matching ribbon, and she carried Noël—also wearing a matching ribbon—in her white-gloved hands.

"Well, lucky me!" Ruston said, a smile of pride on his square face. "I am to dine with the two prettiest girls in England." He held out his hand and Mossy came down the steps to take it. With just a moment's hesitation he held out his other arm for Ann.

She gazed up into eyes the color of darkest amber, and took his arm. They went in to dinner.

From the formality of their entrance, dinner soon disintegrated into chaos. Mossy insisted on keeping Noël with her, and the kitten was irrepressible. From a solemn little gray and white ball of fluff, he could turn into a whirlwind of manic energy in the time it took to blink.

Ann tried desperately to maintain the air of imperturbable calm she intended to employ to convince Ruston he had not upset her equilibrium with his words or kiss, but with Mossy and the kitten, calm was out of the question.

Mossy was enchanting. Ann was completely captivated by the silliness that Ruston not only permitted, but encouraged at his dinner table. From turbot on toast, to cream on chicken, the child had a long list of silly requests.

"Cream on chicken?" he said, making a face and pretending to gag.

Mossy giggled, but Ann put on her best haughty air and said, "My dear sir, do you not know that Prinny himself will eat it no other way? Are you so out of style that you do not know this?"

Her hazel eyes sparkling with laughter, Mossy gazed at her with admiration. In the absurdity stakes, Ann had seen her silliness, and raised the bet to tomfoolery.

Ruston, not to be outdone, said loudly to the footman, "That does it! Albert, cream pitchers for everyone! If Prinny does it then we simply *must* follow. From now on turbot is always to be served on toast, and chicken must always be accompanied by cream pitchers, and . . . and . . ."

"And a kitten on every table," Mossy crowed, putting Noël on the cloth-covered surface. The kitten scampered down to where Ann sat, moved to the edge and with just a brief pause, launched himself at her.

Ruston sat back in his chair and laughed, watching Ann and Mossy playing together with the kitten. What would London say if they could see Lady Ice now? How could he reconcile the stories he had heard of her with this laughing, giggling, breathtaking young woman? Who was she really, the cold, composed creature he had first heard about and met, or this warm, lively woman who would scamper with children and pets with no thought to her consequence?

Ann, when she sat back to take a breath, was thinking much the same thing. Was she mad? If her London acquaintance saw her right now, gloves stripped off, panting and out of breath from having lunged to catch Noël before he fell from the table, they would not know her. Hoydenish behavior, her father would have called it. And he would have been right!

Her eye caught Ruston's warmly appraising gaze. She straightened. A cold wave of fear washed over her. She felt dizzy for a moment, like she was being sucked into a whirlpool, about to drown, and had no way out. This was not right. This was not her life, and she had better not get used to it.

Ruston, watching her with admiration for her sparkling violet eyes and flushed cheeks, saw the transformation. A rigidity stiffened her backbone, and the life died from her animated features. Like Lot's wife, she was turning into something statue-like before his very eyes, but this time he was at a loss to know what had brought it on. He had been looking into her eyes, and there was a brief second of something like terror, and then . . . coldness descended like a veil.

She composedly pulled her chair in and took a sip of wine. "I do hope the weather improves soon, so I may go on to Bath. I would not want Verity to worry," she said in a composed, refined voice.

Mossy, who had chased her madcap kitten into the other room, came back with the squirming pet. She stopped by Lady Ann, stared at her for a moment with a puzzled expression and drew back, sensing the change. Ruston watched with a sinking heart. He could no longer believe that Lady Ann was naturally frigid, which meant she was that way by choice. She chose to be cold and hard; even when some other part of her took over for a while, she returned to the chilliness that she assumed like a cloak. She was as she was because she wanted to be, and that was worse, somehow, than if she had been frosty by nature.

Lady Ice.

Six

Mossy was quiet through the rest of dinner and ate her dessert with an abstracted air. Ruston burned. It was just as he thought. Lady Ice would enchant his impressionable little daughter and then go cold, snuffing her fetching personality like a candle, dousing the lovely light in her eyes just as effectively.

With a sigh of relief, after her last bite of dessert, Mossy asked to be excused. "I'm sleepy," she murmured. "And so is Noël."

She kissed her father good night and then hesitated by Lady Ann's chair, gazing up at her with a searching look.

Ann looked down at her, desperately wanting to take the child in her arms, but so afraid of her own feelings. A child. She *did* want a child, after all. All the years of lying to herself were for naught. One day in this household had taught her everything she had missed and now that it was too late—for after all, one could not have a child without a husband—she understood.

And if she could choose a child in the whole world to be her own, it would be Mossy. She would have just that piquant, narrow face, just those hazel eyes, just that curling blonde hair. And just that sweet, unspoiled personality. She longed to reach out and smooth back one errant curl, but kept her hands folded in her lap.

"Good night, Lady Ann," Mossy finally said. She curtsied, picked up her now sleeping kitten gently from a saucer, where it had nodded off, and left the room.

There was silence, after, but not a comfortable, companionable silence. It was a tangible, accusatory silence. Ann lifted her chin and stared into Ruston's brown eyes.

"I should leave you to your port, my lord," Ann said, rising and shaking out her skirts.

"Yes, I suppose you should."

She turned to go.

Ruston fought with himself for a moment then said, just as she reached the door, "Lady Ann!"

Her hand was on the knob. She seemed eager to leave his presence. He should let her go. But she presented a mystery to him; what made her as she was? Why so changeable, so . . . he searched for the word. So afraid. He frowned, wondering where that thought had come from. Was it an insight into her character or an indication of his own desire to excuse her, to exculpate her from the guilt of deliberate cruelty in raising his child's hopes that she had found a friend, only to dash cold water over them.

"What is it, my lord," she said impatiently, turning the knob as she spoke.

"Will you join me for coffee?"

Her eyes widened, the thin, dark, arching brows raised on her white forehead. "I-I-I . . ."

He suppressed a smile, guessing that her ingrained sense of courtesy was warring with her desire to flee his presence. "Please?" he added.

"I w-would be delighted, my lord."

"I will join you in the gold saloon, then, momentarily."

"I am at your service, my lord." She curtsied, but the look in her eyes was that of a prisoner in the Terror, being wheeled in a tumbril to her death.

Ann paced around the gold saloon. Why could she not have used the polite fiction of a headache or sleepiness to avoid this meeting? The last thing she wanted was to spend the evening making polite conversation with Ruston. And if she did not miss her guess, he was aware of it. If he was a true gentleman he would not wish to inflict his presence . . . ah, but he had already proved that he was not a true gentleman, hadn't he? His kiss burned in her memory. She had never felt one like it, and her cheeks flamed at the thoughts that had plagued her after—indecent thoughts, carnal thoughts, thoughts that even now she would forget if she only could.

She took a chair by the fire, which burned low in the grate, and rubbed her bare arms, wishing she had not stripped off her gloves in the silly games they had been playing. In her hurry to escape Ruston's masculine, magnetic presence, she had left them in the dining room. It was chilly and dim in the big saloon, though the gold colors of the draperies and wall coverings kept it from a cold appearance.

She stared into the glowing embers. She had only known Ruston one day, but he and his daughter had intruded themselves on her mind and heart so that all she could think about was that laughing little girl or her strong, handsome father. The insidious effect of their warmth frightened her badly; she could even admit that to herself, though she wasn't sure of the source of the fear, only that she felt like she was being dragged against her will into their lives.

Would her life have turned out differently if she had married someone like Ruston rather than Reggie?

Idiotic question! Of course her life would be different; that didn't mean it would necessarily be better.

Or would it? Would Mossy be *her* daughter?

Widgeon! she scolded herself. Surely if she did not conceive a child in a year of coupling, when she knew her husband able to sire babies, then she was barren, like rocky soil that could sprout no seed. She leaned her cheek on her hand and watched a coal split with a shower of sparks, the white ash falling from it to the fireplace floor beneath the grate.

She was not meant to have children. Fanny had had a child every year until she had bluntly told her husband not to come near her bed anymore. In one of her whining letters she had complained that other men found mistresses, why couldn't her husband?

At the time Ann had commiserated with her sister. Deep in the misery of her first year of marriage at that time, and suffering Reggie's nightly demands, she would have given anything if he would have left her alone to spend more time with his London whore.

And then, finally, after a miserable year, Reggie *had* left her alone, moving permanently to London with his mistress. He had called her a barren, frigid block of ice, and after a year of fighting him she knew enough not to respond. It only excited him, and she despised him too much for that. She simply agreed with him and he left, calling her a cold bitch. And he had been right. She could not feel as other women did; other women apparently enjoyed men's attentions, but for Ann they were torture.

Ruston opened the door to the gold saloon, expecting to see Lady Ann sitting rigidly on the sofa she had taken the previous night. He glanced around in the dimness, not seeing her at all at first. Then he noticed her, a rosy glow near the hearth, with her elbow on her knee and her cheek resting in her hand. She stared into the fire and her profile presented an almost indescribable look of sadness, or loneliness, or perhaps a compound of the two.

Frowning, he almost decided to leave and send word to her through Stoddart that he had changed his mind and was off to bed. He was intrigued beyond reason by the quicksilver changes of Lady Ann's personality, but he did not want to dive beneath the surface too deeply, for fear he would never come up. He preferred his affairs to be light and frothy, and disengaged himself the moment the woman threatened, as Lydia had, to become clingy or demanding. With Lady Ann he was afraid he would lose the will to detach himself. He turned to exit.

Then he heard her sigh.

It was a ghost-sound that echoed in the still chamber. But there was so much of heartbreak in the sound, so much of unfulfilled longing, and sadness, and a deep, overwhelming desolation, that he was drawn against his own inclination into the room, toward the fire. What did he care if Lady Ice was sad? What did it matter to him if she had suffered heartbreak in her lifetime?

But still, he moved toward her like a clockwork automaton on its well-oiled track.

"This is one of the rooms Celia decorated in the years we

were married, before she died." Of all the things to say, why did he say that?

Lady Ann started and turned, but did not get up. Her expression was solemn.

"I would have guessed that, it is so lovely. Did she also do my room, and Mossy's nursery?"

Ruston nodded and strolled around, touching some of the brass pieces Celia had collected especially for the gold saloon.

"She had exquisite taste," Lady Ann said, her quiet voice soothing, her melancholy tone sweet in its sadness. "You must miss her."

"It has been many years. I . . . to be honest I think I have forgotten a lot about her. There is a painting on the landing that is quite a good likeness, but I cannot animate it with her expression, nor hear her voice anymore. I am often sad about that." His words were an expression of thoughts and feelings he had not even acknowledged before.

"It is natural, I think, to lose those things. It does not mean you are forgetting her."

Ruston came to a halt in front of her. Her face, as she gazed down at her entwined hands, was shadowed.

"Doesn't it? I think it does. I have forgotten a lot of things, important things, but still remember nonsense, like the way she would bite her nails when she was nervous, or how if she was tired she would become sulky, like a particularly irritating child. I hated that about her. And yet it is what I remember."

Lady Ann was silent. Ruston knelt and threw a piece of wood on the fire. He looked up into her face and read the guilt in her eyes, the haunted shadows in the violet depths. How was it that he could read her sometimes, when he never could understand Celia? Or was he only imagining things?

"What about you? What do you remember about your husband?"

Her eyes widened and she half shook her head. Lips compressed, she sat up straight. "I . . . I think I shall go up to bed now, if you don't mind."

He put one hand on her arm, not clutching it, but just to make her pause. "What is it? What are you remembering?"

What could she tell him? That she remembered a year of nightly torture? That she learned to loathe Reggie for his hateful coldness and insensitivity to her pain? And that guilt overwhelmed her that she was so glad when he died she had not even worn mourning. A tear welled in her eye, but she choked it back. It had been many years now since she had cried, and she had no intention of starting again.

"Oh, the usual things, I suppose. As you said, sometimes it is easier to remember the . . . the little faults and flaws."

"And what were those?" Ruston took the chair across from her as a footman entered the saloon with the coffee tray. Silently he set it down on a nearby table and glided from the room.

What could she say, Ann wondered, without revealing too much? It was an old, private pain, one that she had shared with no one, not even her sisters, nor even her mother in the brief time she was alive after Ann's marriage. "I . . . I remember how I hated that he never asked my opinion. He would sit at the end of the dinner table, even when we were alone, and talk. Talk, talk, talk! Never once would he say, 'What do you think, Ann?' 'What is your opinion, Ann?' He . . ."

Ann stopped.

Ruston poured a cup of coffee and handed it to her. "Go on."

Clutching the cup between her cold hands, feeling the steam bathe her face in warmth, she gazed into the fire, the new wood starting to catch and dance with flames.

"I did not exist as a person with feelings and thoughts to Reggie. He . . . he bought me much as one would acquire a brood mare. He wanted to get an heir on me, and for that one does not need a woman, just a vessel."

A sickening taste flooded Ruston's mouth as he considered Ann's words. There was no mistaking the pain and bitterness of her tone. Reggie Beecham-Brooke had been dead three years, and yet she still carried this burden of anger. He had always known there were bad marriages out there—had heard friends complain about their own—but if she was being honest, and he thought she was, Lady Ann's words hinted at an empty life and a bitter legacy of anger.

"I . . . I should not have said that," Ann said, perilously close to tears. "I have told no one that in all the years . . ." She broke off and sipped her coffee.

"He has been dead many years," Ruston said, his voice as gentle as he could make it.

But she stiffened.

"And so I should just forget seven years of pain . . . just forget it even happened and blithely move on?"

"I did not say that." But it had been his intention. It was the easy advice to give, the course he would advise anyone to take after a painful incident. But this was not an incident, this was her life for seven long years. She must have been just out of the schoolroom when Beecham-Brooke wed her. Ruston had met the dry stick a few times in London, and had disliked him on sight. What would it be like to be tied to him so intimately?

It had been widely known that he had a mistress in his keeping, some other man's cast-off wife, and a couple of bastards. Rumor had circulated that Beecham-Brooke was not his mistress's only entertainment. When he was gone, it was said that the lady was not too particular about who slept in her bed. Many jokes had been made about the oldest boy's bright, copper-penny hair.

Had Ann loved him at first, or had she been one of those frightened girls he had seen on the marriage mart who were coerced into marriage with an older man? From her words it would seem she was the latter. For the first time he thought about her reaction to his kiss. She had stiffened, and when he stepped away from her there was such a confusion of reactions on her face he could not pick out one.

Was she frigid, or just . . . just what?

He glanced over at her as he took his own cup of coffee and leaned back in his chair. She was lost in thought, staring into the fire, the bright flickering glow lighting her amethyst eyes with porphyrian fire. Lovely she was, but hurt somewhere deep inside, shattered in the very depths of her soul. Ruston could not believe he was having these thoughts, these musings, about a woman, when he had never even tried in the past to consider a woman's life, what it must be like to be constrained to marry whether one's inclination were to wed or not.

The lot of unmarried women was not enviable. Unmarried

women were ape-leaders, figures of ridicule and pity, and young girls did as their parents commanded. But to marry where one could not love, or even like!

Not his Mossy! Ruston swore that when the time came for her come out, he would make it clear to her that she was to choose as a husband the man who loved her best . . . unless that man was a cad, of course. He reserved a father's right to refuse permission if the man was a bounder.

"I did not realize, when I was seventeen and betrothed to Reggie, that my father had chosen for my husband a man just like himself, just as cold, just as unapproachable." Lady Ann still stared into the fire, and seemed to be talking as much to herself as to him. "Why, I wonder? Because he loved me, or because he *didn't* love me? I will never know."

"I cannot imagine a father not wanting what was best for his daughter."

"Ah, but you *love* Mossy."

"I do. She was the best thing to come out of a marriage that was essentially a friendship."

"You love Mossy, but not enough to stay here, stay with her."

Stung by her attack, he retorted, "I have not abandoned her! I always come back. She knows I love her."

"How?"

"How?" He glared at her, not believing his ears. No one had ever questioned his love for his child, and by God, they were not going to start now. "That is not in question. She knows I love her. I may travel, but when I am here, we dine together, and walk together, and in the summer I am going to teach her to ride. I have promised."

"But in the meantime you will travel again. She told me you are already planning your next trip."

"She doesn't mind. She has everything she could want here, and a staff who dote on her. Celia's parents take her for a few weeks every summer, and when I come back I have promised her a pony of her own. She is completely happy." It was said with anger, and a touch of defiance.

How could he be so blind? Ann wondered. She gazed at his face, ruddy from the heat of the fire. She could not forget

Mossy's voice as she told Ann that she hoped if she was good enough, and if he liked the sampler she had made for him as a gift, he would stay a little longer, or maybe even take her with him. The yearning in her young voice broke Ann's heart, reminding her once more of the desperate need she had felt for her father's love and acceptance.

If she did one thing while she was here, perhaps she could convince Ruston that he was tearing his little girl apart every time he left her for foreign destinations. It was abandonment time after time after time.

"She doesn't need a pony. She doesn't need things, she needs *you!* She only has one parent—you are everything to her."

Ruston's large hand tightened around the handle of the cup, and Ann held her breath, expecting it to snap. From the beginning, his hands had fascinated her. Reggie's hands had been long and narrow, aristocratic. Ruston's were broad and big, with dark hairs on the back. He had encircled her arms with them as easily as he held a riding crop.

"You have been here one day, my lady, and you presume to know everything there is to know about my little girl? You know nothing; you don't even have children of your own, so who are you to judge me?"

Ann felt her heart constrict and a pain shoot through it, a physical pain that she thought she was beyond. His angry words had pierced her like an arrow. She stood and put her cup down on the coffee tray. With a calmness she did not feel, she said, "You are right. What could a barren widow know of children? Good night, my lord."

Head held high, she walked from the room, through the great hall and up the winding stairs. She paused on the landing to stare at the huge painting of Lady Celia Ruston. She felt cold and alone, but those were feelings she was used to and could live with. Much better than the initial pain his words had caused. So much better not to feel at all. After a moment she proceeded on her way, up the staircase to her bedroom, and then to bed.

Seven

Ruston slammed the cup down on the tray and thrust his fingers through his hair. He had reacted badly to her words and had wounded her with his stinging comment that she had no children. He could feel it in the air the moment he said it, her sudden tension, her pain.

But damn it, she had no right to say such things to him! He had been well within his rights to deliver a rebuke after that unbearable bit of righteous indignation. Who was she to say what his little girl, the light of his life, was feeling?

Unless Mossy had told her.

He remembered the cozy scene he had witnessed, with Mossy gazing adoringly up at Lady Ann and the woman's arms tight around his child. That was why he had interrupted; he couldn't bear the thought that Mossy would be hurt when Lady Ann went away . . .

When Ann went away.

Like he went away, hurting his little girl time after time after time.

Was Ann right? She had some experience, after all, with abandonment. Reading between the words she spoke, he thought that perhaps she had been a lonely little girl, never sure of her father's love. But Mossy knew he loved her, didn't she? He told her so often enough.

He leaped to his feet and paced in front of the fire. He had never been the introspective sort, and all of this thought in one night was making his brain ache, but he was no coward. If he was wrong, he wanted to know about it. If he was failing at some elemental part of his role in life as a father, it was best to know now, while there was time to make amends.

His own father had always proclaimed that a man was known by his actions, not his words. Words were easy; it was harder to do the right thing day after day. Value your family, the old man had always said. Ruston sighed and sat down, staring into the fire. Value your family. When he was a boy and home from school on holidays, his father spent a good portion of every day with him, taking him on his weekly visits to the tenants, teaching him what the figures and numbers in the estate books meant, spending valuable time.

At school he had learned that not all fathers were like his own; many sons would not be able to point their fathers out in a crowd. Some only saw the old man if they had done something unforgivably bad.

For Ruston it was different. When he was just three, his mother had died giving birth to a little brother who lived only ten months after her. His little brother had died suddenly in the middle of a dark winter night. Little Charles, as Ruston was known by one and all when he was a child, was just four then, but still he remembered clearly his father holding him and explaining that wee Jonathan had gone to keep Mummy company because she was lonely in heaven. His father's strong arms around him in the darkness had been an anchor in a time of shifting sands, a frightening time when it seemed that anyone might just die in the night, like his mother and little brother had.

Until the day he had gone off to school, his father had spent as much time with him as was possible, given his duties as an active member of the House of Lords, and that he was a landlord with considerable holdings. Did he measure up to the awesome strength of his father? No, he didn't think he did, and that was one more reason why he spent so much time away, wandering the continent. He didn't think he would ever stretch to fit the old man's enormous shadow.

But that was no reason not to try.

* * *

The rain had stopped, but the morning air was frigid and crystalline. Ruston breathed deeply and waited, while Mossy caught up with him.

"And where is your kitten this morning while we are out gathering Christmas greenery?" He smiled and put out his gloved hand, enclosing his daughter's in his own.

"Noël is with Lady Ann." Mossy laughed mischievously. "Only she doesn't know about it!"

Ruston shot her a mock-severe look. "What are you doing to our guest? Are you playing a trick on her?"

Elfin face a picture of innocence, Mossy said, "Oh, no! Noël is. I went to see her this morning in her room, and he followed me. He . . ." She broke into giggles and covered her mouth with one gloved hand.

They walked across the frosted grass, the ice crystals crunching under their booted feet. Snow in the next two days after this icy frost, if local lore were true. Ruston glanced down at his daughter with affection in his brown eyes. "You might as well tell me, young lady. If that madcap little monster is planning a surprise for Lady Ann I should know about it before she rings a peel over my head."

"He wiggled into a shawl that she had laid on the bed. If she picks it up . . ." She dissolved in a fit of giggles again.

"And you never said a word to warn her, you rascal," Ruston said, grabbing her under the arms and swinging her up onto his shoulder as they entered the home wood. "Now you scout ahead and see if you can find us some mistletoe up in the trees."

They walked in silence, followed at a distance by a groom with a sledge to put the evergreen boughs, holly and mistletoe on.

"How was she this morning?" Ruston said finally, unable to refrain from asking. He had spent a sleepless night, part of it worrying that he had been unforgivably rude to Ann when she was right all along.

Mossy didn't answer and he repeated the question, thinking she hadn't heard him. When she still didn't answer, he swung her down and knelt at her side.

"What is it, sweetness?"

Mossy's expression was troubled.

"She's . . . sad. Why is she sad, Papa? When I went to see her this morning, she just looked at me, an' I think she was going to cry, but then the maid came in, an' she had her tea. Lady Ann said she's going this afternoon. She's leaving."

Oh, God, he had chased her away with his unkindness. He gazed into his little girl's hazel eyes, eyes that reflected the sadness she had seen in Lady Ann. He reached up and pulled her to him, holding her in his arms. "I don't know why she's sad, sweetness, but if I can, I'll talk her into staying. Would you like that?"

He released her and watched her expression.

Her small lips pursed, she nodded slowly. "Do you like her, Papa?"

"Of course I do!"

"If she stayed forever, would you stay home?"

"What?" His shock made him abrupt.

"If Lady Ann stayed forever and ever, would you stay here . . . would you not travel again?"

Her face had a pinched, unhappy look, and Ruston was stricken with guilt. Did she think he needed another reason to stay home—that she wasn't enough? Of course she did, he thought. What else could she think? It was what he had taught her every time he went away, just as Lady Ann had said.

Kneeling in front of her on the damp bed of leaves that covered the forest floor, Ruston gazed steadily into her eyes. "Sweetness, I am *not* going away again after Christmas. I'm going to stay here until summer, and then you and I shall go to Brighton, or maybe to Lyme Regis for the sea bathing. I've been spending too—"

His words were choked off as Mossy threw herself at him, throwing her arms around his neck and hugging him as hard as her thin arms could, sobbing with what he hoped was happiness. He was vividly reminded of the first day he had returned, a week ago now. Mossy had stood in the shadows in the great hall gazing at him timidly, until he had pulled Noël out of his greatcoat pocket.

"This is for you, sweetness," he had said, gazing hungrily at his little girl. Until that moment he had not known how much he had missed her and how glad he was to be home again.

To his shock, as she moved forward and took the small, sleepy kitten, she had given an inarticulate sob and burst into tears, clasping the small animal to her bosom.

"You remembered," she had cried, her hazel eyes shining.

"Remembered?"

She eagerly explained, "When you went away last time, you said you would think about whether I could have a kitten or not. I waited and waited, but none of your letters ever said I could. But you *did* remember! You wanted to surprise me."

A chill ran through him. What kind of a father was he not to even remember something that was evidently so important to his only child? Not only had he not remembered, he still didn't! Staring into her eyes, filled with the bright light of adoration, he knew that forever after she would remember his casual, thoughtless gesture of bringing home a kitten that he didn't know what else to do with, as the gift of a loving father. He didn't deserve that.

But he would; he swore that he would. Someday he would be worthy of the love she bestowed on him so freely. He would become his father's son. He thanked a forgiving God that he had not lost his child's affection; this opportunity for a fresh start would not be thrown away or ignored.

Gently, he disengaged her arms from around his neck. "Let's get the greenery now, honey. We have a lot of work to do if we're going to get the manor dressed up for Christmas. Maybe we can talk Lady Ann into helping us."

The night had been so long! Ann hugged her arms around herself and stood at the window looking over the frost-spangled lawn. It had stopped raining the previous night, and she knew for certain that her carriage was repaired. Ellen was better too, and had returned to work, though Ann had told her not to. The girl had insisted, and was now packing Ann's toiletries.

She was leaving. She didn't care whether she went on to Bath or back to London, she just had to go. She had spent hours fighting the tears she had thought she was past, only to be overwhelmed by them near dawn. It was as if through all the years, the tears she had not cried had built up, waiting for release, and once started, she could not stop the flood. Remembering was too painful, and looking ahead to her dreary future was unthinkable.

Who did she think she was, that she could presume to judge Ruston and find him wanting? And to think that she could heal Ruston and Mossy's relationship? He had had a wife he loved, and a daughter who adored him, despite his frequent defections. He must be doing something right in life.

Ann had nothing.

She took a deep breath and steadied herself against the windowsill. It was a little late in the day to start feeling sorry for herself. She had nothing? Untrue. She was very fortunate. She had money, her home, her music and serenity. She would return to that and be grateful.

Looking down at the scene below her, she saw a groom pulling a heavily laden sledge burdened with greenery, and behind him was Ruston, with a laughing Mossy on his shoulders. Ann smiled, ignoring one last tear that trickled down her cheek.

Ruston paced restlessly in his library, confused by the swarm of feelings that buzzed in his head and his heart. Lady Ann was leaving. She had calmly announced it at luncheon, her icy mask in place, her demeanor cool and collected.

She had been kind to Mossy, but adamant that her friend, Verity, would be worrying about her if she did not arrive in Bath soon.

Why did he care? Mossy would get over her sorrow, now that she knew her father was home to stay. It was his own emotions that puzzled him. He felt there was unfinished business between him and Lady Ann, and yet what that unfinished business was he could not say. Tomorrow was Christmas Eve day. She could stay one more day and still get to Bath in time for Christmas Eve.

A scratch at the door.

"Yes!"

"Jacob Lesley, my lord." Stoddart ushered in Lady Ann's driver.

Lesley, looking supremely uncomfortable, stood on the carpet turning an ugly brown cap around and around in his hands. The butler closed the door.

"Ah, Lesley, thank you for responding to my request."

"I would 'ardly refuse, milord."

Ruston grinned. He liked the hint of humor in the man's words and the fact that the man, though obviously ill at ease in the luxurious surroundings, looked him straight in the eye.

"I am going to ask a favor, something extremely odd, of you, Lesley. But first I need to know how your working relationship with her ladyship stands."

"Beg parding, sir?"

"Does she take your advice?"

The man snorted. " 'Ardly, sir. Lady Ann is a rare feisty one, begging your parding, milord, and seldom takes my word. 'Twere why we was traveling so late. I was all fer stopping over at the inn in the last town but one, but milady does not like inns. Sez there's impertinink people there."

Ruston frowned. "You know that she wants to leave this afternoon?"

"Aye, sir. She sent word to the stables that we would be a'leaving arter tea."

"I want a delay."

The grizzled man frowned.

It went against the grain, but Ruston found he would have to explain himself to the driver if he wanted his cooperation. He paced around his desk and sat on the edge, gazing into eyes so pale blue they were almost white. "My daughter has an affection for Lady Ann, and I . . . *we* would like her to stay for at least another day. But she is set on going." He looked down at his boots. "I'll be honest with you. I said something that hurt her, and I need time to find a way to make it up to her."

There was silence, but when he looked up he found the driver studying him with a piercing stare.

"Beg parding, milord, but she is my mistress, an' I do what she tells me, e'en when it goes agin the grain."

"I am only asking for prudence, Lesley. The roads really are not good yet, and I would not see her harmed; I know you share my concern. This is *my* responsibility. I shall send one of my men out, he will discover that the road both ways is still impassable, and shall tell you that. You may tell her ladyship the truth—that you have been informed the road is not safe for carriage travel." Ruston straightened. "That will be all."

Jacob grinned, showing a row of dark teeth. He touched his forehead and turned to go, but paused and glanced back at Ruston. "She were a bonny lass when Sir Reggie got 'is hands on her, milord, with the sweetest smile I ever did see. 'E broke her spirit, but she got it back arter he died, only wi'out the sweetness. But I do believe it still be there somewhere, a'waiting fer the right man. I do believe that, sir."

Eight

Ruston watched Ann's long white fingers deftly working with the red velvet ribbon, twisting it into bows for the decoration of the Manor. There was something sensuous about the capable, feminine hands, bare of gloves, manipulating the soft ribbon, pinching and twisting until the bow was perfect. She had hesitated before agreeing to help with the decorations for the Manor, but seemed to be enjoying herself, sending Mossy off on a scavenger hunt with Sarah for pine cones and dried clusters of berries.

She had resigned herself to a delay of one day, she said, when she announced that Jacob refused to take the horses out when a groom had checked and found the road still in abysmal condition.

One day. He had one day to figure out what was between them, if anything. It had seemed to be acrimony and anger mostly, but there were occasional flashes of something else. The night before, in front of the fireplace, they had both spoken of things they had told no one else. Surely that meant something. Or was that just two lonely people unburdening themselves of their guilt to strangers whom they did not think they would have to face again after a short while?

She glanced up and smiled. "Someone is not a very good worker," she said archly. "I have done twelve bows to your three, my lord."

"See here," he said, smiling and leaning across the table and covering her hand with his own. "I am not overly fond of 'lord' and 'ladying' every time I speak. Can you not call me Charley, as my friends do?"

The smile died from her lips and she pulled her hand away with a quick movement. She was going to freeze up again, he knew it.

But just then, Mossy raced into the room with a basket of pine cones and clusters of berries, wizened and puckered from being the last on the vine. She eagerly danced over to Lady Ann. "Will these do, Lady Ann? Are these good enough?"

As his daughter and the baroness culled through Mossy's pickings, he watched. Ann's eyes, when they rested on his daughter, had a softness of expression, much as a mother's. Mossy clambered up on Ann's lap, seeming to have forgotten her shift into iciness the previous night. Children were forgiving, Ruston thought, a good thing for him since he had some ground to make up in being a dependable, worthy father.

For the rest of the afternoon they moved through the house, using fresh-scented evergreen boughs to decorate mantels and doorways, and holly to adorn tables. The mistletoe Ruston held back until they were almost done. He knew what he wanted. He desperately wanted to kiss Ann's lips gently, not in anger. The feelings that had coursed through him the first time he touched them needed to be explored, understood. But she would never stand for a kiss between them. She had made her feelings plain.

And so he would employ a little chicanery, a ruse that would involve the entire household.

"I think the whole Manor looks splendid," Ann said, admiring the great hall, the last area to be decked. "What a lovely house you have!" The staircase had garlands winding up the banister and the great arching doorways were adorned with wreaths of holly, ivy and clusters of red berries.

"Ah, but we are not done yet!" Ruston knelt by Mossy and whispered in her ear. She giggled and dashed off.

Ann glanced at him apprehensively. She felt that she had done admirably in finding and maintaining just the right tone of cheerful, impersonal behavior. On the morrow she would ride out herself and check the road if Jacob said it was still bad.

There were just two days to Christmas, and she longed to be away. But Ruston had not stepped over her invisible line once, all afternoon, since suggesting she first-name him.

And that, in itself, was suspicious.

Albert, the tallest of the footmen, brought in a ladder and set it under the grand chandelier. "The household has been alerted, my lord," he said, bowing before Ruston.

Mossy danced around, first on one foot and then on the other while the household, even down to Ann's maid Ellen, filed into the great hall.

Ann frowned. What was going on?

When they had all gathered, Ruston ascended a few steps up the ladder with some of the greenery in his hands. "Attention everyone!" he called. The buzz of voices hushed, and all eyes turned toward him, some with a puzzled gaze, others with the imperturbable look of a well-trained servant.

"It is Christmas, that time of year when every person, man and woman, servant and master, sets aside their differences and rejoices in the bounty of the season, remembering that the baby born on Christmas Day grew up to be the man who exhorted us to love one another."

Where was he going with this? Ann felt a small hand steal into her own and glanced down to find Mossy at her side. But her gaze returned to Ruston, who stood a few steps up on the ladder with a lazy grin on his handsome countenance. He looked straight into her eyes and the warmth of his expression sent a shiver down her back.

She had felt at times, in the past few days, as though he was toying with her. She had started her journey to Bath angry at London society, but not unhappy with her lot in life. But in two days she had learned to question her life and whether she had attained true happiness. Ultimately she decided she had resigned herself to serenity rather than happiness, but that serenity was not such a bad thing to have.

But was there more for someone like her? She did not have that capacity to inspire love that some women seemed to have. She did not think that anyone had ever really loved her, had they?

Mossy leaned against her, and she found herself putting her arm around the child's thin shoulders. Ruston had been rattling on about the season for a minute, but now he was gazing into her eyes again, and his warm regard caused a blush to rise through her body. She really should look away. But she found that was not so easy to do when all she wanted was to keep gazing into brown eyes that held in their depths secrets of life she could not even guess at.

Ruston had had it all. A wife who must have loved him, a child who very obviously adored him, and the regard of everyone, even down to the lowest servant. He had the touch to make even Lady Ice melt. He had kissed her twice—first on the sole of her foot and then on her lips, and both times she had felt his warmth and vitality spread from that point of contact until it felt like her very blood was heated.

Ruston was farther up on the ladder now, and fastening one of the great swags of evergreen they had prepared to the majestic chandelier. He then tied on some greenery of his own, leaves and pale berries.

He descended, jumping the last few steps down to the floor.

"There are very special berries up there, gentlemen," he said, glancing around at his gathered household. "It is the age-old tradition of Russetshire Manor that every woman or girl in the house must be kissed under the mistletoe to ensure that the next year is a happy and healthy one for everybody who resides here. This, of course, is where that must happen, and now is the moment."

Ann frowned and started to move away, but Mossy had her arms wrapped around her waist and would not move. She certainly could not drag the child away, but surely Ruston was not serious. A buzz had gone up amongst the servants, and much laughter ensued. Teasing glances were exchanged, and Ruston was beaming.

"The trick is, that it is the female who will choose who shall have the honor of kissing her under the mistletoe!"

Laughter again.

"I have made sure there are enough berries up there, for the chosen gentleman must climb the ladder, pluck a berry and present it to the fair maid before the kiss can be completed. What brave lass will choose first?"

Pandemonium broke out among the distaff members of the household, but finally Mrs. Bowles, the housekeeper, stepped forward. Ruston looked like he was ready to choke with suppressed laughter. Ann, caught up finally in the merriment, watched with wide eyes as the black bombazine-clad woman, lips primmed, step forward.

"I can't say as I approve of this pagan nonsense, my lord, but if it will allow me to return to my duties that much more quickly, I shall go first. I must register my disapproval though, sir. Never has such licentious behavior been tolerated in this household. I think that the girls will be impossible to manage for a time."

Ruston glanced over at Ann, who looked back at him with raised eyebrows. Age-old Russetshire Manor tradition?

"Mrs. Bowles, you have caught me out. I am merely reviving an ancient fertility rite, to ensure good crops in the coming year."

Ann knew by the quirk of his grin that his intention was to shock, and he had succeeded. Mrs. Bowles turned scarlet as the younger members of the household giggled and guffawed.

"Come, Mrs. Bowles. Whom do you choose as your champion?"

To everyone's shock and with much accompanying laughter, the august woman chose the head groom, a sturdy older man much shorter than she, but with large strong hands and a twinkle in his gray eyes. He turned beet red himself, but scaled the ladder like a boy a quarter his age and plucked a berry.

Mrs. Bowles, still red in the face and with the expression of a martyr, moved to stand under the chandelier. Jem Standish, surveying the tall, formidable woman he was expected to kiss, took her hand in his and pulled her over toward the ladder, where he went up a step and bussed her enthusiastically on the lips.

Applause and laughter broke out, and Mrs. Bowles, face still aflame, curtsied to Ruston and retreated, presumably to the safety of her office. Her swain, meanwhile, strutted away from the ladder like the cock of the walk, to much hooting from the other men.

After that a succession of chambermaids chose handsome footmen, though one, a pretty, buxom woman in her thirties, was daring enough to choose Stoddart. He good-naturedly went along with it, but their kiss was rather lengthy by any standards, and he moved away from the woman with a thoughtful expression. She appeared dazed, and touched her lips with gentle fingers. Ruston winked at his butler.

"Well done, Stoddart, old man. I think . . . Iris, is it? I think you left Iris with something to remember! Who is next?"

Ann was surprised to see Ellen move timidly forward. Ruston glanced over at Ann, and then smiled at Ellen.

"Has one of my young men caught your fancy, then?"

She curtsied and murmured a name.

"I couldn't hear you, my dear," Ruston said. "You will have to speak up."

"Cobb, sir!" Her voice rang out loud and clear.

"Well! My gentleman's gentleman has caught the maiden's fancy! Step up, Cobb, you have made a conquest!"

Ruston's valet shot him a dark look, but stepped forward, scaled the ladder and plucked a berry, presenting it to Ellen. She took it and lifted her face trustingly to his, but she was doomed to disappointment. He merely brushed her lips quickly and stepped away.

"I demand a better attempt than that, Cobb, old man," Ruston said, glancing over with a grin at Ann. "We must show our visitors that Russetshire men have what it takes to woo and win the fair maids. Try again!"

With much laughter from the remaining staff, Cobb kissed Ellen again, this time taking her in his arms and sweeping her almost literally off her feet. The girl was red-faced when he was done, but a smile lingered on her curved lips.

"Well done! Who else is there?"

A tiny scullery maid stepped forward and chose one of the groom's boys as her champion.

"And whom will you choose?"

The voice in her ear nearly sent her skittering across the floor.

Mossy had danced away from her some time ago, and she should have taken the opportunity to slip away, she realized, before Ruston approached her.

"You don't expect *me* to . . . oh, no! I couldn't!"

"Oh, yes you will! Think about who, in this room, you would like to kiss. You will be called in about three minutes. And don't even *think* about slipping away, or I will make an embarrassingly large fuss when I find you and carry you bodily back."

Ruston moved back toward the ladder and called on the cook, a plump, cheery individual of about fifty who blushingly refused to name a man. To Ann's surprise, she saw her own driver, Jacob Lesley, step forward.

"Might you be wantin' a volunteer, milord?" he asked, slapping his cap against his leg.

The cook threw her apron over her face, but Ruston, laughing, ushered the driver over to the woman. "May I provide a willing fellow for you, Mrs. Jasper?"

She nodded shyly, and Jacob scaled the ladder, plucked his berry and was back in front of her in seconds. He presented the berry to her and, wrapping his arms around her rotund waist, planted an enthusiastic kiss on her plump lips. She shrieked, threw the apron back over her face and scuttled off to the kitchen, almost bumping into the wall and doorway a couple of times.

"Now me, Papa!" Mossy said, dancing eagerly around, her kitten in her hands.

Ruston stood, hands planted on his hips and feet apart, gazing down at her. "And what gentleman have you chosen, young lady? Might I hope to be your champion?"

"I choose Noël," she giggled, planting a kiss on the kitten's pink nose. Noël sneezed, and wiped his paw across his nose.

Ruston expressed disappointment. "I suppose I have been supplanted in your affections by that little monster, even though he can't be expected to scale the ladder and pluck a berry . . . just yet, anyway. So be it. There is only one lady left." He turned his gimlet gaze on Ann.

She felt her stomach lurch. How could she kiss him again? And yet how could she choose someone else? The whole thing was ridiculous, but she did not want to appear as Lady Ice this once. She shot a panicked glance around the rest of the room, and got an idea. She stepped forward boldly, and smiled inwardly at the gleam in Ruston's brown eyes. "I choose . . . Jacob!"

Her driver was still watching the proceedings with great interest. His pale eyes widened and he shook his head.

Ruston, who had been stalking toward her, stopped abruptly. He looked genuinely disappointed, Ann thought with amazement. His eyes narrowed then, and he considered.

"You cannot choose someone who has already been chosen!" he announced.

"But Jacob was not chosen, he volunteered!"

"Ah, but he did kiss a woman, so the point is in dispute. Choose again!"

He moved toward her, and she wanted to back away from the warm amber light in his eyes.

"I-I-I . . ."

He was right in front of her, looking down into her eyes.

"Choose me," he said, his voice deep and low. "Choose me, Ann. You won't regret it."

Mesmerized by his stare, she said, before she thought, "I choose you."

A collective sigh swept through the room. Many of the giddy chambermaids and handsome footman had stayed to watch, happy to suspend their numerous duties for a break. A high giggle broke out from Mossy.

Ruston, his athletic form showing to great advantage, scaled the ladder, and then jumped back down. He beckoned Ann, who walked toward him even though her knees felt weak. He offered her a berry.

She took it and looked up at him as he put his hands on her shoulders. She wished she could read the expression in his golden-brown eyes. He watched her even as he lowered his face toward hers, but then her eyes closed instinctively, and the first touch of his lips was experienced as a sweet moment of bliss.

Without releasing her, he deepened the kiss, and her hazy awareness that there were people watching drifted away. Sensation throbbed through her body, a body she had thought devoid of natural feeling. A giddy dizziness swept over her, and she was no longer sure if she stood or sat or what. All she knew was his lips were soft, his kiss tasted like cinnamon, and he was . . .

She gasped as she felt his tongue touch her lips, tickling and teasing with delicious darting movements. And then he released her.

They had the rapt attention of the small crowd, including Jacob. Ann felt a fiery blush steal over her body. She had not wanted that moment to end, although she was still puzzled by what she had felt in his arms. It was as if her body, deep down to some secret core, was awakening from a long slumber.

He held out his hand and she glanced down. He had a fistful of berries—at least twenty, and maybe more.

"Shall I redeem these all at once, or shall I take my kisses one by one, through the evening and night?"

Nine

Ann dressed slowly. Ellen fussed around, laying out the right gloves to go with the deep amethyst gown her mistress had donned for dinner, and finding a shawl to go with the gown.

She shrieked and Ann whirled to find Noël blinking up at the maid from under a pile of discarded dresses. He skittered away, a whirlwind of energy, finally burrowing into Ann's reticule.

She laughed. "That is what that little demon did to me this morning. He had gotten himself buried in my shawl on the bed and when I went to put it on, he jumped at me." She dumped the kitten out of her small evening bag, and the little animal sped across the room and out the door.

"Green-eyed little devil-cat," Ellen said.

There was silence for a moment.

"And so you chose Cobb to kiss you," Ann said, watching her lady's maid tidy the vanity table.

Ellen huffed and tossed her head. "Little did I know the man was a cold fish!"

"You didn't feel anything when he kissed you?"

"I . . . I wouldn't say that. But I was that embarrassed that the master . . . I mean *his* master, had to tell him to do it proper! You'd think I was an antidote!"

"He was just on his dignity, Ellen, that's all. Some . . . some of us find it hard to thaw, you know."

"Still!"

There was silence for a moment. "Isn't Lord Ruston the

handsome one, though," Ellen said, sneaking a sly glance at her mistress's face.

"And I think he is aware of it," Ann said quellingly.

"Do you think him vain? I have heard Cobb complain in the servants' hall that the master does not think enough of his appearance. It is Cobb's bane in life, he says."

Ann did not answer. No, she did not really think Ruston conceited. She was trying to find excuses not to like him. If that was the best she could come up with . . .

"I will go down now."

Ann heard laughter as she descended, and she followed the sound to the rose parlor. She entered to find Ruston on the floor, with Noël on his stomach, worrying frantically at his waistcoat buttons. How the creature had gotten from her room down to the rose parlor so quickly was beyond her, but the little devil seemed to be everywhere at once, sometimes.

Mossy gaily grasped her kitten and danced away. "I'm going to take him upstairs now. He hasn't had his dinner yet."

"Please, don't let me interrupt," Ann said.

Ruston clambered to his feet as Mossy skipped from the room. "Let her go." He brushed himself off. "Cobb would be mortified to see me like this," he muttered, straightening his cuffs and smoothing his breeches.

Ann realized she was watching his broad hands straighten his breeches, and quickly looked away. She was shy, suddenly, not knowing what to say after the frivolity of the afternoon.

He stepped in front of her, reached in his pocket, took her hand and placed one berry in it. "I think I will claim one kiss now."

"Why are you doing this?" she moaned, looking away. She didn't think she could bear another of his soul-shattering kisses just then . . . or ever. They left her feeling weak and strange.

He clutched her shoulders and drew her near, not answering. He tipped her face up with one hand and kissed her, possessing her lips with a gentleness that seared her soul. She shivered, and despite all her resolutions found herself responding, opening to him like a flower to warming sunshine.

When he released her, he gave her a long, searching look in

the dimness of the rose room. "How could anyone call you Lady Ice?"

She pulled away from him. "I despise that name," she cried.

"How did it happen?"

She crossed to the harpsichord in the corner and touched the keys, desperate to stay away from him. She shot him a glance. "You must know! If you have heard the name, you have heard the story!"

"I was only in London for three days after arriving from the Continent, but yes, I heard the story. I heard that you crushed young Madison like an insect under your heel after leading him on for months. I heard you humiliated him in public, and he had to slink away on his 'grand tour' to escape the laughter." His words were harsh but his tone curiously neutral.

"Ah, yes," she laughed, a bitter, sharp sound that echoed. She hit a discordant note, and walked away from the instrument. "Poor, young Madison. Poor lovesick boy who dogged my every step for months, no matter what I said to him. Poor love-starved fellow, who laid his hands on me one night when I was walking in my garden, bundled me into a waiting carriage and abducted me!"

Ruston's dark brows shot up. "Abducted you? Whatever was he thinking?"

"You tell me! He said we would be married at Gretna, and that I would learn to love him."

"What happened?"

"We stopped at an inn outside of London to water the horses, and I screamed for help. I was able to bribe the innkeeper, who was greedy and could see where the best possibility of money lay. I was able to obtain his help, at the cost of my diamond earrings, and get back to London. Only Madison's immediate friends knew about it, and I threatened them by saying I would charge Madison if they opened their mouths."

"But I heard that you publicly humiliated Madison, and that *that* is what sent him to the Continent," Ruston said.

Ann slapped her palm down on a table. "The fool had the temerity to approach me at Sally Jersey's Christmas Ball to ask me to dance. I had had enough; I could not bear the thought of him touching me with his damp sweaty hands, hands so wet even gloves could not disguise it. No longer was I going to be confined by courtesy. I told him that if I ever desired public humiliation, I would dance with him, clumsy oaf! After all I had been through, that was what finally sent him away! Being laughed at by the *ton!*"

And that was the explanation for the infamous Lady Ice, Ruston thought. It showed what happened when one knew only a part of the story.

"Is that why you are leaving London over Christmas?"

"Yes. I could not bear the whispers, the . . ." She shook her head.

Ruston wondered, was her icy demeanor her way of protecting herself, insulating herself from the ravages of a cruel world? Instead of being frigid, was she only *too* vulnerable? He would soon know.

He approached her and stripped off her long lavender gloves one by one as she watched with wide violet eyes. Ah, yes, her flesh was warm and her elegant long-fingered hands as subtly arousing as he had remembered. He placed another pale berry in the palm of one of her naked hands and raised the other to his mouth, turning it so the palm faced him. He watched her eyes as he laid a soft kiss in the middle of her palm, and then curled her fingers around it. If he was not mistaken, her breathing was faster and her cheeks just slightly flushed.

He hoped this evening lasted a long, long time, because he intended to get to the bottom of the mystery of Lady Ann Beecham-Brooke before the end of it.

They had talked about everything, Ann thought, but each other. Mossy had returned to eat dinner with them, and conversation had been lively and diverse. Formality between them was absurd, she decided, and so Ann started calling him Charles, and he called her Ann back, with a significant look, as if daring her to object.

But she didn't. The sound of her name on his lips gave her

a little thrill. His voice had a deep timbre when he said it, and it pleased her much more than it should have.

He was well-traveled, she learned. At the end of the war he had been in Brussels, and talked about the euphoria after Napoleon's defeat. Since then he had been to Switzerland, Germany and Italy, and she watched his eyes light with enthusiasm as he spoke of the art treasures of Italy, the museums he had seen, the majesty of the Vatican.

And now, as he had planned, he would go on to the Balkans and then to Greece, Ann thought, leaving behind his child once again. She could not forgive him for his blindness there, for not seeing how his leaving would affect his precious daughter. Mossy was resigned to it, no doubt, Ann thought, watching the girl's wide-eyed fascination with her father's stories.

Dinner was done. "It is time for your bed, Mossy," Ann said after the child's fourth yawn.

"Will you come up with me?" she said.

Ann glanced at Charles, who nodded, and said, "I will. Let's go."

Catching her eye, Charles said, "Meet me in the rose parlor after you put her to bed."

She hesitated, remembering the pocketful of berries he still had, but in the end acquiesced. It was what she wanted to do, after all, and she would be leaving in the morning. She had come to enjoy his company too much for her future tranquillity, but she would indulge herself this once and be with him.

Up in Mossy's blue and white chamber, Ann dismissed Sarah with a smile and helped the little girl into her nightie. A child seemed such a fragile thing, she thought, and yet their sturdy hearts and bodies survived all the insensitivity of adults, and they grew into the men and women who would shape the future.

Noël pounced out from under the bed and attacked Mossy's bare toes, and she collapsed on the bed in a fit of giggles. Ann picked up the tiny kitten, which immediately started to purr, the sound a vibrating rumble in its tiny body. She held him and sat down on the bed beside Mossy.

"Do you say prayers at night?"

"Sometimes, when I remember."

Ann put the kitten up near Mossy's neck, pulling her covers up so they were tucked around her snugly against the chill of the room. Noël circled twice and tucked himself into a tight little ball after one quick lick to his hind leg.

"What do you pray for?" Ann looked down into the hazel eyes that sparkled in the dim light of the candle.

"For Papa to stay home. For him and Grandfather Chase and Grandmother Chase to be safe, and . . . and other things."

For Papa to stay home. Ann felt the anger again, and quelled it with difficulty. She had said all she could to Charles, and now it was time for her to go.

"Thank you for helping me with Papa's sampler." Mossy said. "Do you think he'll like it?"

Ann glanced over at the framed sampler, sitting on a table by the bed. Together they had washed it, dried it and framed it with a frame found in the attic. Nothing could correct the slanting stitches or misspelling, but to Ann it was the more precious for all of the love and effort that went into it—all the hopes and dreams and prayers.

"He will adore it and treasure it forever. I wish I could be here when he opens it Christmas morning."

Mossy's tiny face pinched with unhappiness and Ann wished she had not mentioned having to leave. In just a couple of days this child's happiness had become so very important to her, and she was torn apart inside, knowing she could do nothing about her coming sadness.

"It's time for you to sleep, honey," Ann said, blowing out the candle. She bent down and touched her lips to the child's smooth forehead, wishing, yearning to hold her in her arms and tell her she would be there for her whenever she needed a friend. If only she had that right.

"Good night, Lady Ann."

"Just Ann, honey."

"Good night, Just Ann Honey," Mossy said with a tiny smile. Ann ruffled her silky hair. "Scamp."

As the door closed, Mossy touched the soft fur of her kitten, and felt the reassuring rumble of a purr start in the tiny figure.

"Noël, we have to keep her here somehow. Papa likes her,

an' I like her, and she's . . . she's sad. We could make her happy again. We'll have to think of something. We'll have to think of something *quick.*"

The rose parlor was dimly lit, with only one branch of bees-wax candles and the embers of the fireplace lighting the dusky reaches. Ann entered uncertainly. He *had* said the rose parlor, had he not?

And then she felt his presence. She wasn't sure where he was yet, but she could feel something in the air, some vibration that touched her and enveloped her.

"Charles?"

"Ann."

His voice was almost in her ear and she whirled, startled. He reached out for her, steadying her.

"I'm sorry; I did not mean to startle you."

"But you did!" she snapped.

"Again, I apologize. Please, come and sit by the fire. It is a desperately cold night."

He led her to the fire, but when she started to sit on a chair, he pulled her down, onto a deep, soft rug on the hearth.

"I-I-I cannot sit on the floor!"

"Of course you can. It is warmer here, and . . . snug."

And dangerous, Ann thought, eyeing him nervously, tucking her gown securely around her ankles. He sat down by her, so close she could feel the animal warmth emanating from his body. He smelled delicious, like spice, and she had an absurd urge to nibble at his neck as if he were a gingerbread man. She shifted, trying to move away a little, but found that was not practical, for she moved away from the warmth of the fire if she did. It was as if he had placed her strategically, knowing what her next move would be and countering it.

But he would have to be unbelievably devious to do that, would he not? She glanced up at him from under her lashes. The flicker of the fire cast a ruddy glow over his handsome countenance. What a lucky woman Celia Montrose had been. Even though he had made it clear theirs was a marriage based on friendship more than love, his amity would be worth more than many men's *amour*.

He caught her look, and the warmth of his return gaze blossomed in her heart. Never had she felt so . . . so close to a man. His hand went to his pocket, and this time she was not surprised when he pulled out a berry and presented it to her.

"How long do you intend to keep this up?" she asked, finding she could do nothing but smile at him, though she knew she ought to be angry or insulted that he would casually kiss her like this.

"As long as I have berries," he said with a mischievous grin.

He must have looked like that as a boy, she thought, looking at the rumpled, dark hair and quirked mouth. So would his sons look, if he had had any.

"You have kissed me on my foot, on my mouth three times, and on my hand. Where else do you intend to claim a kiss?" she asked.

Only when his grin deepened into a sensuous, smoldering gaze did she realize the danger behind her innocent question. She swallowed. "I-I-I . . ." She had to say something to divert his attention.

But it was too late. He moved closer to her, leaning toward her with a look that was softening into something she had never seen in any man's eyes before. Gently, he kissed her on the neck just behind her ear and tugged on her earlobe with his teeth, setting her pulse racing and her thoughts spinning wildly out of control. It seemed that when he touched her she was no longer her own woman; he could toy with her senses and soften her until she was a puddle of heated desires. It wasn't her! It just wasn't, and it had to stop.

Why was he doing this to her?

"You are so beautiful, Ann. Why have you never married again?"

She stiffened. "That is an impertinent question!"

"I like being impertinent."

There was that lazy, sensual grin again, and it gave her the same quivering thrill in her stomach every time. She stiffened her backbone and drew herself up as much as possible considering her undignified position.

"You do it well," she observed wryly.

He chuckled and said, "I think you are even more beautiful when you get huffy."

Exasperating man!

She rolled the berry around in her hand. It was firm and white and glowed like a translucent pearl. The others he had given her she had tossed away or discarded somewhere. She glanced down at the small, round troublemaker.

"Why?" she asked, hearing her voice echo in the parlor as if it were a stranger's.

"Why? Why what?"

She held up the berry, turning it in her fingers. "Why are you doing this? This elaborate scheme, all for some kisses? I would not think you a man who would need to resort to trickery for that. Many women would be eager to kiss you."

He caught her hand in his and kissed the tips of her fingers and the berry too. She opened her mouth to protest but he held up his hand. "I know; that was not in the bargain. Why don't you try it?"

"Try what?" He was talking in riddles.

"Give me a berry and take a kiss."

She gasped. "I-I-I . . ."

"Try it! Are you, too, frightened?"

Infuriating man!

"I will! Take this berry, Charles Montrose!"

He took the berry from her and glanced coyly up at her from under his long dark lashes. "La, my lady. And now you will demand a kiss from me!"

She smothered the laughter that welled up in her at his imitation of a coquette. She moved toward him, kneeling on the soft rug, kicking the folds of her skirt out of the way. She placed her hands on his broad shoulders and lowered her face toward his. He closed his eyes and she found herself seeing things from a different perspective.

His lips were inviting, slightly parted, and he moistened them with his tongue. She took her kiss. She felt him sink back, and by the time she was midway through the kiss, found herself lying on top of him on the floor. He was a big man, and she could feel the muscles and sinews of his body though the thin fabric of her skirts before she lost herself in what she could only imagine was a kind of delirium.

His hands caressed her waist, and then moved around to her back as she deepened the kiss when he opened his mouth to her. She felt, nestled against her in the V of her thighs and body, something hard that her body cupped. He moved his hips and she gasped at a surge of desire through her dormant body.

His big hands roamed, down her back and to her bottom, cradling her buttocks and squeezing with gentle strength. Hunger overwhelmed her as she felt him stir, pushing her up with a powerful movement that lifted her whole body on his. And still their lips were joined, sealed, as she dared to touch her tongue to his mouth. His response, another thrust with his body, rocked her, the intensity of her answering push against him shocking her into some semblance of normalcy.

She rolled off of him and scrambled to her feet. How could she have allowed herself this shameless abandonment? What was she thinking?

He lumbered to his feet and towered over her, his brown eyes glittering strangely in the firelight. "Ann, Ann! Come, sit back down."

He moved toward her and she backed up.

"No! Charles, stay away from me. That should never have happened, that, that . . . whatever that was! That wasn't me!"

His low chuckle was soft. "Oh, yes it was. That was you on top of me, kissing me, moving on me." He reached out, but she evaded him.

"No, it was not."

Her words were uttered with a chill finality, and he straightened, sighed, and his smile died. "Ann, I never thought to say these words again, but I see no option. Marry me."

Ten

"Marry? You?"

In twenty-eight years never once had a request taken her so aback. Even being kidnapped had not amazed her like this—if she had heard him right.

"Yes. Marry me, Ann."

"Why?"

"Do I need to tell you? You were there just now." He took her hands in his. "We're good together, Ann. And then there is Mossy."

She shook her head, trying to clear the fuzziness in her mind. "Mossy?" It was all she could do to repeat his words in the form of questions.

"Yes, Mossy. You love her, don't you?"

Of course she did, with all her heart. How many people had she loved in her life? It was a sad question—one she had never had occasion to ask herself before. She supposed in some involuntary way she loved her family, but that was not the kind of love she was wondering about. How often had she felt love steal over her in imperceptible degrees, taking over her heart and mind? Only now. And all in two days!

He patiently awaited her answer, and she stared at him, her fingers flexing in his warm grasp. This was ludicrous!

"I do love Mossy, but you are asking me to marry *you!*"

"Well you can't marry her, can you?"

His wry grin infuriated her. For him this was a grand game, and she was one of the playing pieces—though not the queen. More like a pawn.

"And I cannot marry *you!*" She jerked her hands away from him.

His grin died, and she was glad. A burning core of anger was threading through her body, and she was grateful. It crowded out other painful feelings. Would she only ever be asked for her hand to be useful to someone? Charles Montrose only wanted her to marry him so he could gallivant to the Continent with a clear conscience, knowing a woman who would be a mother to Mossy was there to care for her and raise her. He would marry her, make love to her, and then take off for foreign countries. It was abominable, and she would not have believed it of him if he hadn't made such a nonsensical offer. All of the kissing and talking and laughter had been offered with but one aim in mind.

"Why not?"

"Why not? Why not?" Her voice was raising to a screech, and she reined in her emotions with difficulty. At least that smug grin was off his face, his too handsome, ever-smiling face. She took in a deep breath and with all the dignity she could muster when she felt like crumbling into a ball and crying, she said, "You are not right for me; I am not right for you. Good night, Charles."

She turned and left the room, not stopping until she reached her bedchamber, where she dismissed Ellen so she could lie on the bed and cry. At twenty-eight years of age she had done something as foolish as any maiden of sixteen could. She had fallen in love with a cad.

In the weak morning light of Christmas Eve day, Ann's carriage moved out of the stable at a sedate pace, and she gazed out the window, taking one last look at Russetshire Manor as she left. On the table beside her bed were two letters, one for Charles and one for Mossy, the one for the child folded around her silver locket, her Christmas gift to a little girl who could never be hers, but would be the daughter of her heart forever. She would pray that by leaving she was giving Mossy her best chance at keeping her father at the Manor. He would have no sop for his conscience, no easy way out.

Goodbye, little Noël. Goodbye, sweet Mossy. Goodbye, Charles, beloved.

Weary and morose, Charles sat and stared into the fire in the parlor, remembering back just twenty-four hours. He had sat with Ann on the rug his feet now rested on, kissing her ear and teasing her. And then he had dared her to give him a berry back and take the initiative. It had surprised him when she did, and he thought it surprised her too. But when she had kissed him, and they had fallen together down onto the soft rug, her pliant, shapely form pressed down on him, he had wanted nothing more than the right and the privilege of carrying her up to his bedchamber and removing her clothing, one silky piece at a time, and lying with her in his big bed, touching her everywhere until she was shivering with desire. He wanted to make love to her and then lie with her until dawn peeked through the curtains on Christmas Eve day. He wanted to be lying with her again when Mossy raced into their room to share her joy of another Christmas morn the next day, and every day after that.

He wanted to marry her.

The thought had come to him suddenly, and just as impulsively he had asked her. Perhaps that was his mistake. Her rejection should not have surprised him, but she had been horrified by the very idea of marriage, he thought, not just marriage to him. What had her married years been like? He remembered Reginald Beecham-Brooke slightly, though the man was older than he, and he had heard the stories; there was some scandal attached to him, whispers that the sport he took in London brothels involved some unsavory aspects. It was said he needed to get angry to become aroused. Disgusting, if it was true.

He should have approached Ann delicately, given her some time, not rushed her. And now what? She had made her feelings plain, and he had no excuse to follow her. He didn't even know if she had gone on to Bath or back to London, and he didn't know the last name of this woman Verity, her friend.

He buried his face in his hands. The day had started with the realization that Noël was missing. Mossy had been distraught and had raced through the house crying and calling for her pet. It was not until about eleven A.M. that they had thought that perhaps the kitten was in Lady Ann's room.

Immediately, Ruston had raced to her room, followed by Mossy. What they found behind the carefully closed door was an empty wardrobe and two letters. His had simply said that for reasons she did not feel he needed to know, she must reject his kind offer.

Mossy's had expressed how Ann would never forget a little girl that she would want for her very own, if she could ever be blessed with such good fortune. "Your father loves you very much," it had continued. "Take care of him, and always know that if you ever need me, I will be there for you." A silver locket had been enclosed, with the instructions that she would like Mossy to wear it always.

It had been a long, dreary day after that, for Noël seemed to have disappeared completely, and with Lady Ann gone too, Mossy was distraught. At seven she had gone to bed and had cried herself to sleep as her father watched, helpless to soothe her pain.

He had been sitting for hours now, unable to think, unable to do anything. Such profound depression was unlike him and he frowned into the fire, wondering what was wrong with him. So the kitten was gone and Mossy was sad. He would get her a new one, and she would forget soon enough.

It was Lady Ann's defection that was destroying him. He missed her. He dug into his pocket and pulled out a berry, one of the fifteen or so he had left, and had not allowed Cobb to throw out. He thought over his acquaintance with Ann, brief though it had been. Far from being the Lady Ice of London gossip, she was the warmest, most beautiful woman he had ever known.

He had seen her eyes alight with so many kinds of . . . of what? Of love. She loved Mossy, she had said so, and had repeated it in her note to his daughter.

But he had seen another light in her eyes, and it had been when he kissed her. She had glowed, evanescent with a lovely flame that torched his body with heat and touched his soul with longing. Longing for her . . . yearning to have her near him always, so he could spark a permanent light in those gorgeous eyes, one that would not extinguish when sad memories came to haunt her.

She had made him see that home was where he belonged. His daughter needed him, and, yes, needed her, the mother she had never had and the mother he had thought never to give her. The truth was so simple and so profound.

He loved Lady Ice.

His heart throbbed with acceptance. It was true. He swallowed hard. Was it too late? Would he never be able to kindle the love light in her eyes and prove to her that loving did not always bring pain?

A noise behind him made him start, and he turned in his chair.

A ghost!

But no, not a ghost. Lady Ann, standing in the shadows holding something close to her.

He stood and strode toward her.

"I . . ." Her voice trembled and she cleared her throat. "I found him in my bag. He was in my sewing bag, and I knew Mossy would be so sad, and I couldn't bear the thought of that, so I had to bring him back, even though I was ever so far away and—"

"What? What are you talking about?" Charles heard his own voice, harsh with suppressed emotion.

Ann held out her hands. Noël was curled there, sleeping. He didn't take the animal.

"I . . . I have to go," Ann said. "Please, take him to Mossy. She must be frantic, and I just couldn't bear . . ."

"Ann!"

She stopped talking, but would not meet his eyes.

He put one finger under her chin and pushed it up. He dug in his pocket and pulled out a berry and showed it to her. She shook her head, but did not say anything.

"Please, Ann. Just once."

He lowered his face to hers, and poured his heart into the kiss he gave her, his first given with the knowledge that he loved a woman. When he stepped back, he could see the dazed surprise on her face.

"Why . . . ?"

He put his hands on her cloaked shoulders and pulled her close, careful not to crush the kitten. "Because I love you. I didn't know it until just now, but I love you." He resisted asking her if she loved him. He wanted her to know that he gave her his love freely, without needing anything in return.

Her eyes welled, and one tear trickled from the corner. "You . . . are you sure?" She sounded disbelieving, as if it were a trick.

"I'm sure," he said, gently.

"I . . . I love you too. I do! I wasn't sure at first if that was what I was feeling but it was, and I love you. I was so afraid to come back, once I knew. I was so afraid . . ."

He put one finger on her lips. "You mustn't ever be afraid again. Ann, marry me. Not just to be Mossy's mother, but to be my wife."

His words spread a budding, quivering tendril of hope into Ann's heart. Not just to be Mossy's mother? He wanted her for himself? Just to love?

He kissed her again and again—no berries exchanged this time—and she felt his love on his lips and in his whispered words and in her heart.

"You found him!" Mossy, tear-reddened eyes wide, raced into the room. "You found him and you came back!" She threw her arms around the two adults, standing so close together in the dying firelight.

Noël awoke, mewing his displeasure at the jolting.

"He was in my sewing bag when I left, the little devil!" Ann's voice trembled with love. She knelt in front of Mossy and gave over care of the kitten.

Charles knelt beside her and gave her a conspiratorial glance. "Mossy, how would you like it if Lady Ann were to live with us always?"

"Always?"

"Always," Ann answered. "Would you . . . could I be your . . ." She could not say it. The words were too precious and the answer too important.

"Sweetness, you have never had a mother, except for the one

in heaven." Ruston smiled over at Ann. "What if Lady Ann were to marry me and live with us and be your mother?"

"Forever?" Mossy's voice held a note of awe. Noël yowled just at that moment, and Mossy broke out laughing. "Noël says yes! Noël says that was what he planned from the beginning! That is why he got into your bag, so you would come back!"

Ann and Charles gazed at each other in bemused silence.

"I didn't know how I was going to find you," Charles said. "I don't have your friend's last name, and I didn't know how long you'd be in Bath, or even if you would ever want to see me again!"

"I was so afraid!" Ann admitted. "Too afraid to even tell myself the truth, that when you asked me to marry you, I wanted to say yes, even though I thought you just wanted a mother for Mossy so you could go back to the Continent and not worry about her."

"But I wasn't going back to the Continent! I told Mossy that a couple of days ago. I plan to stay here."

Mossy shook her head as if to say, silly adults! "Noël knew! I wished on a falling star that Papa would stay home from now on. But I bet Noël wished for a mama! And both our wishes came true."

Charles stood and took Ann in his arms as the clock struck midnight. "It's Christmas," he whispered. "And I have the loveliest gift I could ever hope for in my arms this minute."

It was one year later, exactly. The clock struck midnight as Charles carried Mossy in to his wife's bedchamber after the midwife had gathered her things and left with a pocketful of gold. Noël, now an elegant and beautiful cat, raced ahead of them and sprang in a graceful arc to the bed, where he circled and curled into a purring ball.

Charles put Mossy down, and she tiptoed to the bed, fingering the silver locket she wore around her neck.

Ann looked up and smiled. "Come and see your little brother, sweetheart."

Mossy moved forward and gazed down at the small bundle held in Ann's arms as Charles sat down on the bed near his wife's head. He wiped back the damp curls on her forehead and leaned down to kiss her.

His daughter had a dissatisfied look on her face.

"What's wrong, sweetness?" Charles asked.

"He's . . ." She screwed her face up into a look of distaste. "He's kind of ugly."

Ann laughed weakly. "He was just born two hours ago! It takes a while for them to get as beautiful as you."

"I guess he's all right. But next year, could I have a baby sister for Christmas?"

Ann smiled up into her husband's laughing brown eyes. After thinking herself barren for so many years, the miracle of bearing her husband's heir was almost too much happiness. But she wasn't afraid anymore. At first, after she and Charles married on New Year's Day, she had been so afraid it would all go away that she had crept unhappily around, worrying she would find that it was all a dream, and that her husband really did not love her as much as he said and with such gentle fire. But he had proved it to her every day for three hundred and fifty-eight days now, and she was finally convinced.

And now they had the proof of that love.

Charles winked at her, and then gazed down at his daughter, who was peering at her baby brother with a critical eye. "We'll have to see what we can do about that. With any luck at all, you'll get your next Christmas wish."

"And Noël, too!" Mossy said.

The cat looked up at the sound of his name, his green eyes blazing jade in the candlelight. He yawned, meowed and stretched, digging his claws into the counterpane. Then he curled back up to sleep.

"I think he said he already got his wish, and he's happy."

Mossy nodded in agreement with her father. "Me, too," she said. "I think I like Noël's Christmas wish best of all," she said, her hazel eyes alight with love as she stared at Ann.

Charles gathered his family to him. "I couldn't agree more."

More Zebra Regency Romances